GILLBERT

THE ISLAND OF ORANGE TURTLES

ART BALTAZAR

PAPERCUT Z

New York

#4 "The Island of Orange Turtles"
By Art Baltazar
Production – Lily Bilgrey
Managing Editor – Jeff Whitman
Jim Salicrup
Editor-in-Chief

Papercutz books may be purchased for business
or promotional use. For information on bulk pur-
chases please contact Macmillan Corporate and
Premium Sales Department at
(800) 221-795 x5442.

Hardcover ISBN: 978-1-5458-0717-0
Paperback ISBN: 978-1-5458-0718-7

Printed in China
March 2022

Distributed by Macmillan
First Printing

AW YEAH, PAPERCUTZ PRESENTS...

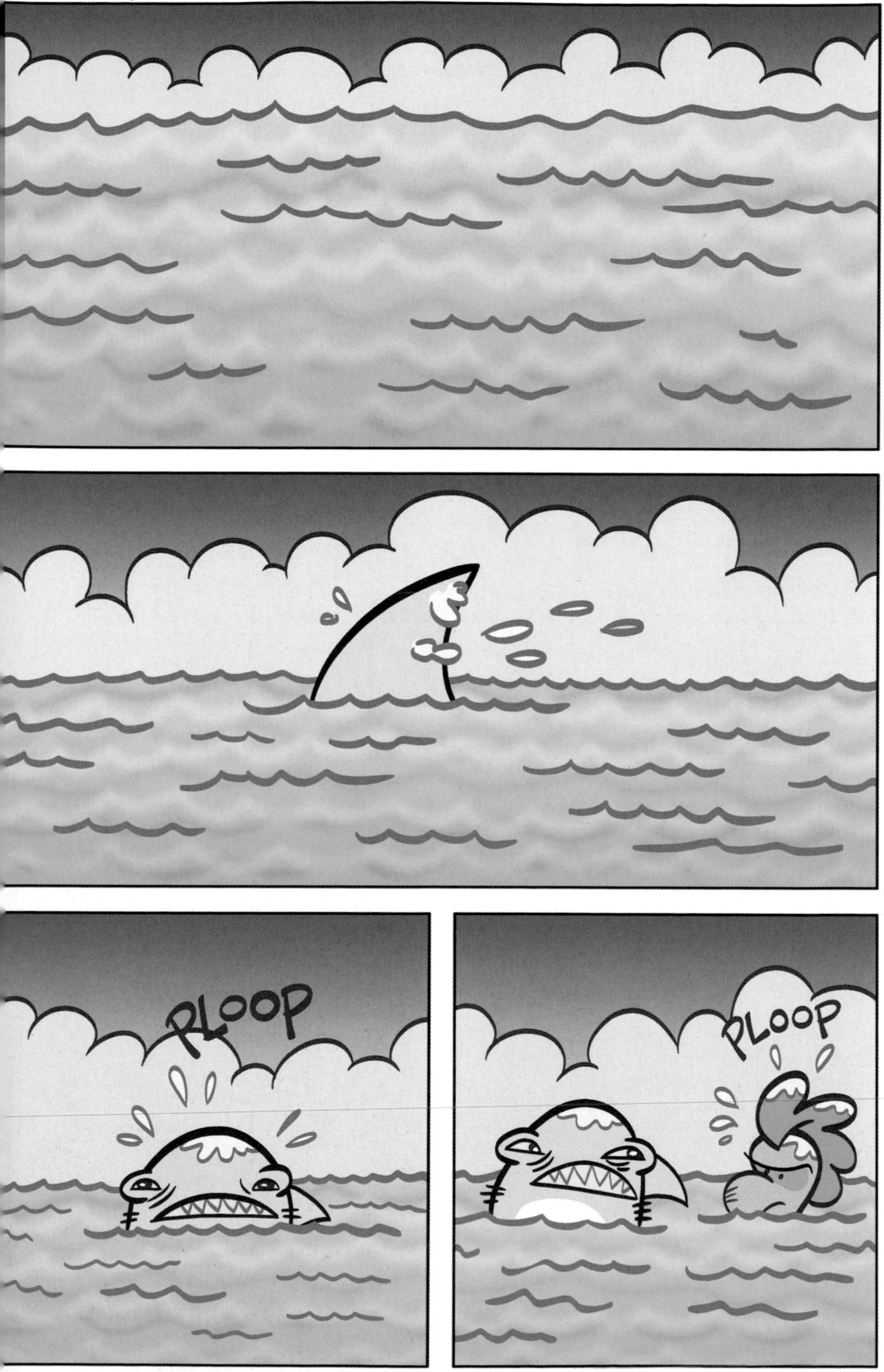
PLOOP
PLOOP

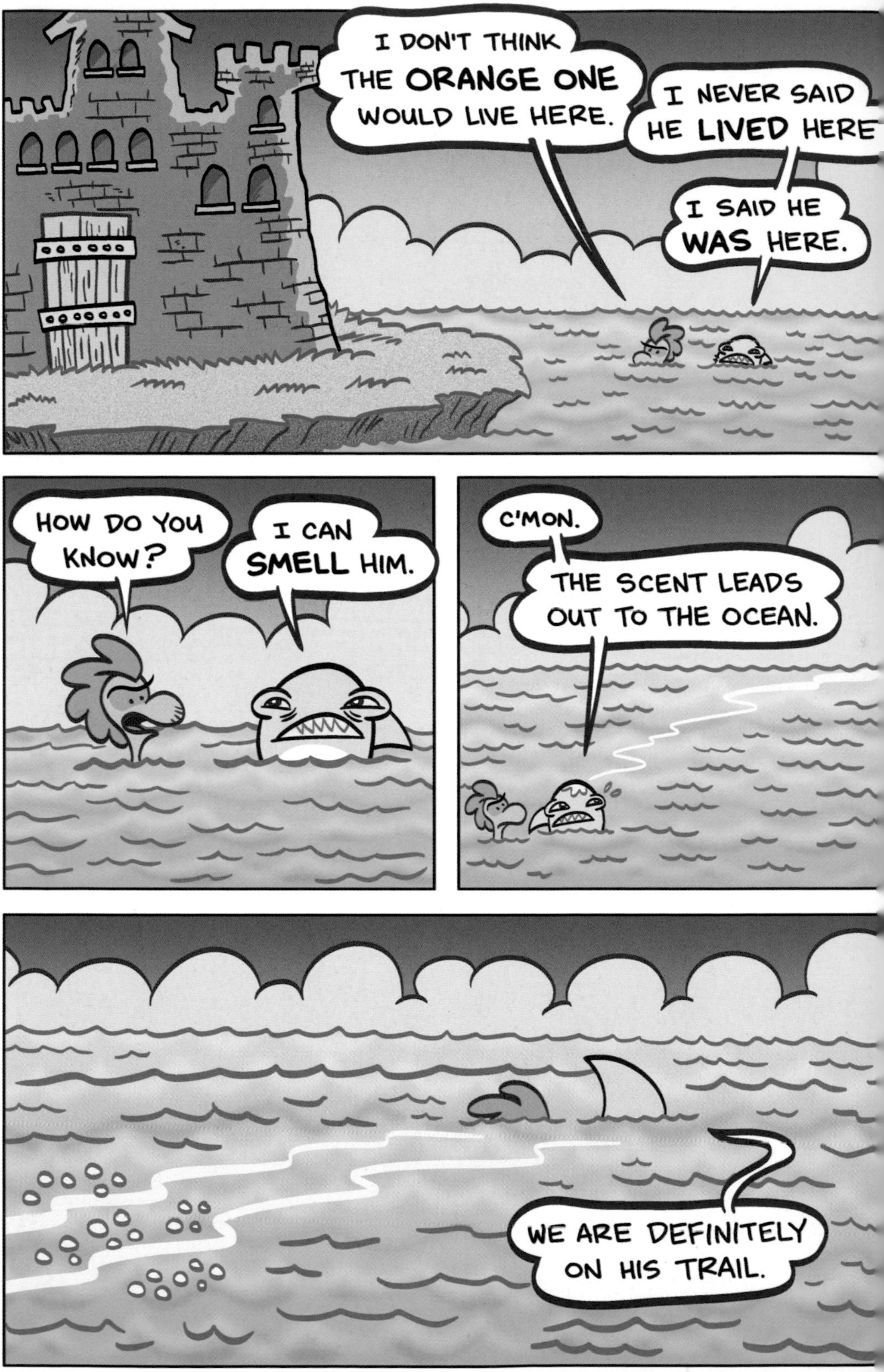
I DON'T THINK THE ORANGE ONE WOULD LIVE HERE.
I NEVER SAID HE LIVED HERE.
I SAID HE WAS HERE.
HOW DO YOU KNOW?
I CAN SMELL HIM.
C'MON.
THE SCENT LEADS OUT TO THE OCEAN.
WE ARE DEFINITELY ON HIS TRAIL.

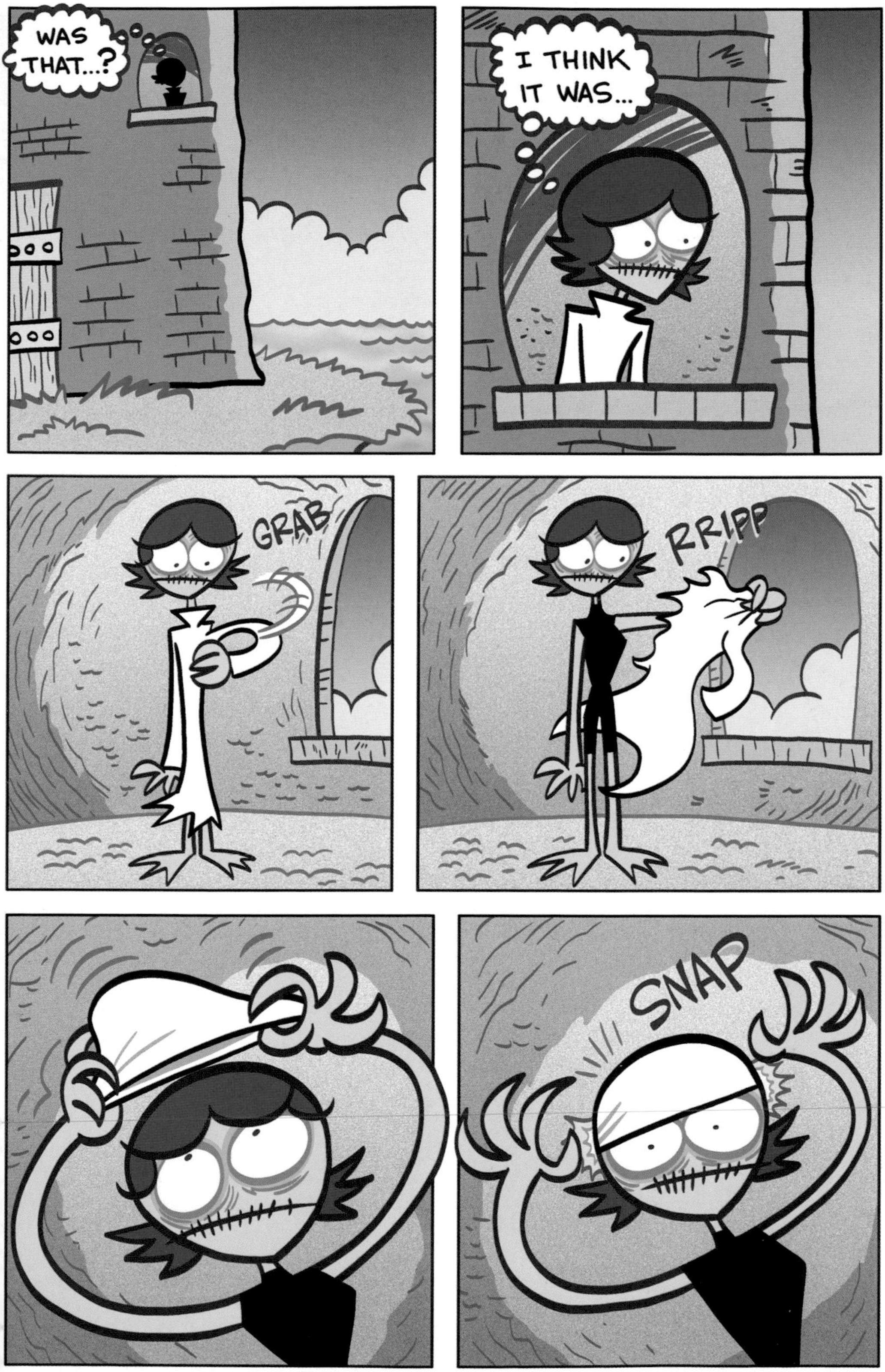
WAS THAT...?
I THINK IT WAS...
GRAB
RRIPP
SNAP

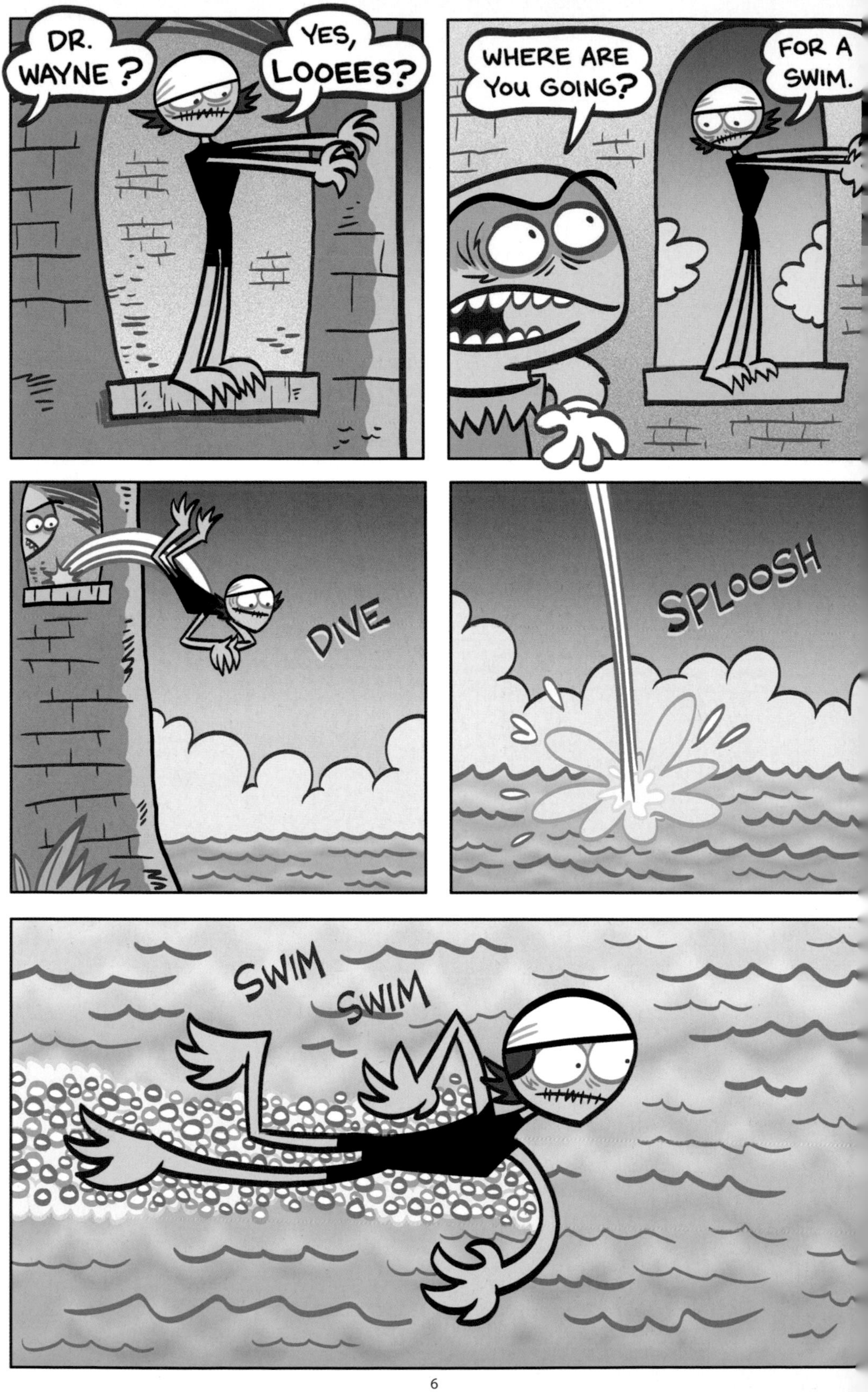
DR. WAYNE?
YES, LOOEES?
WHERE ARE YOU GOING?
FOR A SWIM.
DIVE
SPLOOSH
SWIM
SWIM

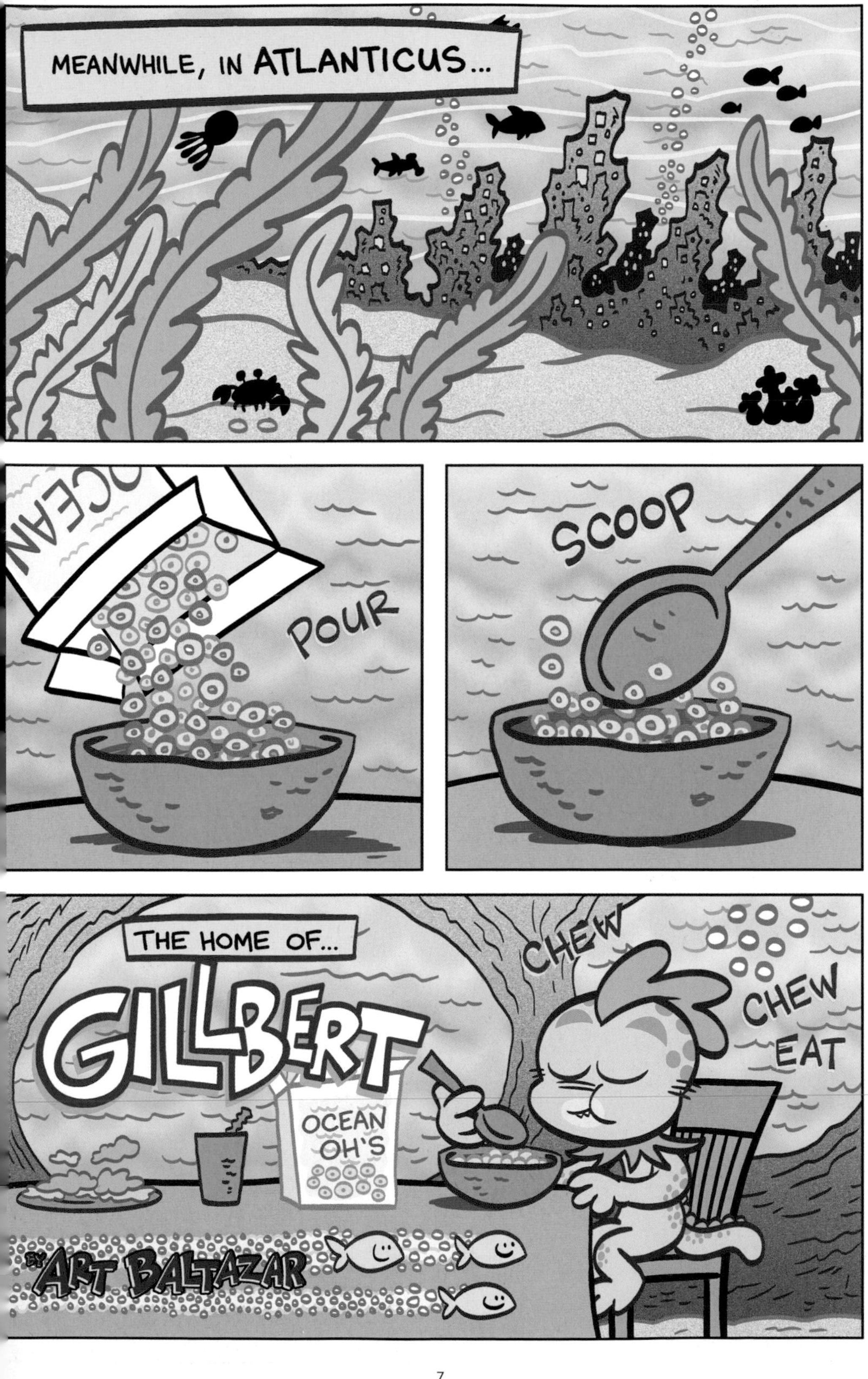
MEANWHILE, IN ATLANTICUS...
OCEAN
POUR
SCOOP
THE HOME OF...
GILLBERT
CHEW
CHEW
EAT
OCEAN OH'S
BY ART BALTAZAR

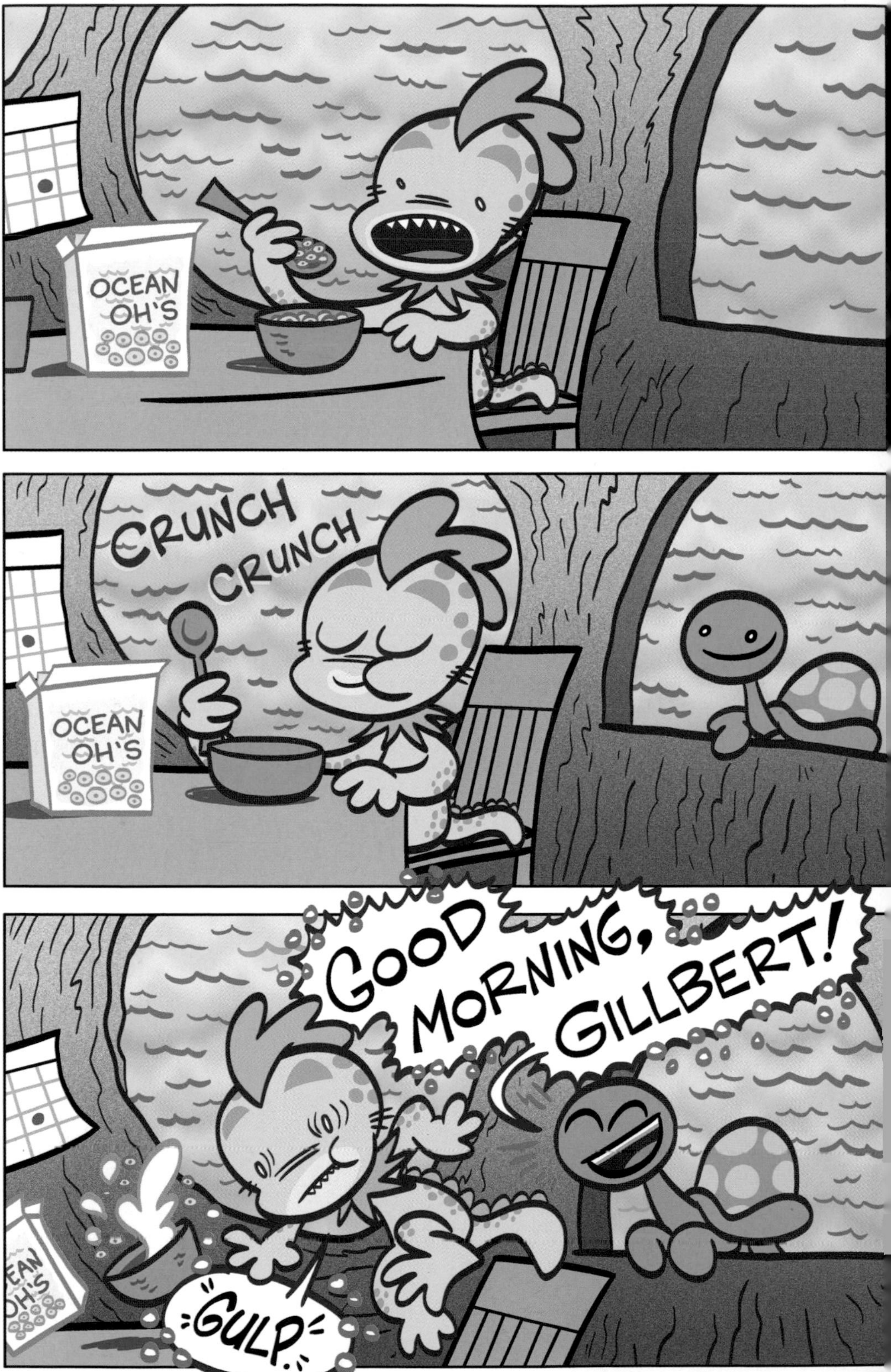
OCEAN OH'S
CRUNCH
CRUNCH
OCEAN OH'S
GOOD MORNING, GILLBERT!
GULP.

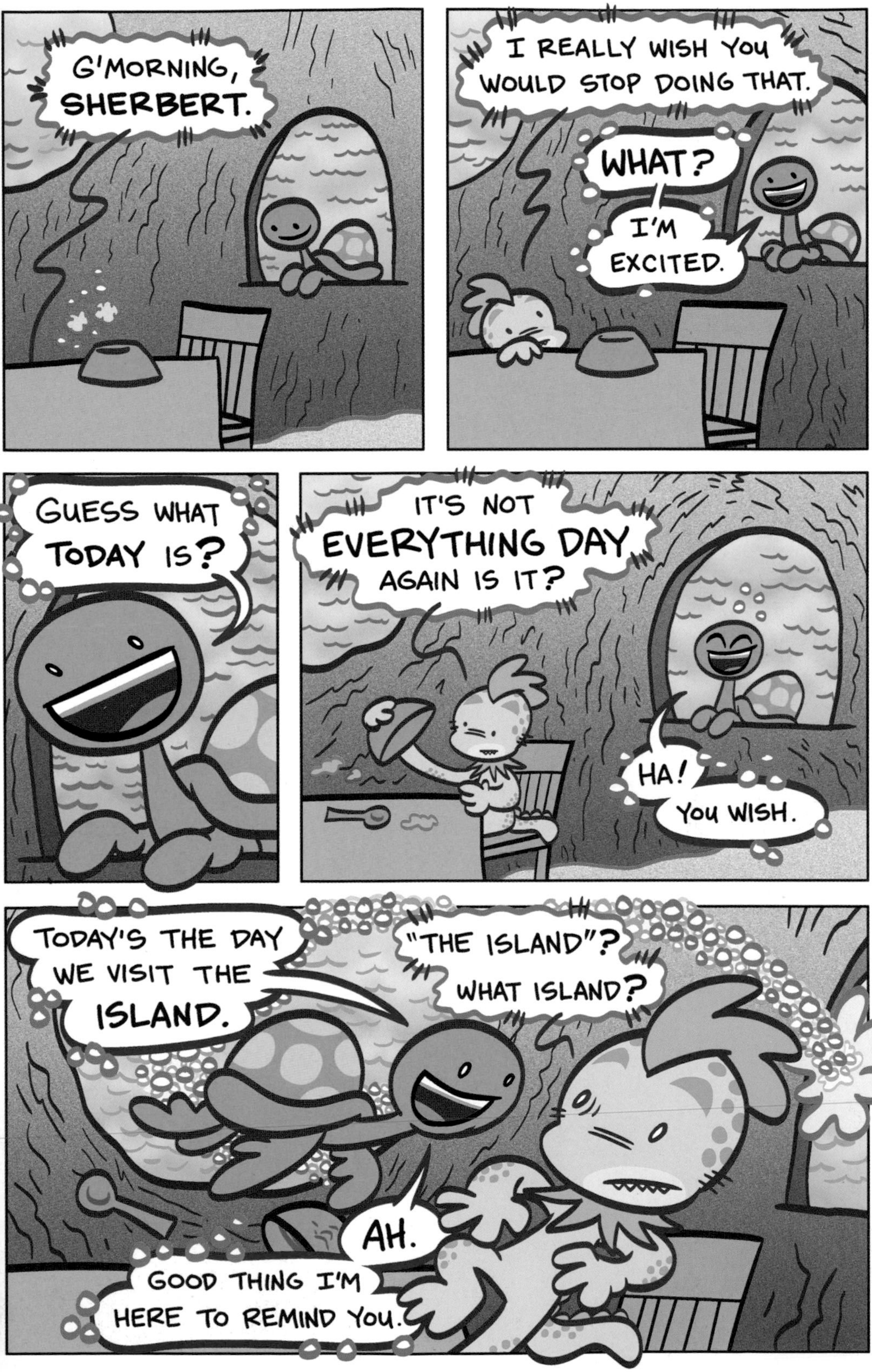
G'MORNING, SHERBERT.
I REALLY WISH YOU WOULD STOP DOING THAT.
WHAT?
I'M EXCITED.
GUESS WHAT TODAY IS?
IT'S NOT EVERYTHING DAY AGAIN IS IT?
HA!
YOU WISH.
TODAY'S THE DAY WE VISIT THE ISLAND.
"THE ISLAND"?
WHAT ISLAND?
AH.
GOOD THING I'M HERE TO REMIND YOU.

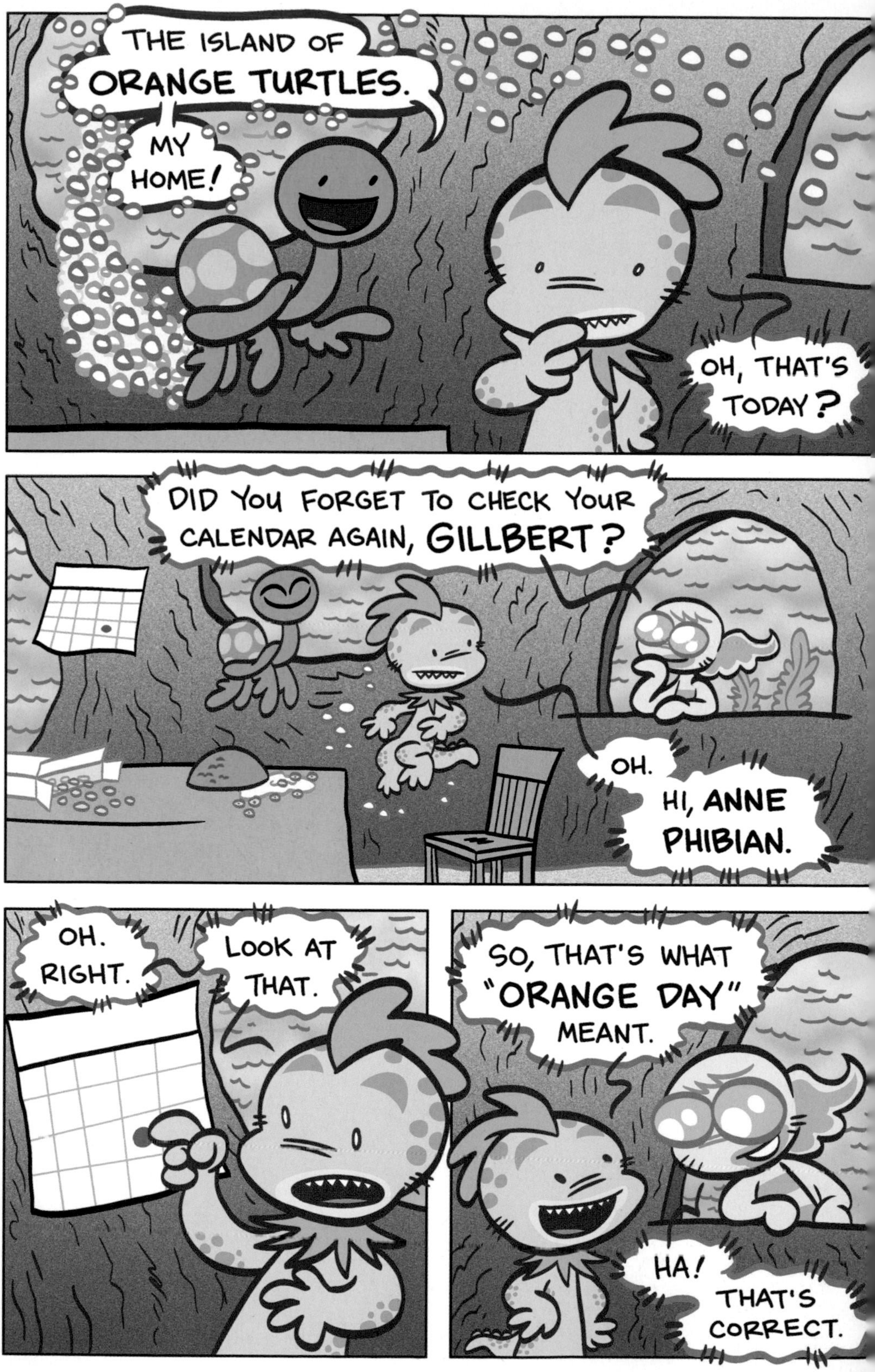
THE ISLAND OF ORANGE TURTLES.
MY HOME!
OH, THAT'S TODAY?
DID YOU FORGET TO CHECK YOUR CALENDAR AGAIN, GILLBERT?
OH.
HI, ANNE PHIBIAN.
OH. RIGHT.
LOOK AT THAT.
SO, THAT'S WHAT "ORANGE DAY" MEANT.
HA!
THAT'S CORRECT.

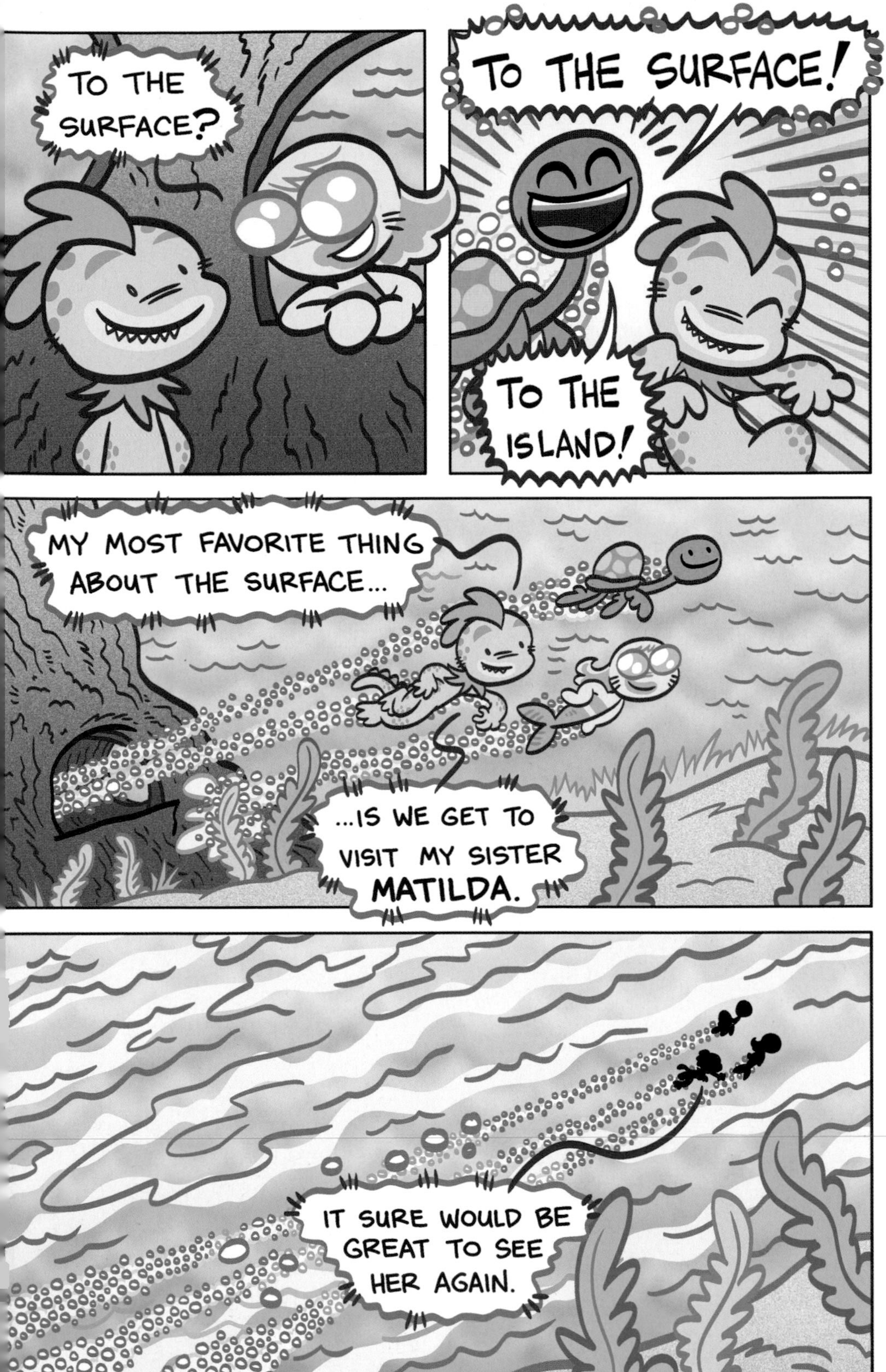
TO THE SURFACE?
TO THE SURFACE!
TO THE ISLAND!
MY MOST FAVORITE THING ABOUT THE SURFACE...
...IS WE GET TO VISIT MY SISTER MATILDA.
IT SURE WOULD BE GREAT TO SEE HER AGAIN.

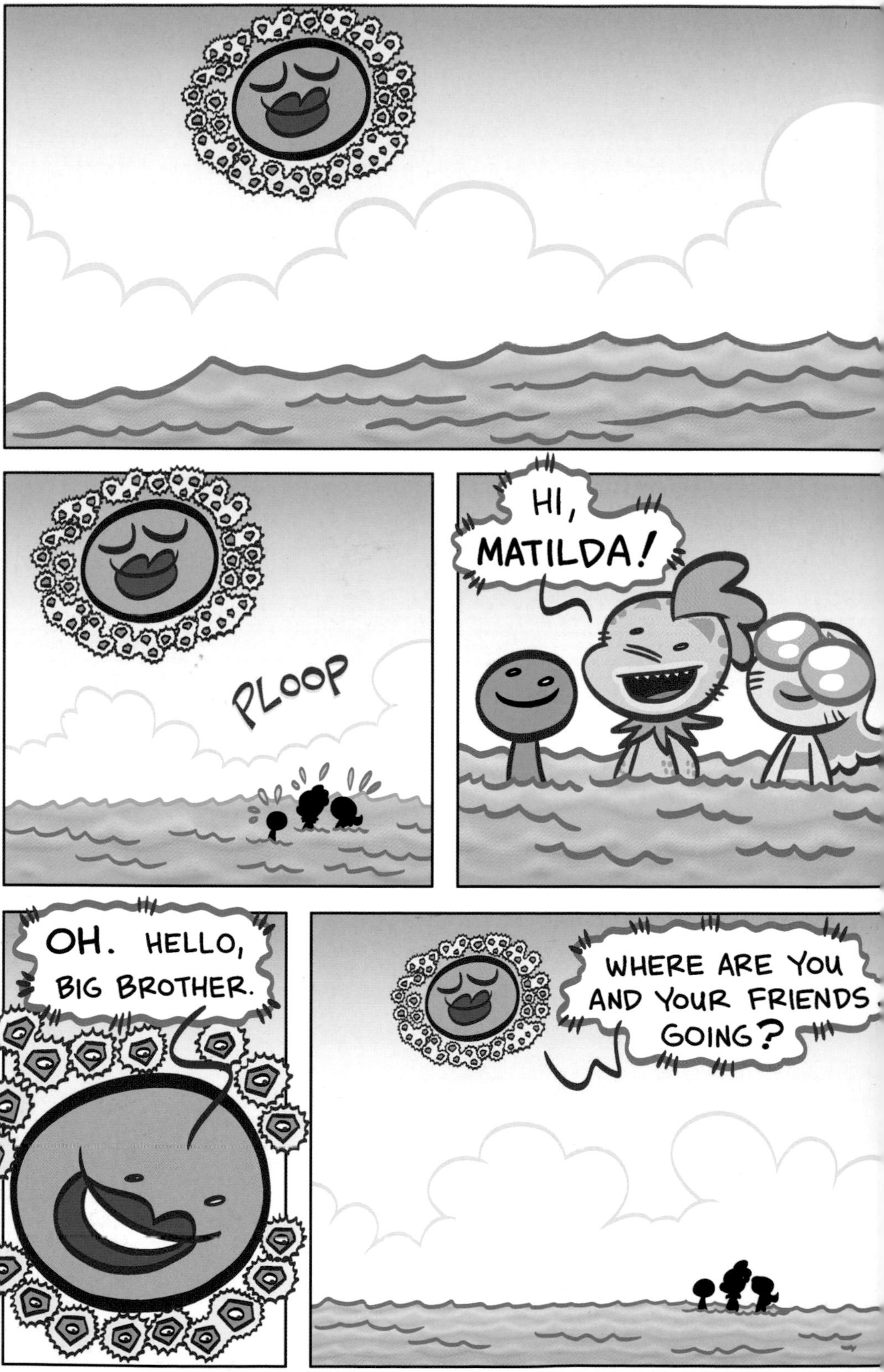
PLOOP
HI, MATILDA!
OH. HELLO, BIG BROTHER.
WHERE ARE YOU AND YOUR FRIENDS GOING?

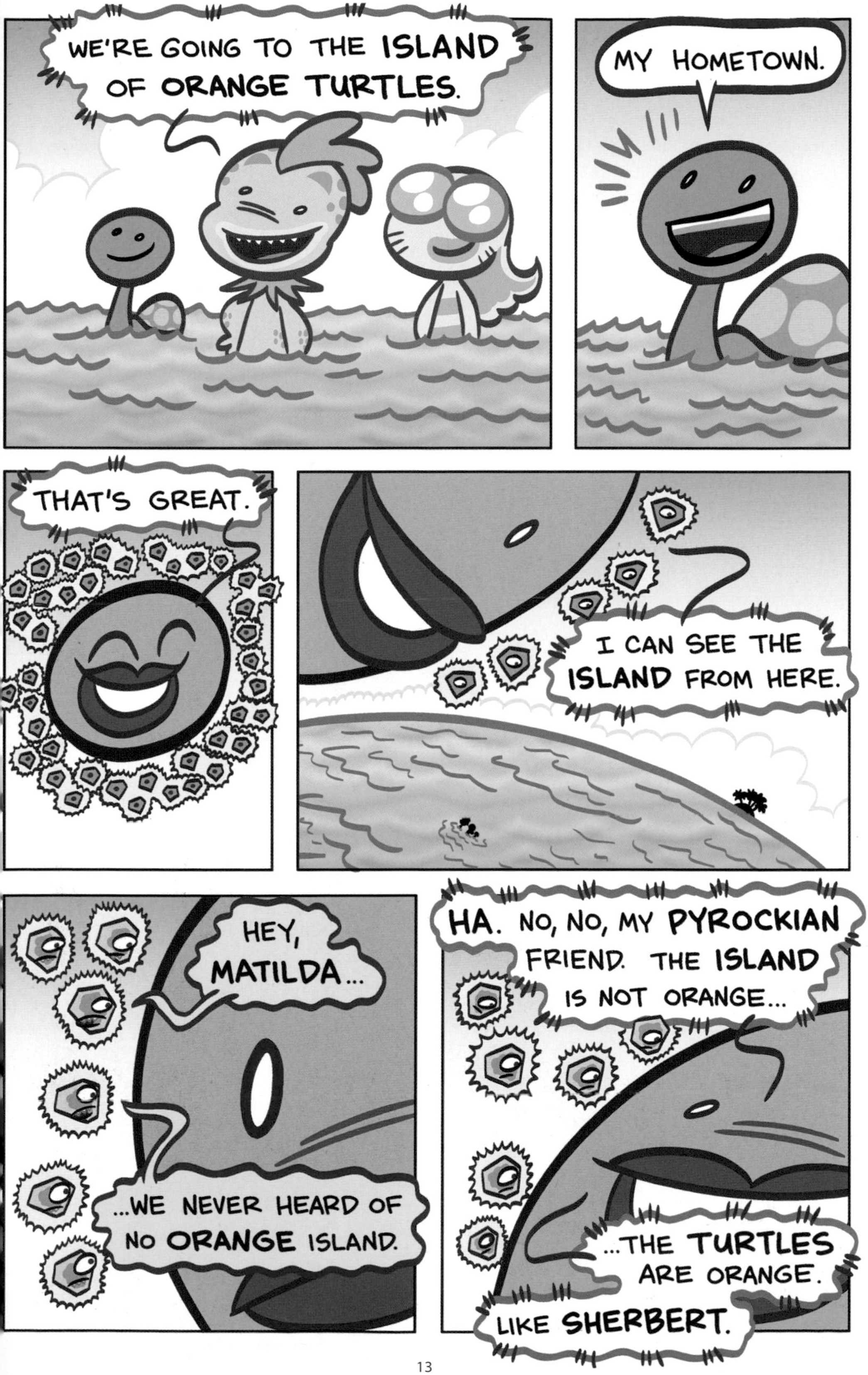
WE'RE GOING TO THE ISLAND OF ORANGE TURTLES.
MY HOMETOWN.
THAT'S GREAT.
I CAN SEE THE ISLAND FROM HERE.
HEY, MATILDA...
...WE NEVER HEARD OF NO ORANGE ISLAND.
HA. NO, NO, MY PYROCKIAN FRIEND. THE ISLAND IS NOT ORANGE...
...THE TURTLES ARE ORANGE.
LIKE SHERBERT.

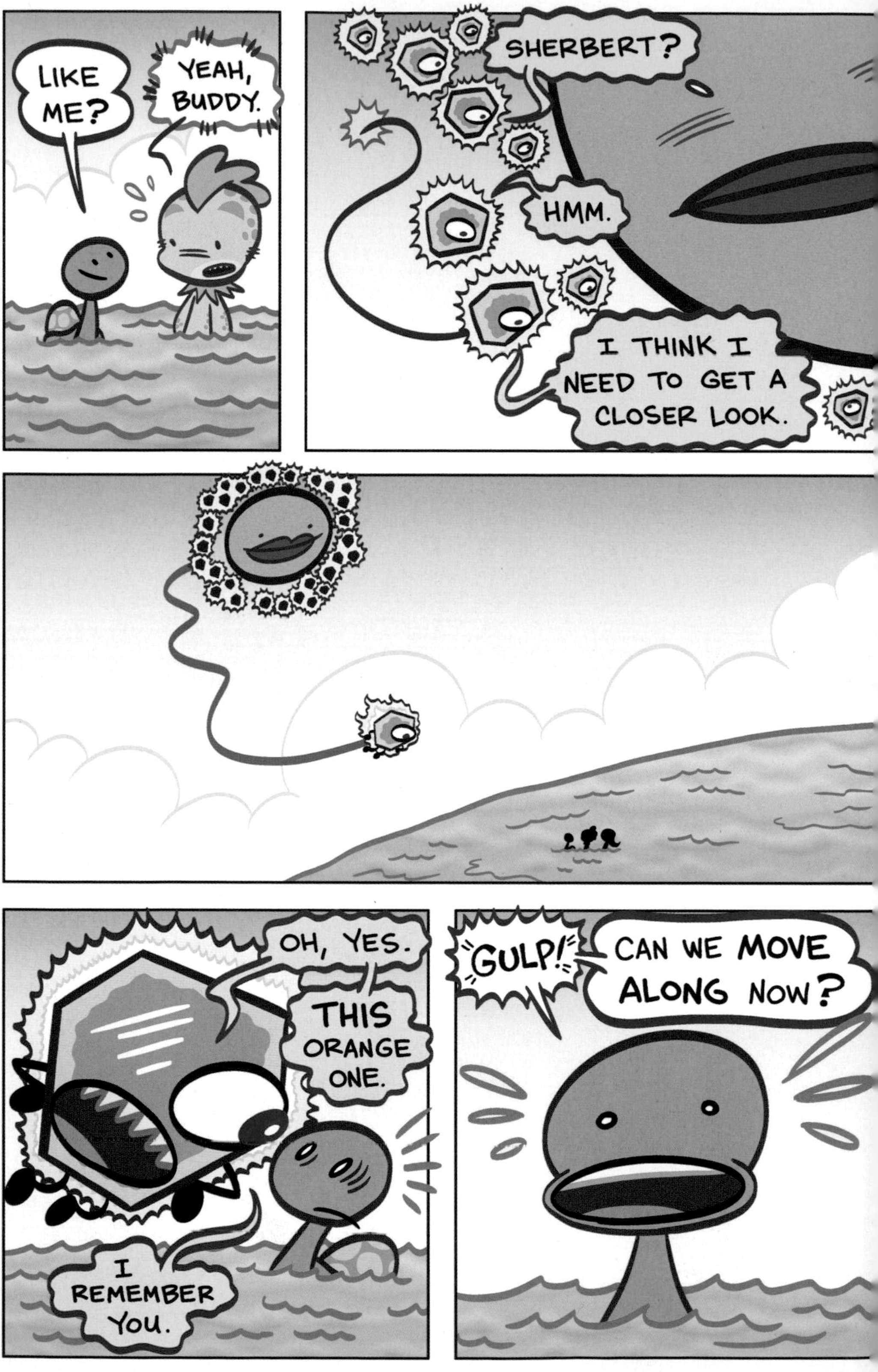
LIKE ME?
YEAH, BUDDY.
SHERBERT?
HMM.
I THINK I NEED TO GET A CLOSER LOOK.
OH, YES.
THIS ORANGE ONE.
I REMEMBER YOU.
GULP!
CAN WE MOVE ALONG NOW?

ELSEWHERE...

I DON'T SEE THE ORANGE ONE.

HE WAS HERE.

ALONG WITH OTHERS.

SOME FRIENDS.

SOME **NOT** FRIENDS.

ENEMIES?

PERHAPS.

THE TEMPERATURE OF THE WATER HAS BEEN ALTERED HERE.

COME.

OUR SEARCH CONTINUES.

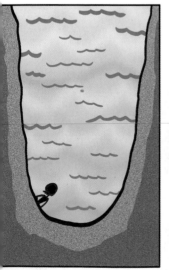

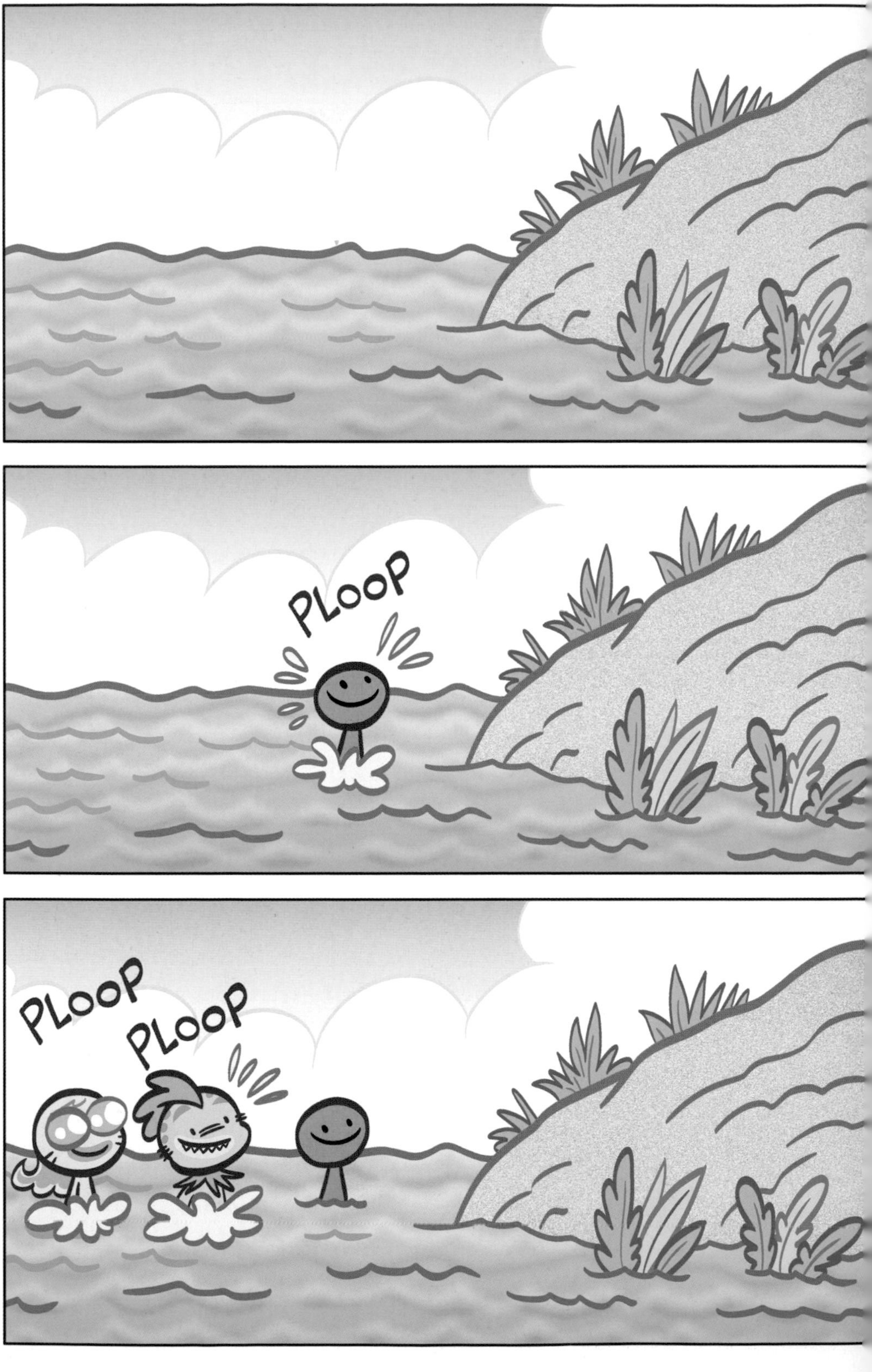
PLOOP
PLOOP
PLOOP

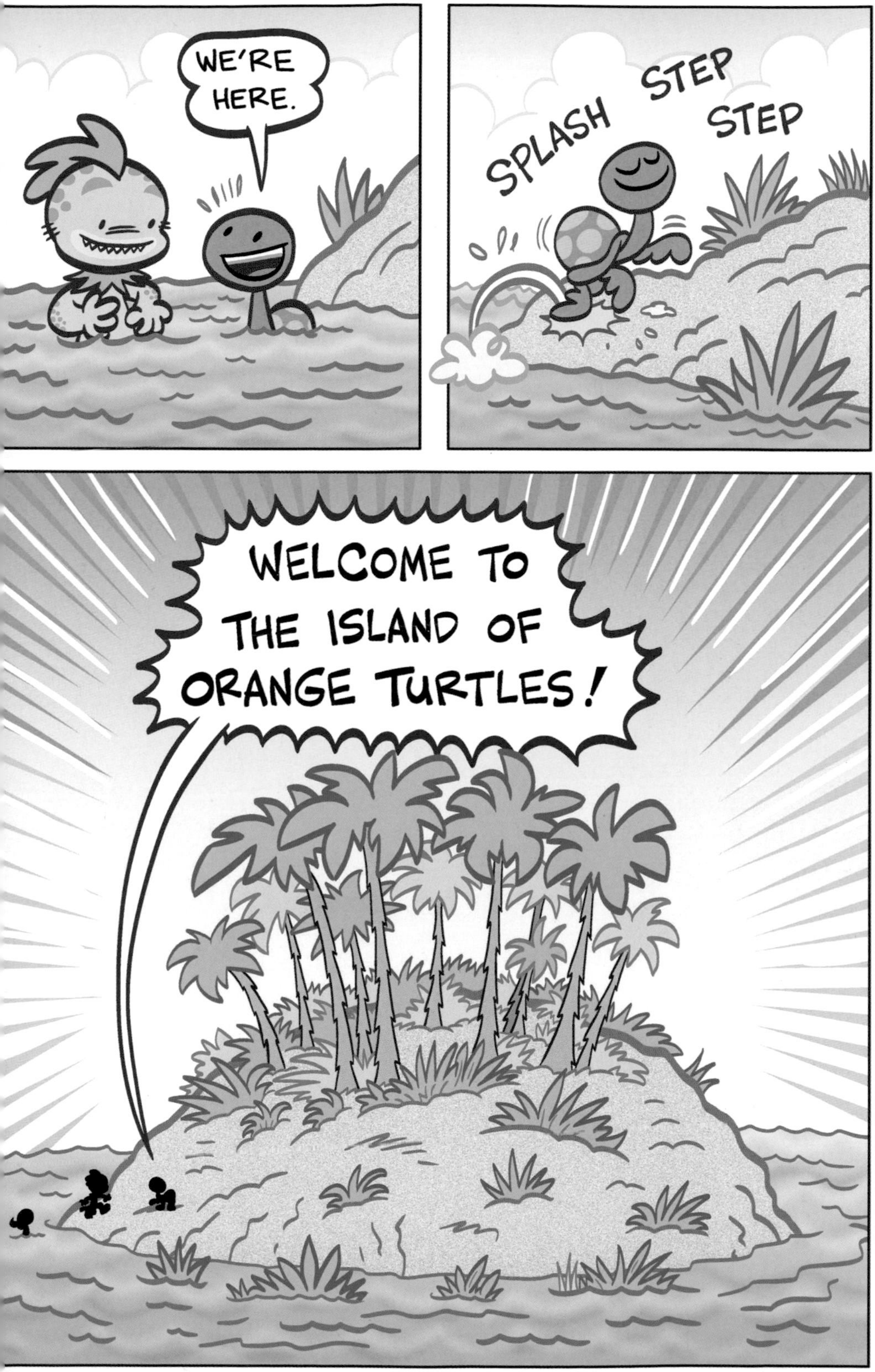
WE'RE HERE.
SPLASH
STEP
STEP
WELCOME TO THE ISLAND OF ORANGE TURTLES!

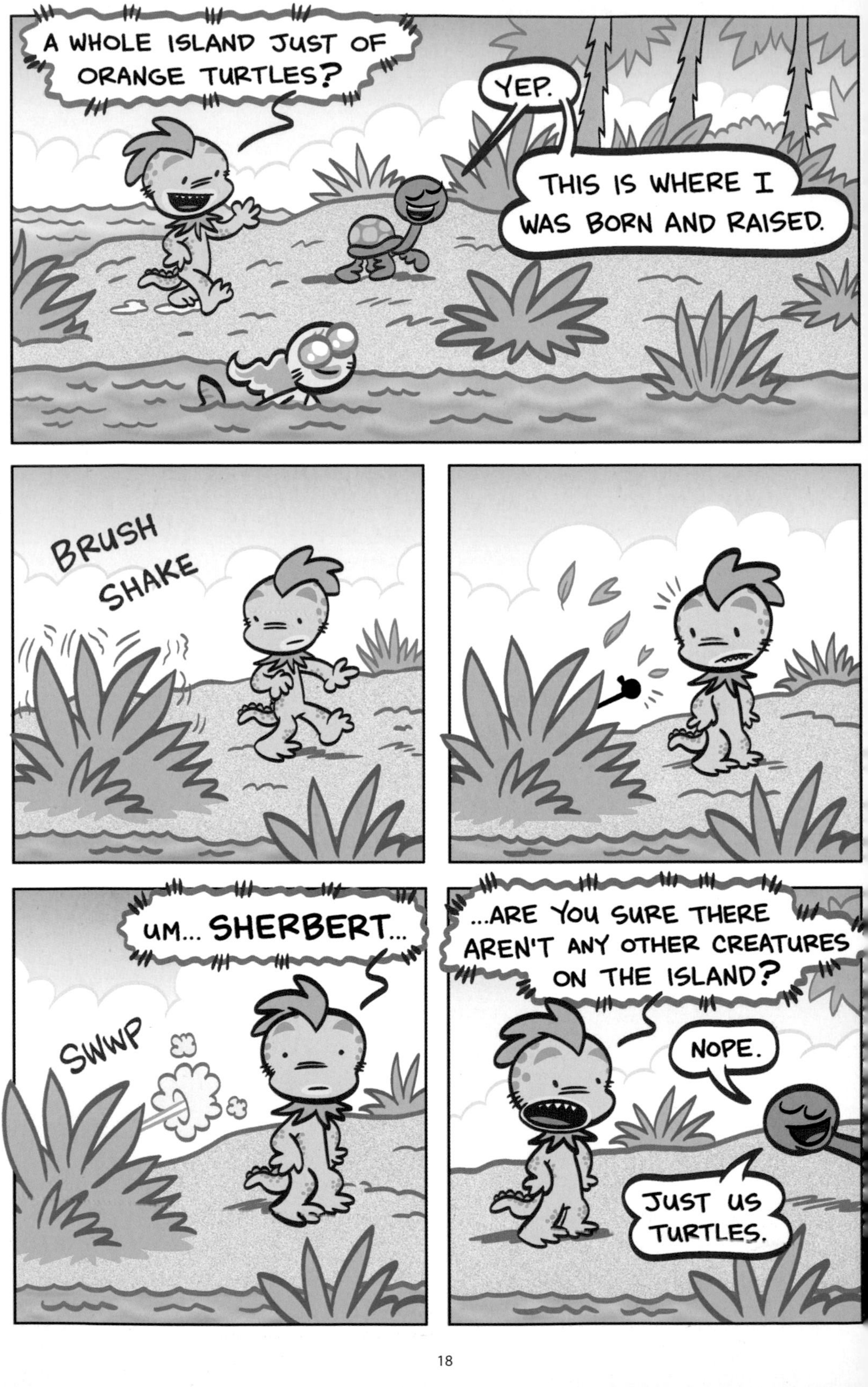
A WHOLE ISLAND JUST OF ORANGE TURTLES?
YEP.
THIS IS WHERE I WAS BORN AND RAISED.
BRUSH
SHAKE
UM... SHERBERT...
SWWP
...ARE YOU SURE THERE AREN'T ANY OTHER CREATURES ON THE ISLAND?
NOPE.
JUST US TURTLES.

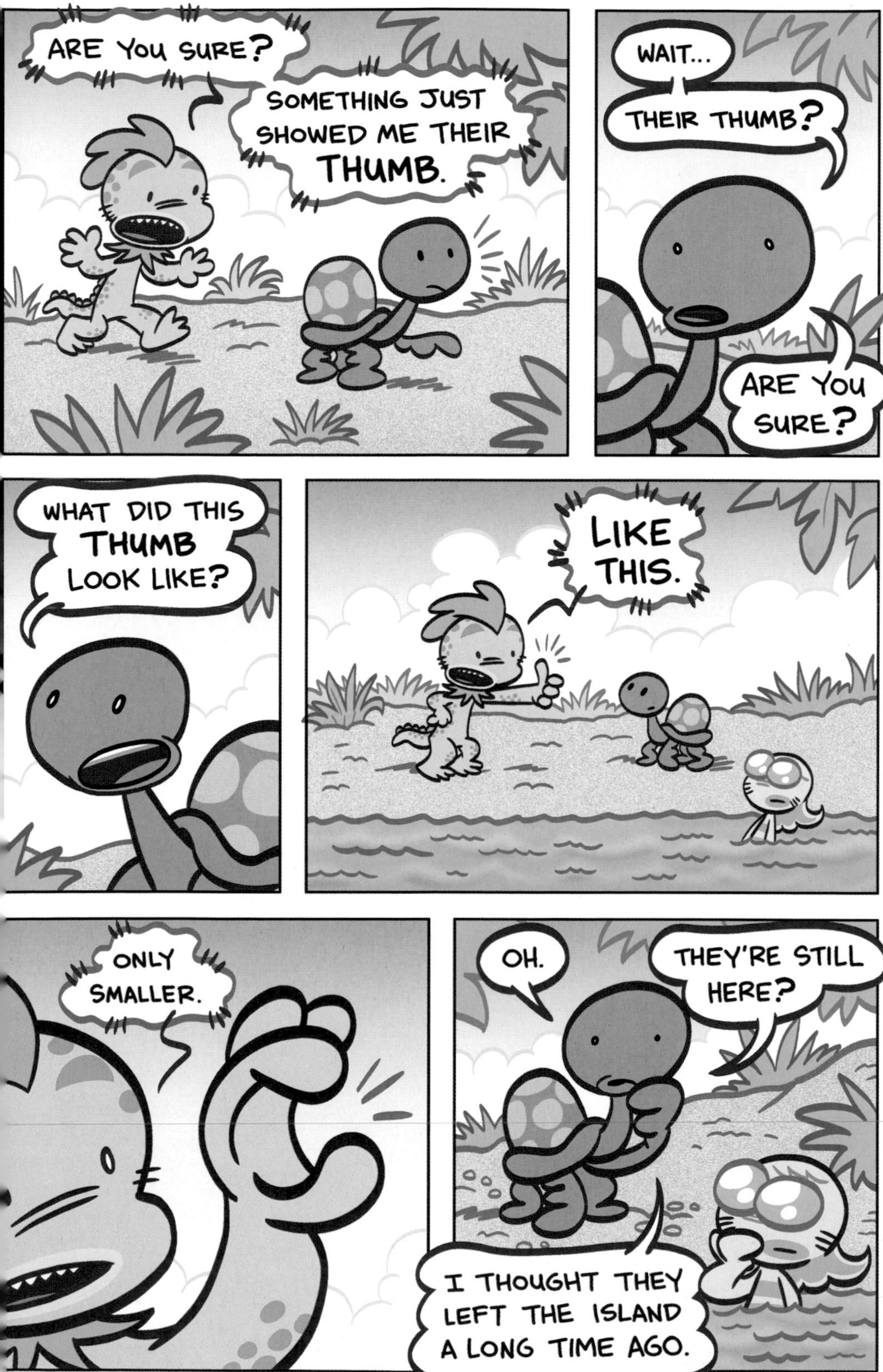
ARE YOU SURE?
SOMETHING JUST SHOWED ME THEIR THUMB.
WAIT...
THEIR THUMB?
ARE YOU SURE?
WHAT DID THIS THUMB LOOK LIKE?
LIKE THIS.
ONLY SMALLER.
OH.
THEY'RE STILL HERE?
I THOUGHT THEY LEFT THE ISLAND A LONG TIME AGO.

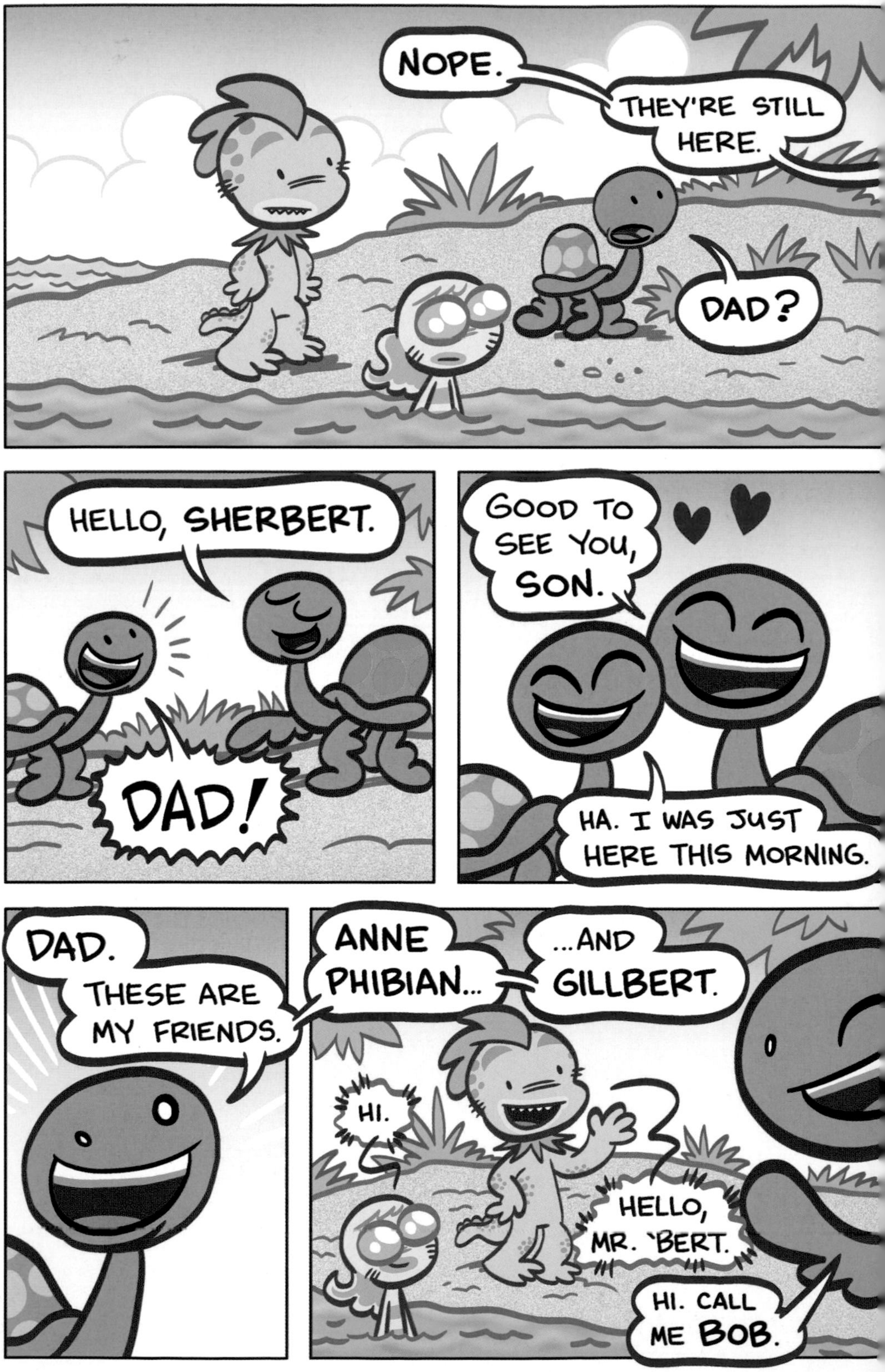
NOPE.
THEY'RE STILL HERE.
DAD?
HELLO, SHERBERT.
DAD!
GOOD TO SEE YOU, SON.
HA. I WAS JUST HERE THIS MORNING.
DAD.
THESE ARE MY FRIENDS.
ANNE PHIBIAN...
...AND GILLBERT.
HI.
HELLO, MR. 'BERT.
HI. CALL ME BOB.

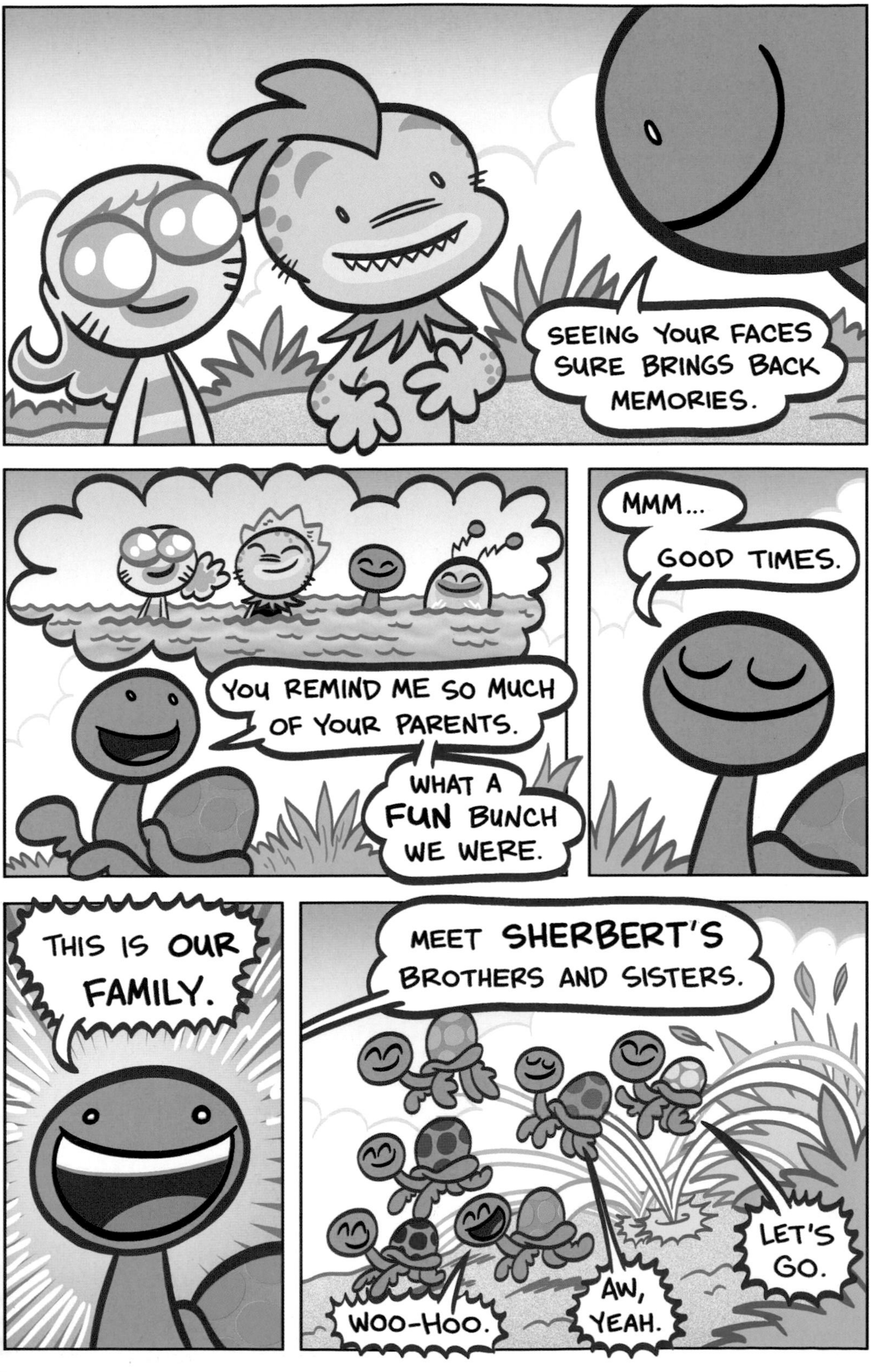
SEEING YOUR FACES SURE BRINGS BACK MEMORIES.
YOU REMIND ME SO MUCH OF YOUR PARENTS.
WHAT A FUN BUNCH WE WERE.
MMM...
GOOD TIMES.
THIS IS OUR FAMILY.
MEET SHERBERT'S BROTHERS AND SISTERS.
WOO-HOO.
AW, YEAH.
LET'S GO.

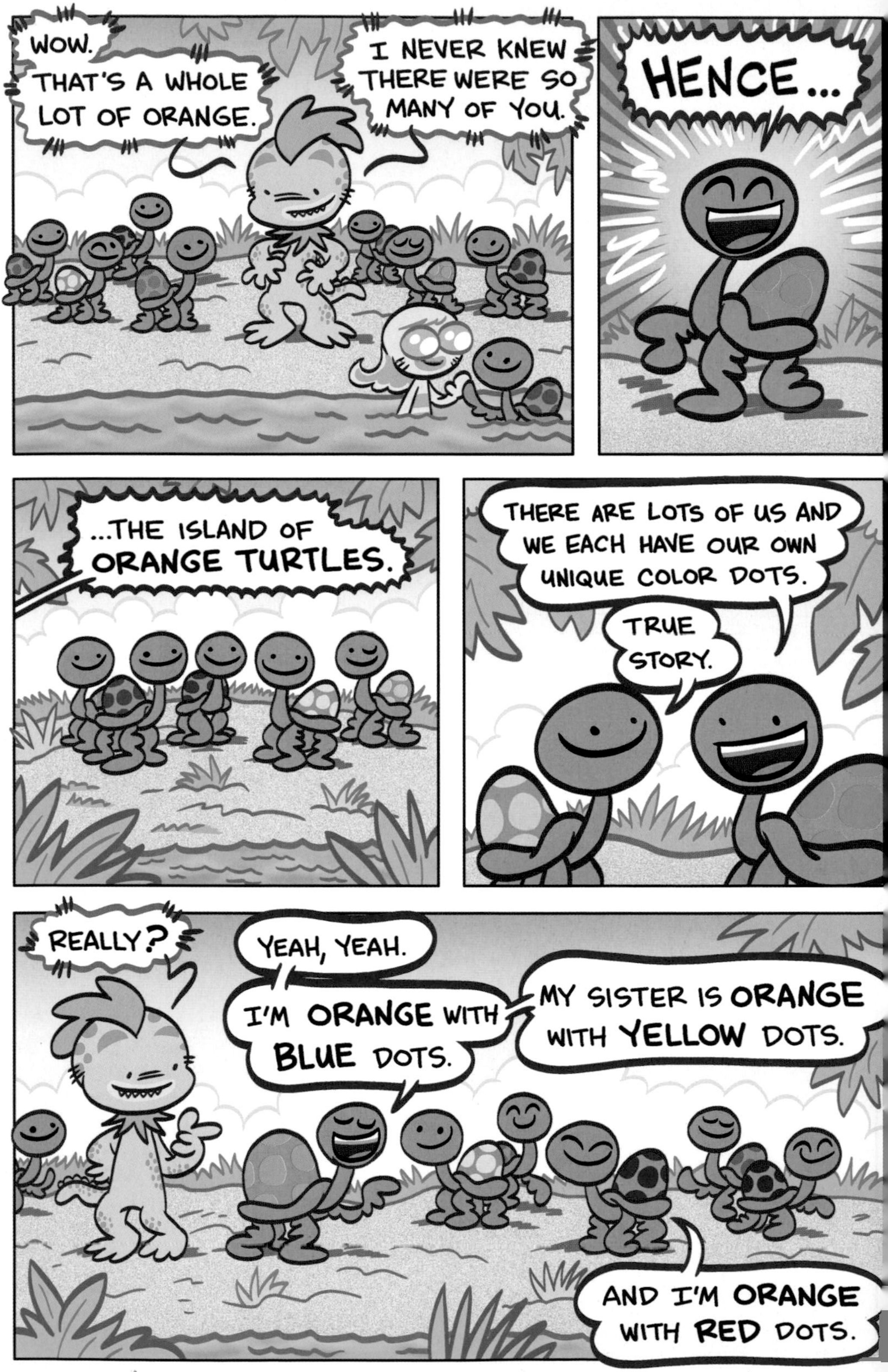
WOW.
THAT'S A WHOLE LOT OF ORANGE.
I NEVER KNEW THERE WERE SO MANY OF YOU.
HENCE...
...THE ISLAND OF ORANGE TURTLES.
THERE ARE LOTS OF US AND WE EACH HAVE OUR OWN UNIQUE COLOR DOTS.
TRUE STORY.
REALLY?
YEAH, YEAH.
I'M ORANGE WITH BLUE DOTS.
MY SISTER IS ORANGE WITH YELLOW DOTS.
AND I'M ORANGE WITH RED DOTS.

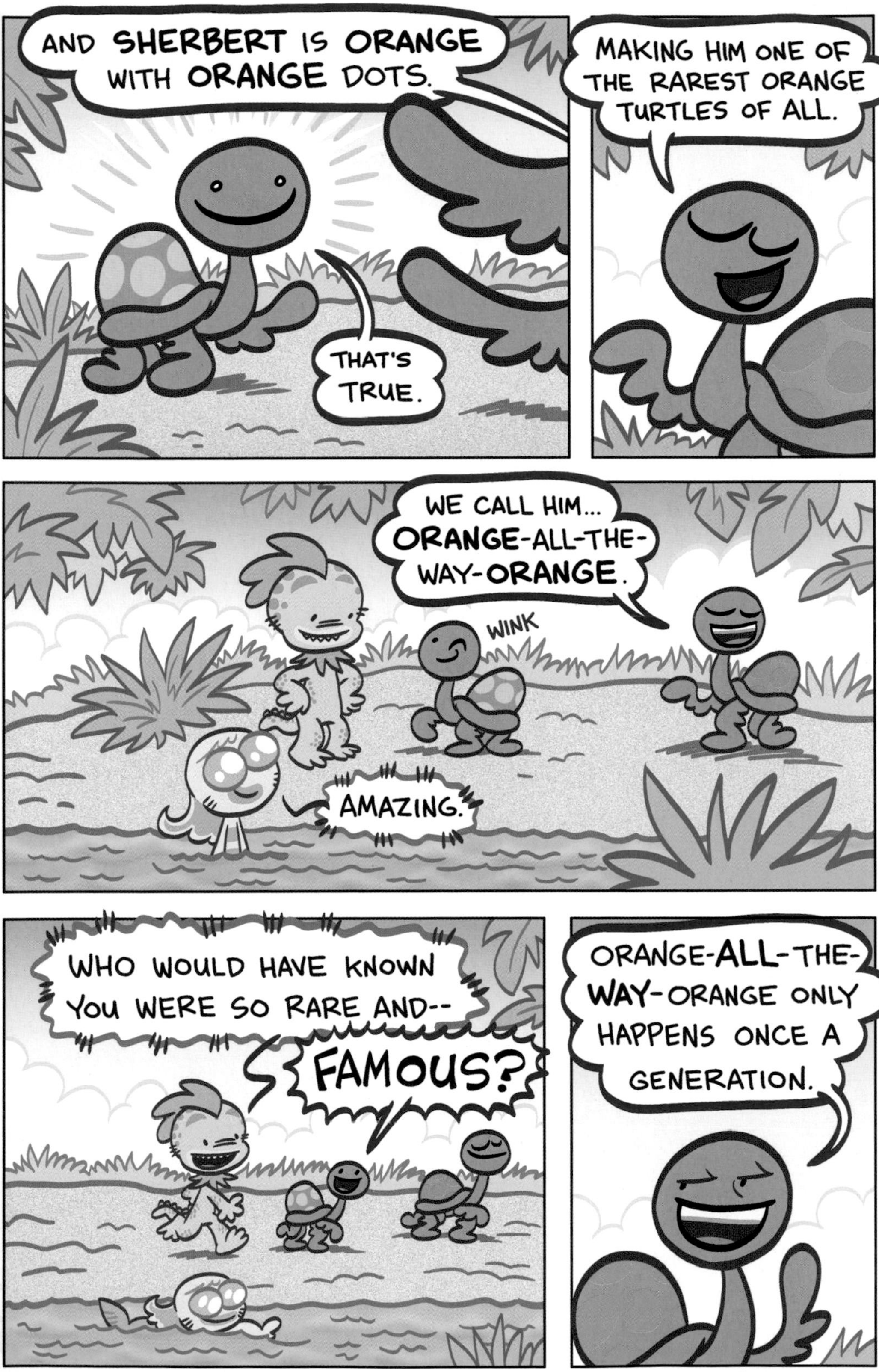
AND SHERBERT IS ORANGE WITH ORANGE DOTS.
THAT'S TRUE.
MAKING HIM ONE OF THE RAREST ORANGE TURTLES OF ALL.
WE CALL HIM... ORANGE-ALL-THE-WAY-ORANGE.
WINK
AMAZING.
WHO WOULD HAVE KNOWN YOU WERE SO RARE AND--
FAMOUS?
ORANGE-ALL-THE-WAY-ORANGE ONLY HAPPENS ONCE A GENERATION.

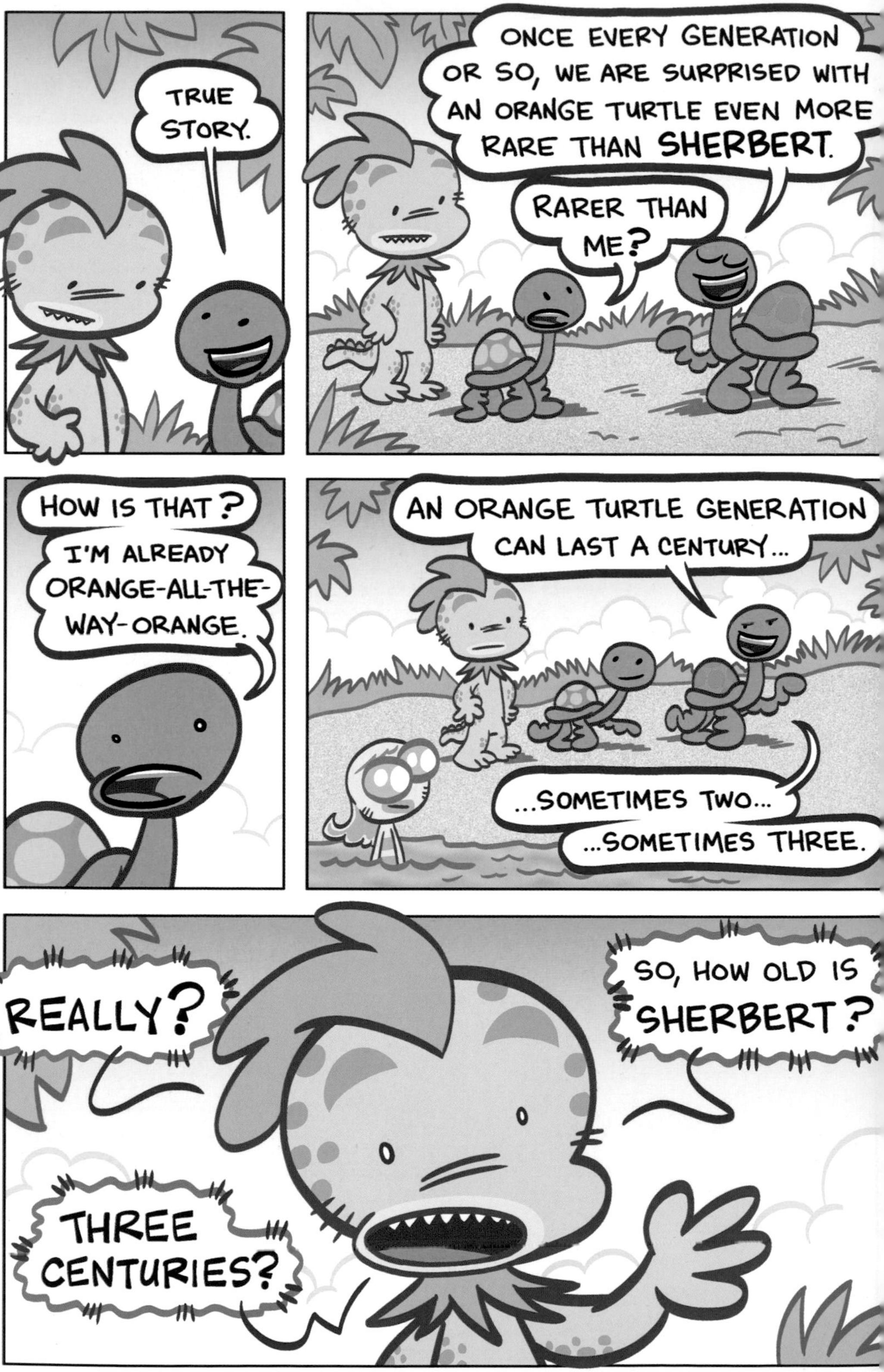
TRUE STORY.
ONCE EVERY GENERATION OR SO, WE ARE SURPRISED WITH AN ORANGE TURTLE EVEN MORE RARE THAN SHERBERT.
RARER THAN ME?
HOW IS THAT?
I'M ALREADY ORANGE-ALL-THE-WAY-ORANGE.
AN ORANGE TURTLE GENERATION CAN LAST A CENTURY...
...SOMETIMES TWO...
...SOMETIMES THREE.
REALLY?
SO, HOW OLD IS SHERBERT?
THREE CENTURIES?

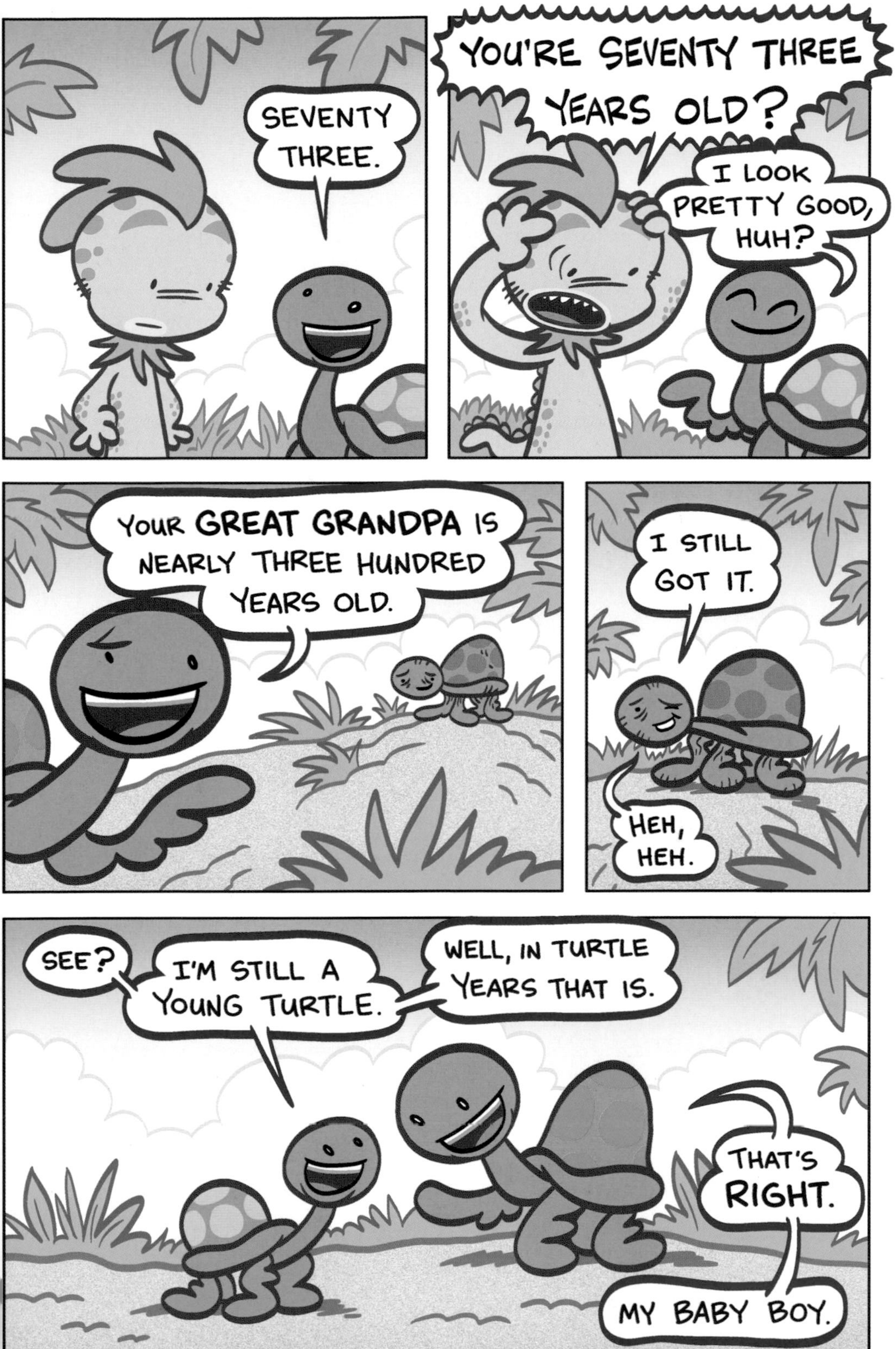
SEVENTY THREE.
YOU'RE SEVENTY THREE YEARS OLD?
I LOOK PRETTY GOOD, HUH?
YOUR GREAT GRANDPA IS NEARLY THREE HUNDRED YEARS OLD.
I STILL GOT IT.
HEH, HEH.
SEE?
I'M STILL A YOUNG TURTLE.
WELL, IN TURTLE YEARS THAT IS.
THAT'S RIGHT.
MY BABY BOY.

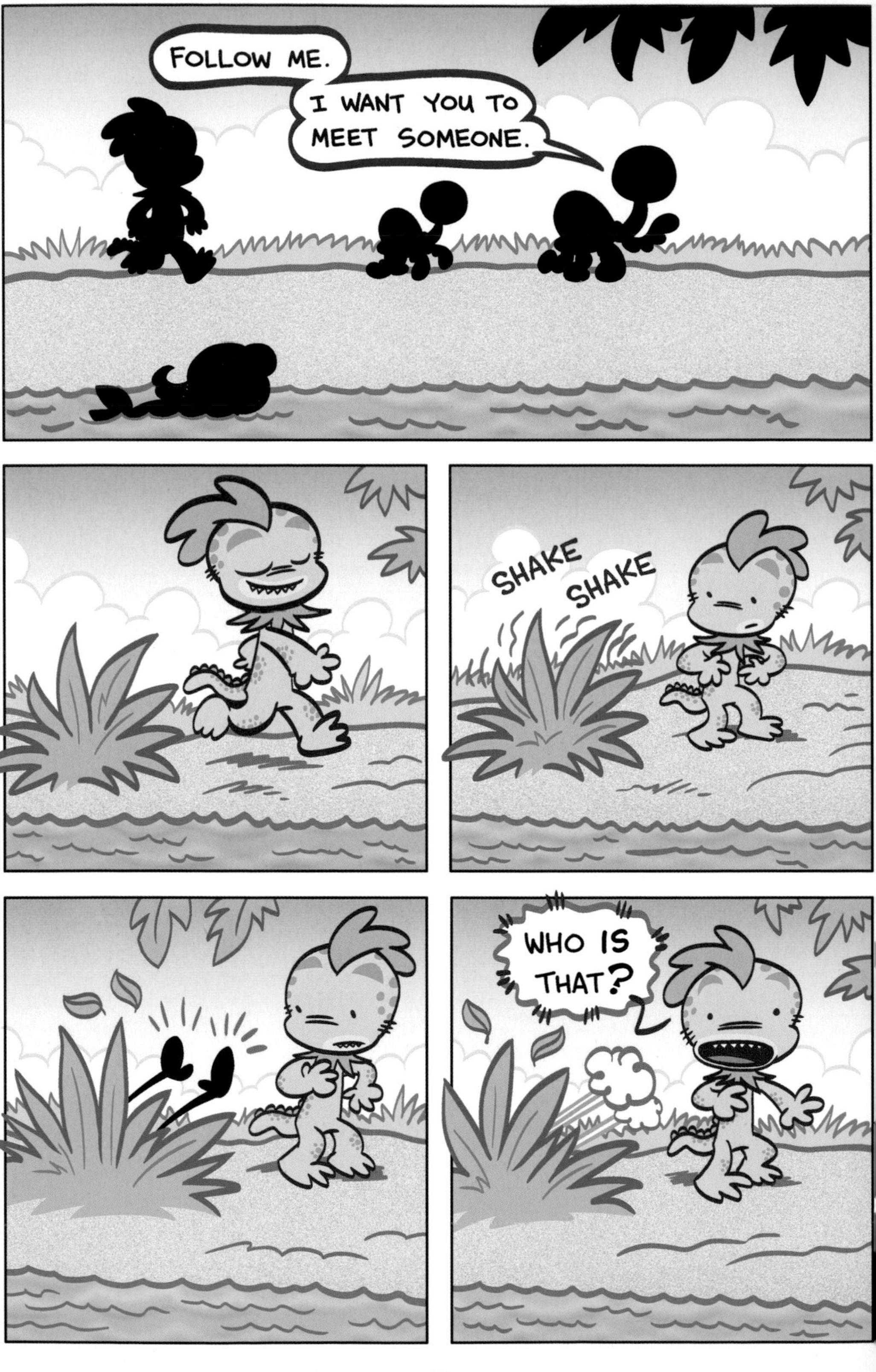
FOLLOW ME.
I WANT YOU TO MEET SOMEONE.
SHAKE
SHAKE
WHO IS THAT?

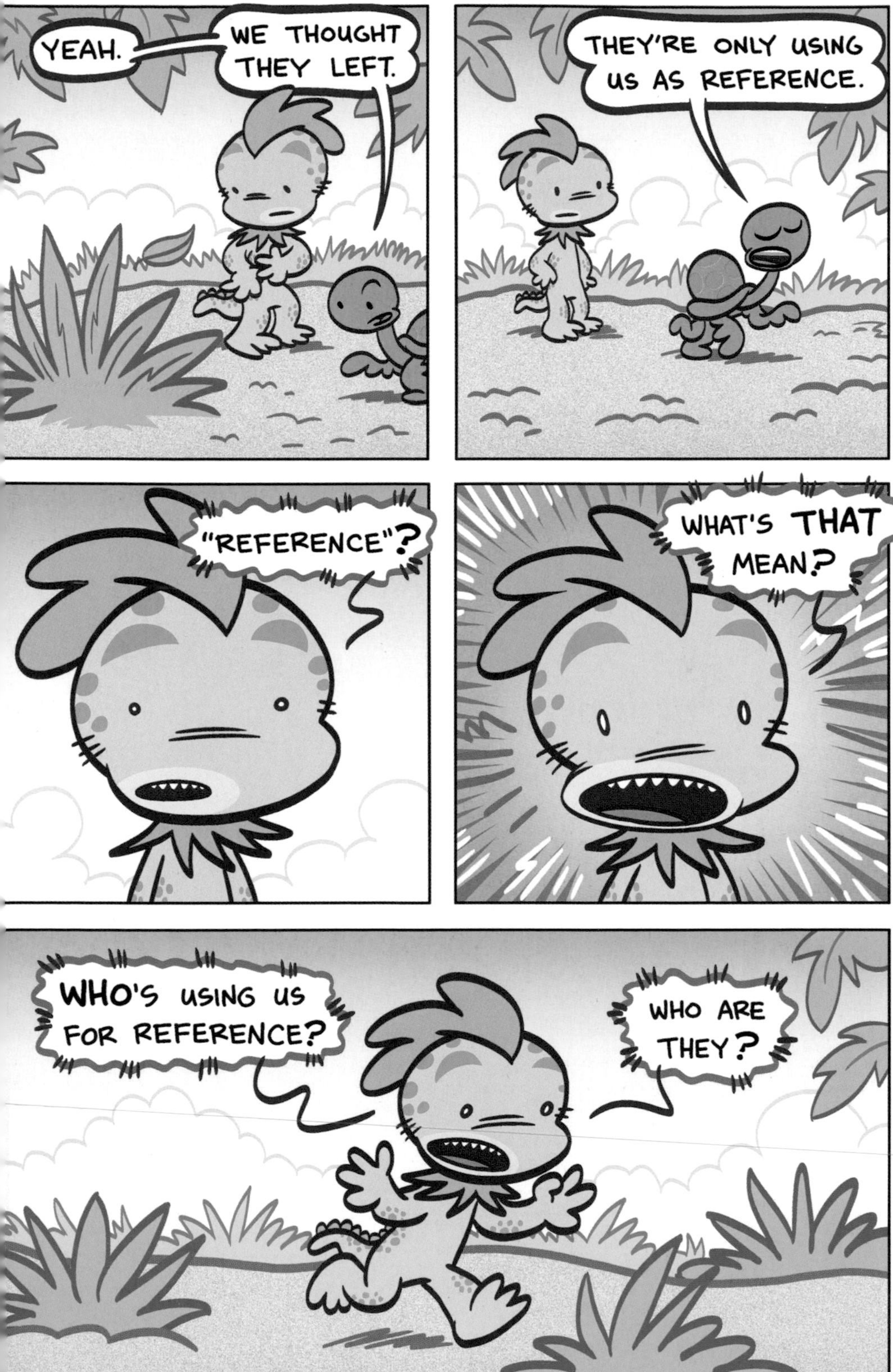
YEAH.
WE THOUGHT THEY LEFT.
THEY'RE ONLY USING US AS REFERENCE.
"REFERENCE"?
WHAT'S THAT MEAN?
WHO'S USING US FOR REFERENCE?
WHO ARE THEY?

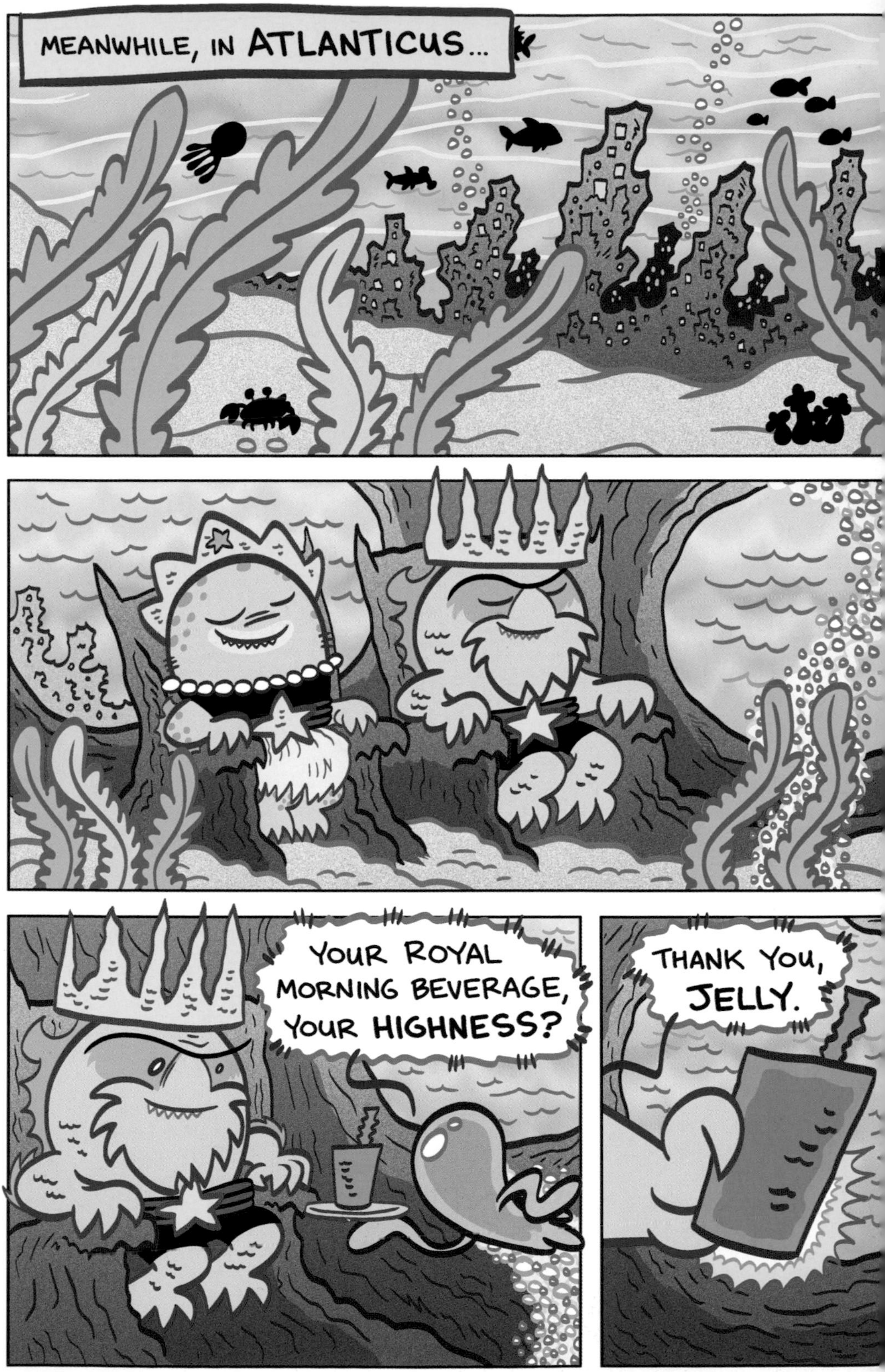
MEANWHILE, IN ATLANTICUS...
YOUR ROYAL MORNING BEVERAGE, YOUR HIGHNESS?
THANK YOU, JELLY.

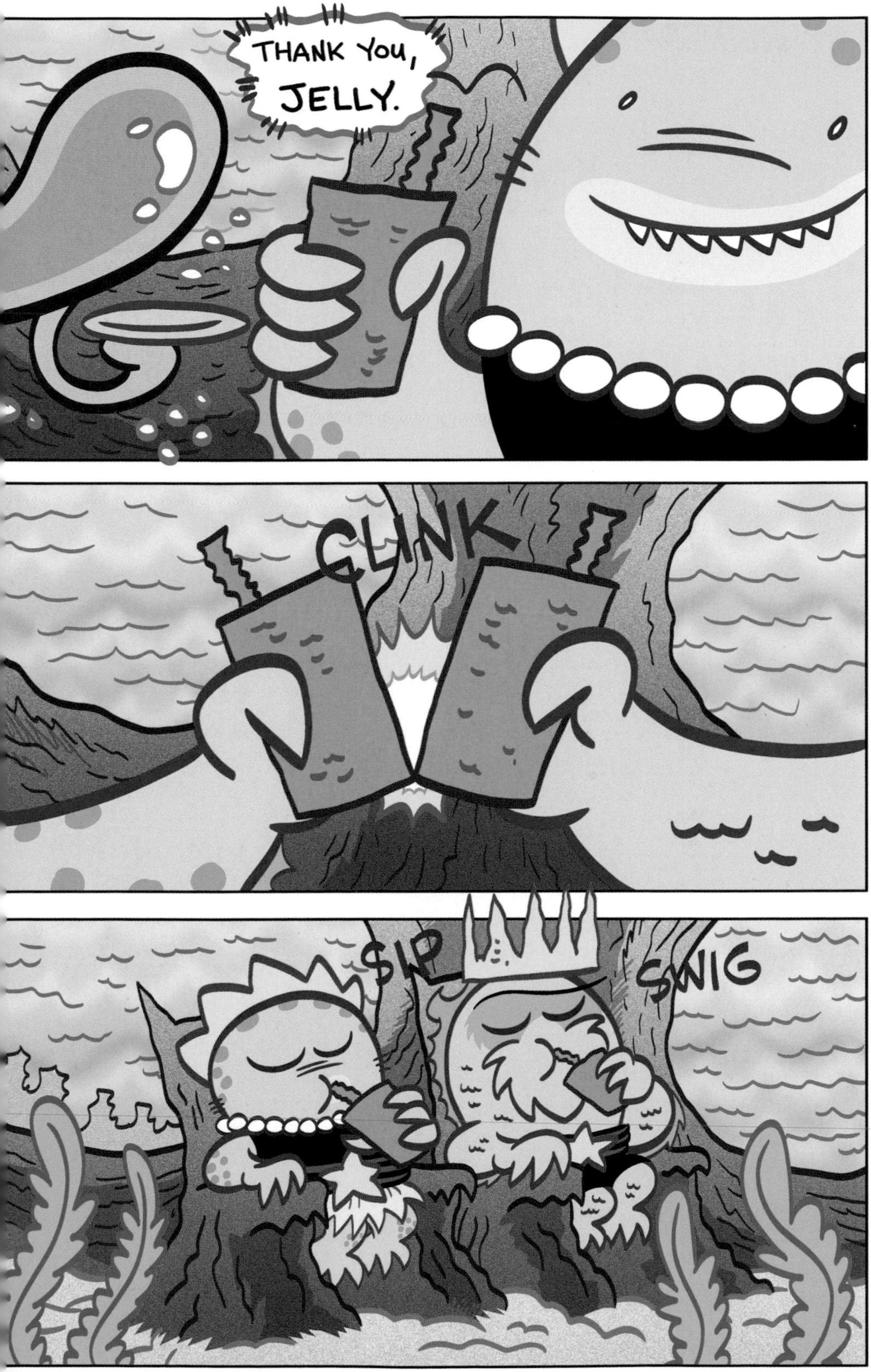
THANK YOU, JELLY.
CLINK
SIP
SWIG

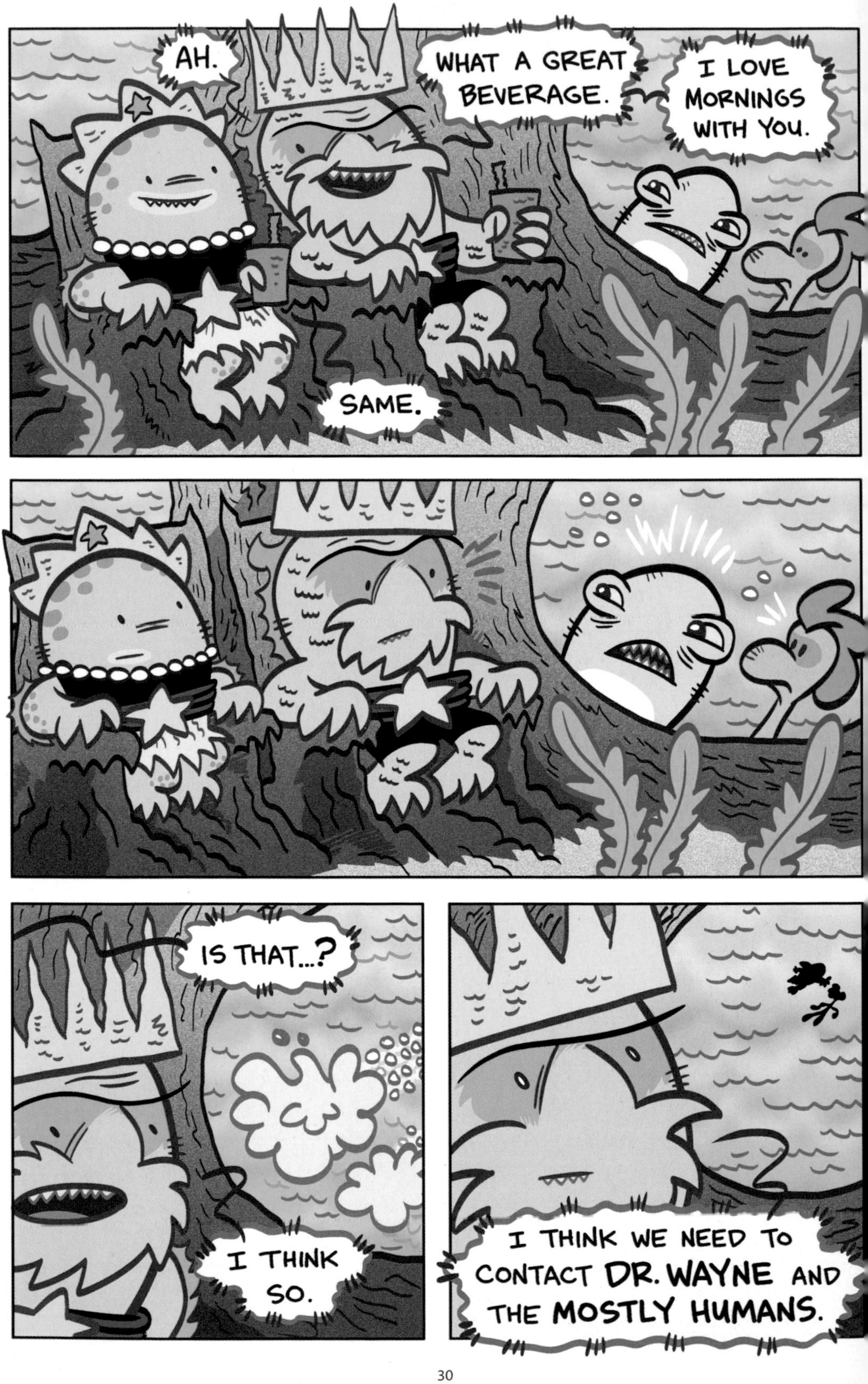
AH.
WHAT A GREAT BEVERAGE.
I LOVE MORNINGS WITH YOU.
SAME.
IS THAT...?
I THINK SO.
I THINK WE NEED TO CONTACT DR. WAYNE AND THE MOSTLY HUMANS.

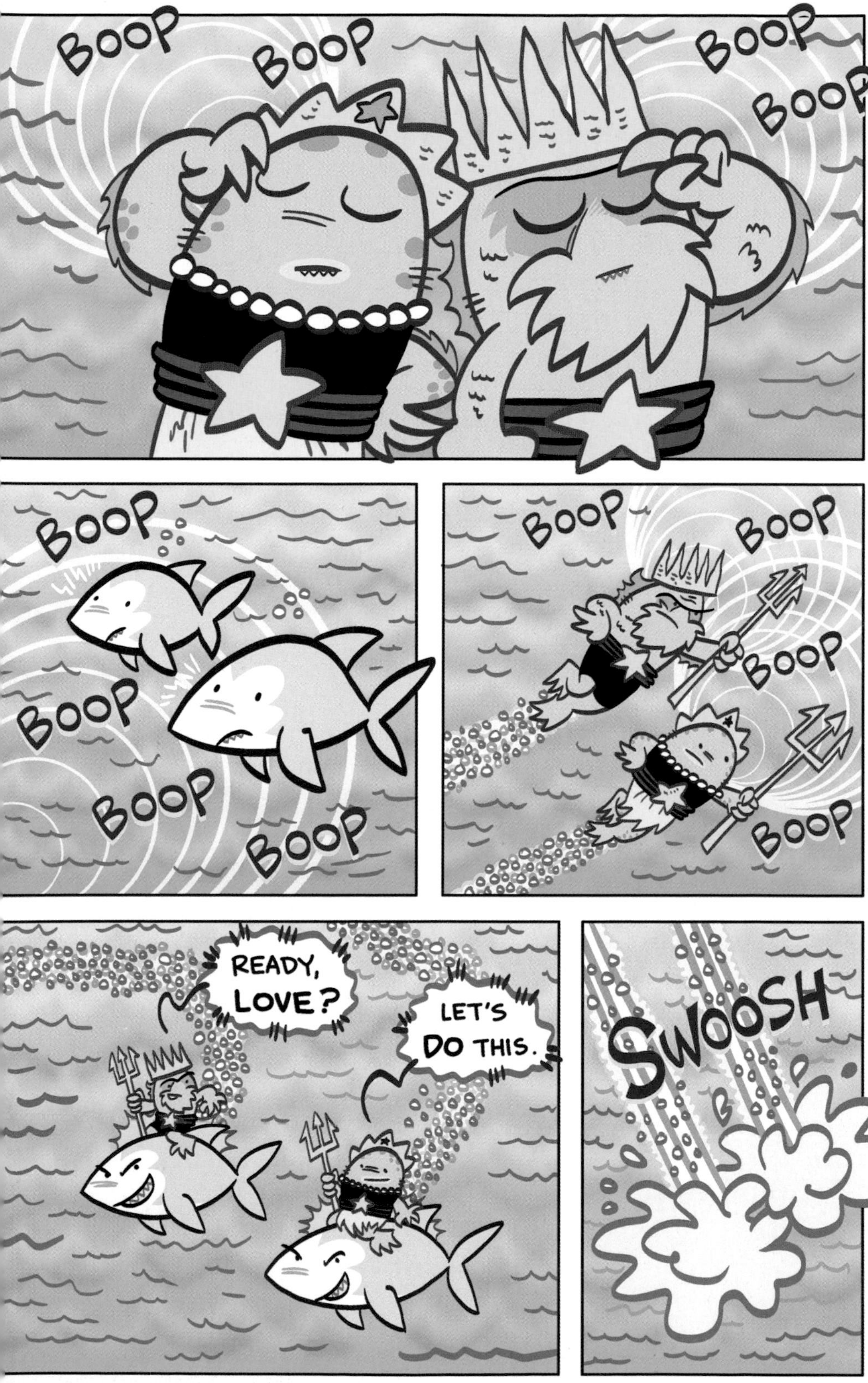
BOOP
BOOP
BOOP
BOOP
BOOP
BOOP
BOOP
BOOP
BOOP
BOOP
BOOP
BOOP
READY, LOVE?
LET'S DO THIS.
SWOOSH

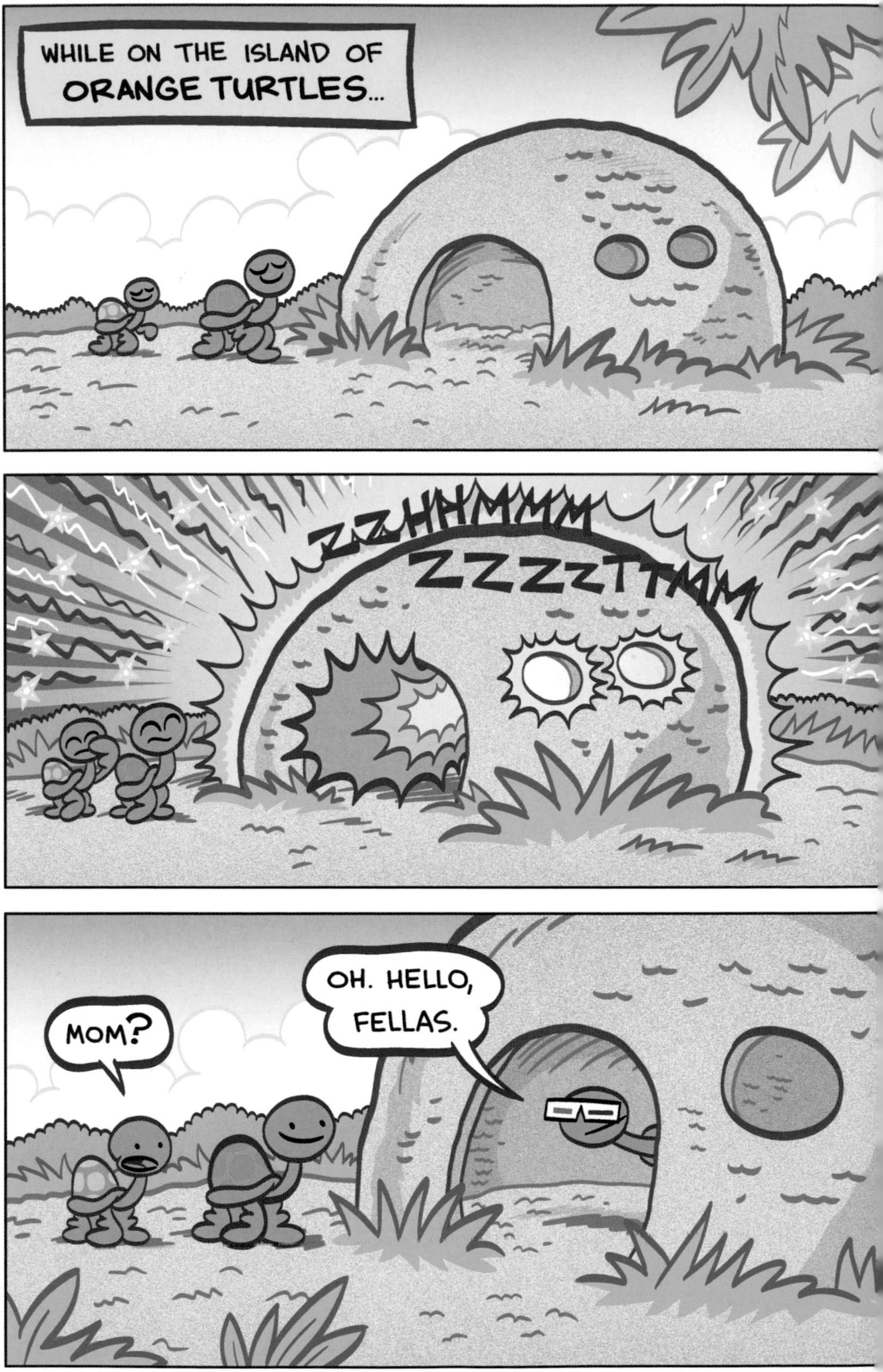
WHILE ON THE ISLAND OF ORANGE TURTLES...
ZZHHMMMM
ZZZzTTMM
MOM?
OH. HELLO, FELLAS.

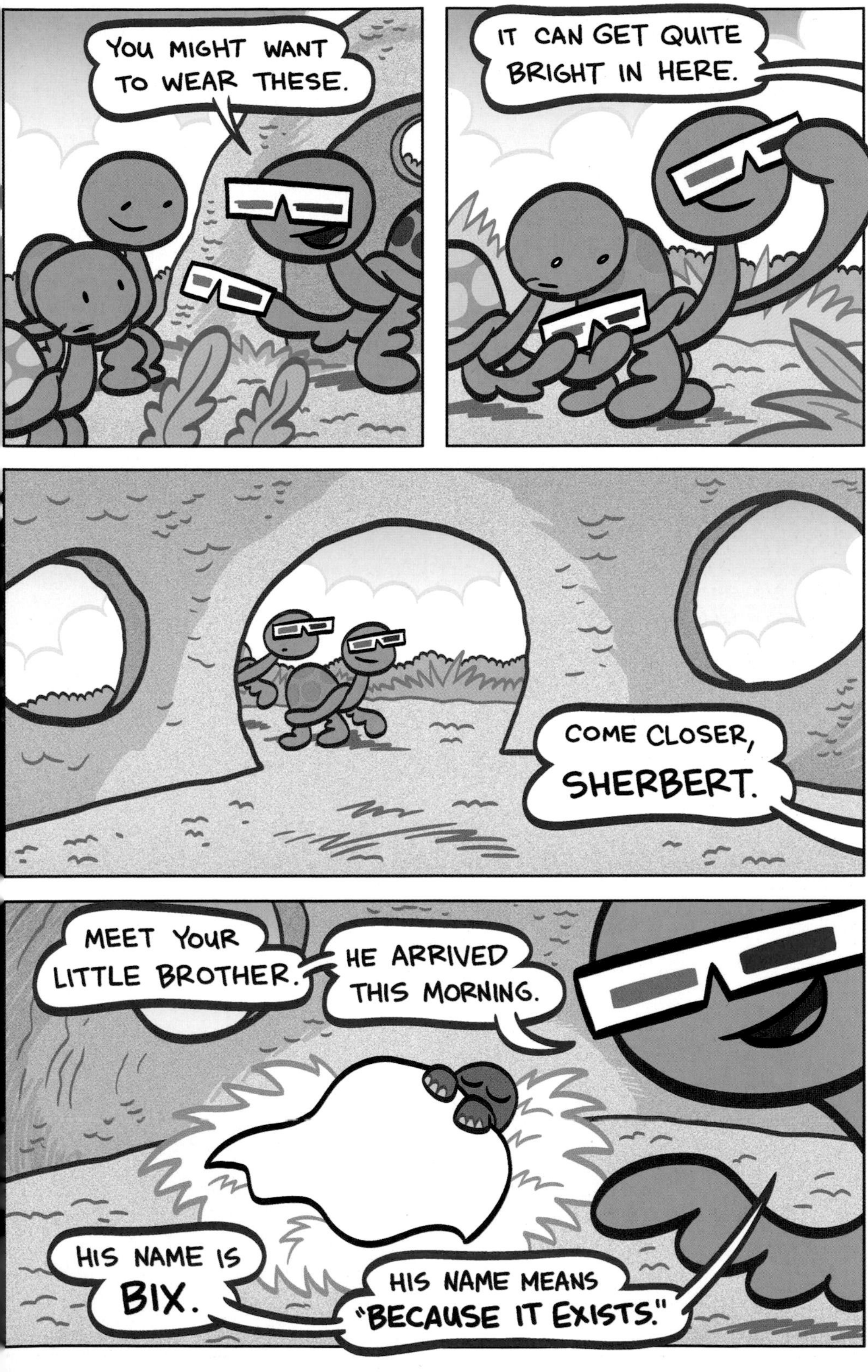
YOU MIGHT WANT TO WEAR THESE.
IT CAN GET QUITE BRIGHT IN HERE.
COME CLOSER, SHERBERT.
MEET YOUR LITTLE BROTHER.
HE ARRIVED THIS MORNING.
HIS NAME IS BIX.
HIS NAME MEANS "BECAUSE IT EXISTS."

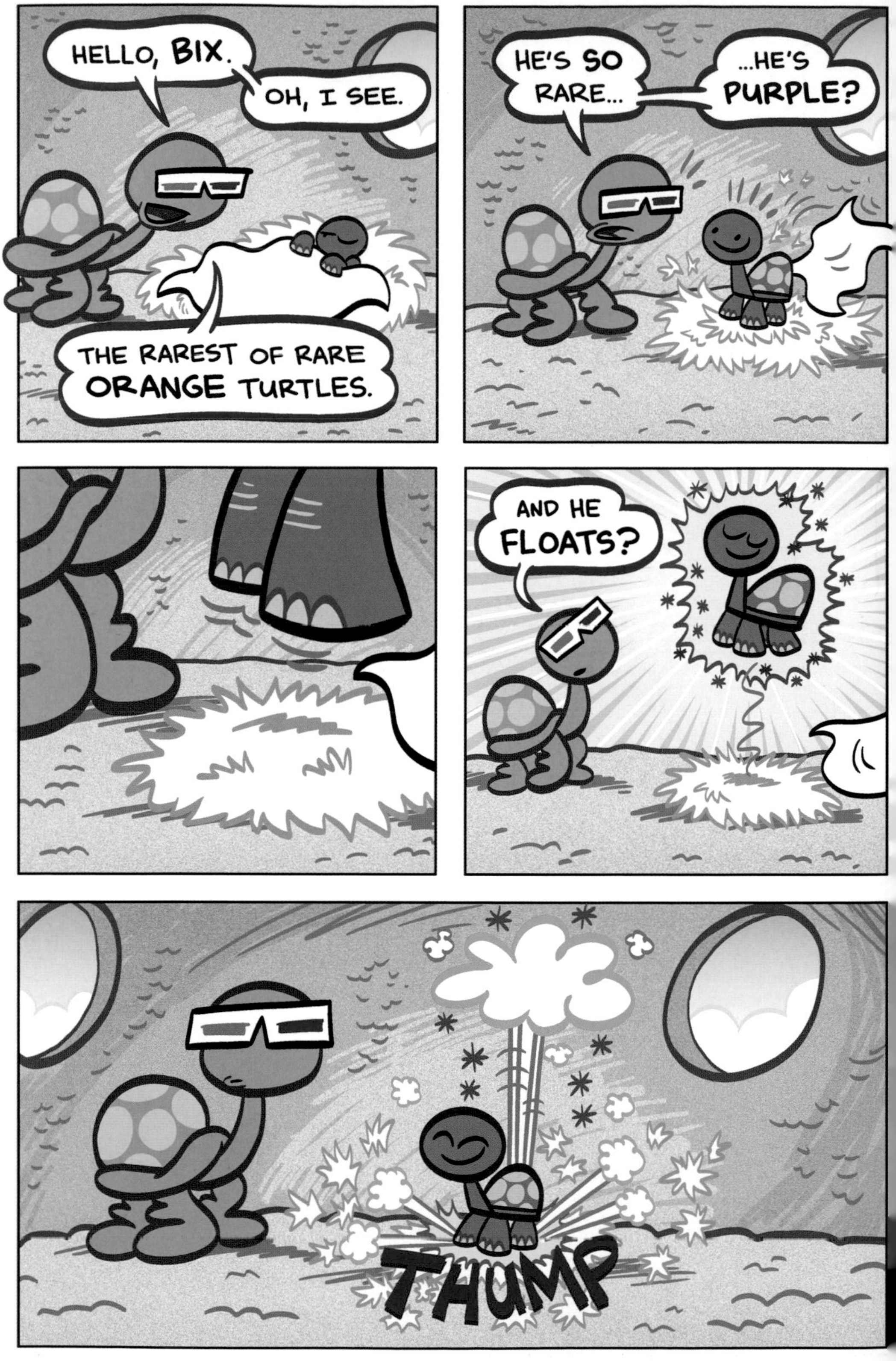
HELLO, BIX.
OH, I SEE.
THE RAREST OF RARE ORANGE TURTLES.
HE'S SO RARE...
...HE'S PURPLE?
AND HE FLOATS?
THUMP

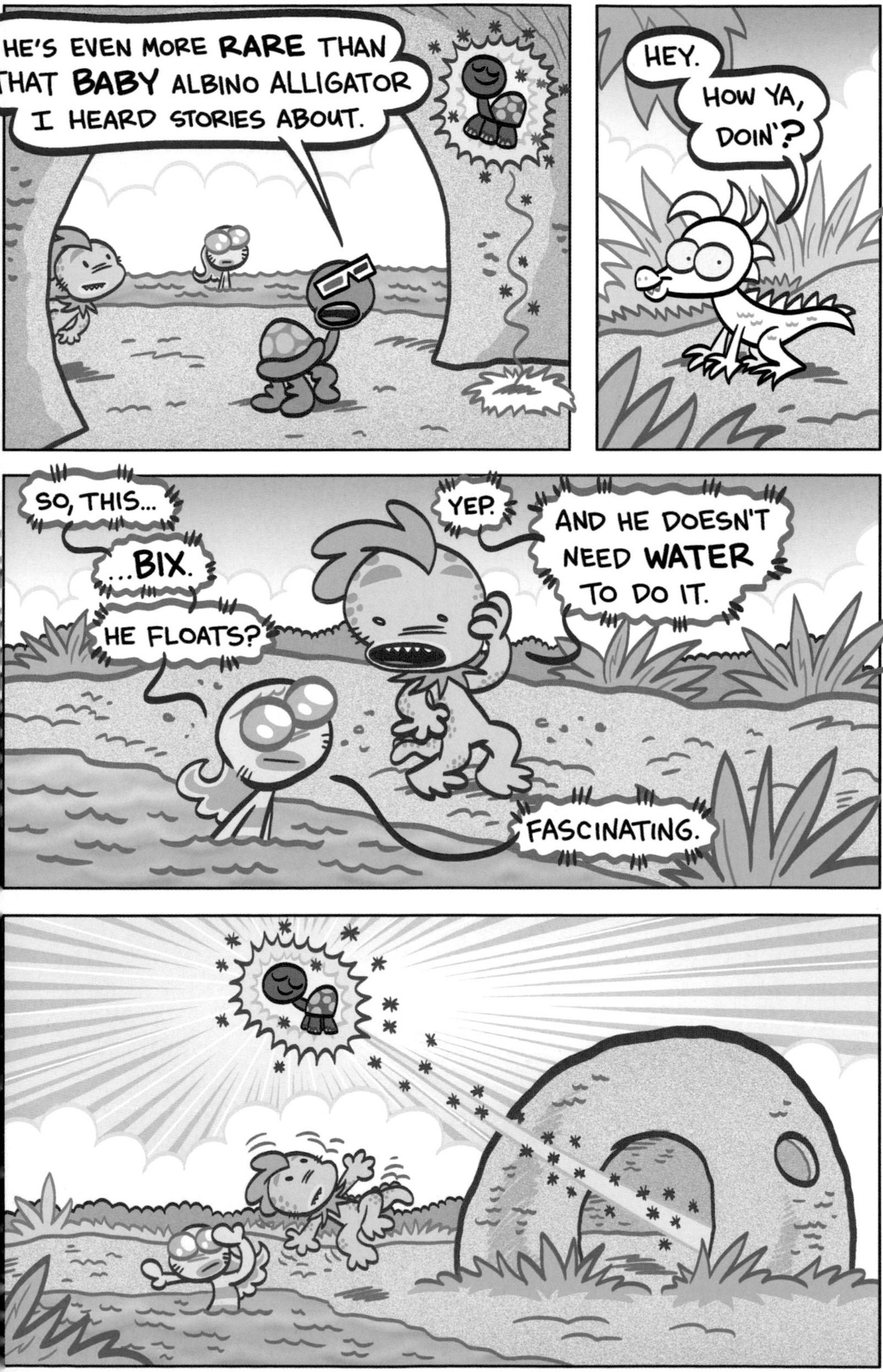
HE'S EVEN MORE RARE THAN THAT BABY ALBINO ALLIGATOR I HEARD STORIES ABOUT.
HEY.
HOW YA, DOIN'?
SO, THIS...
...BIX.
HE FLOATS?
YEP.
AND HE DOESN'T NEED WATER TO DO IT.
FASCINATING.

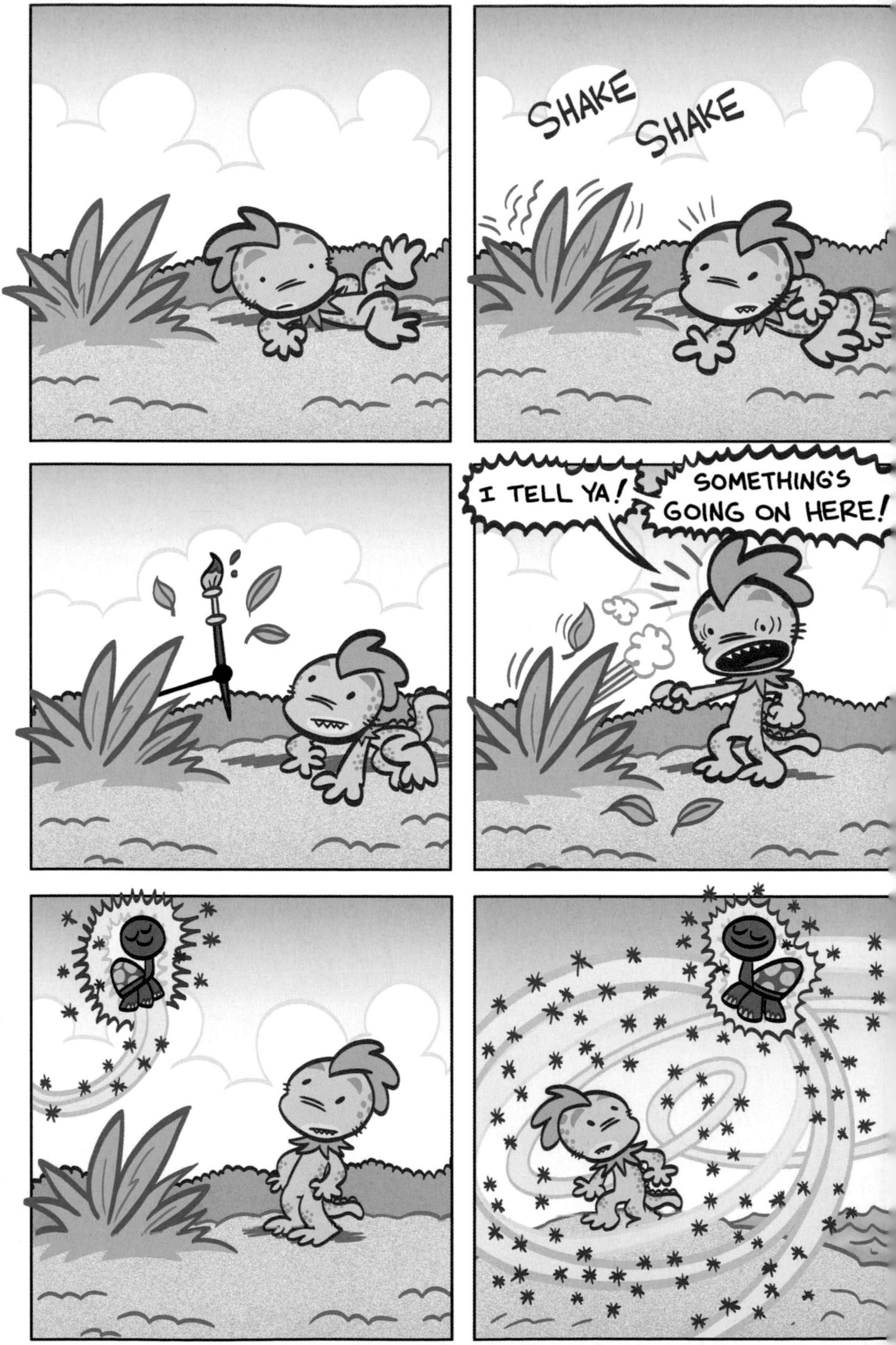
SHAKE
SHAKE
I TELL YA!
SOMETHING'S GOING ON HERE!

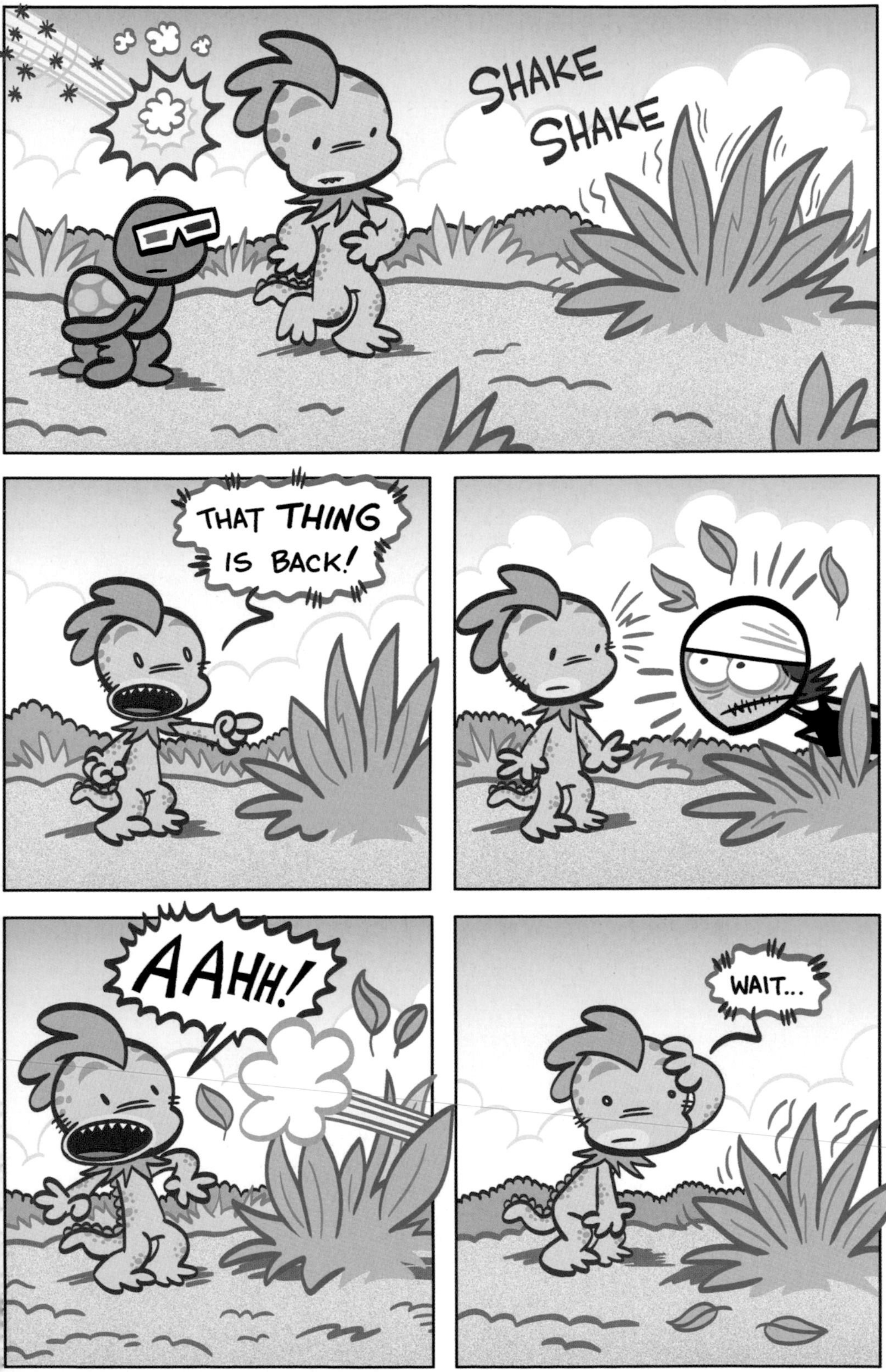
SHAKE
SHAKE
THAT THING IS BACK!
AAHH!
WAIT...

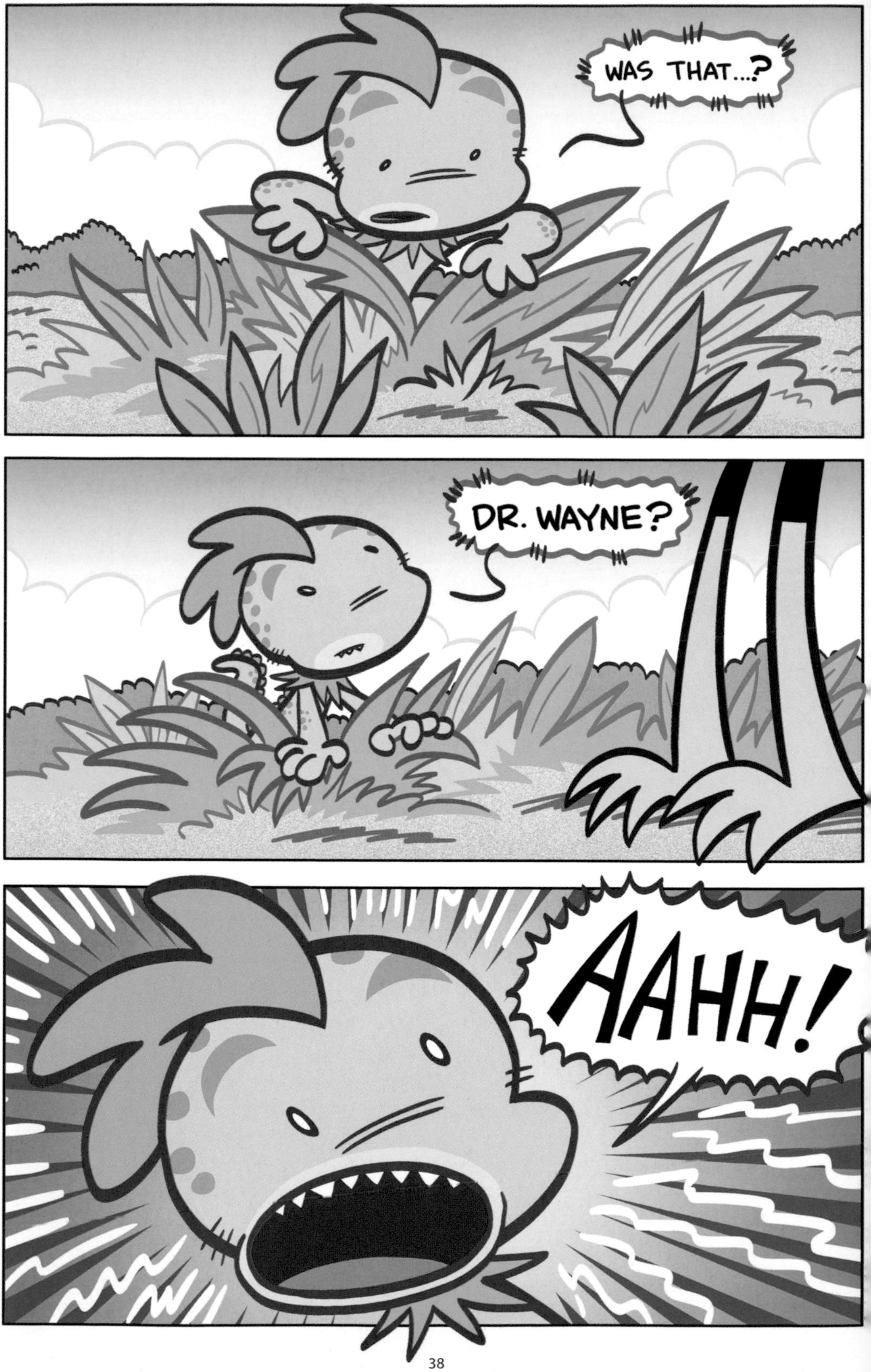
WAS THAT...?
DR. WAYNE?
AAHH!

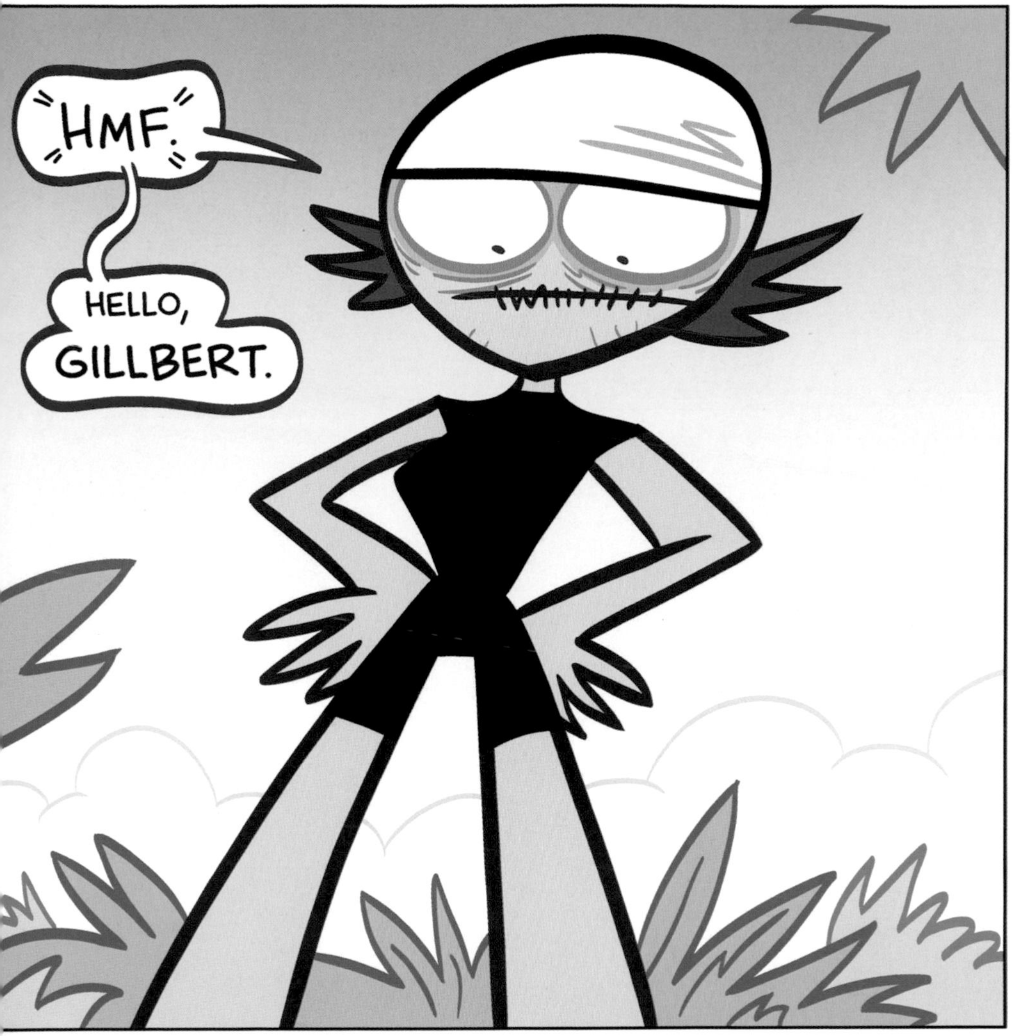
HMF.
HELLO, GILLBERT.

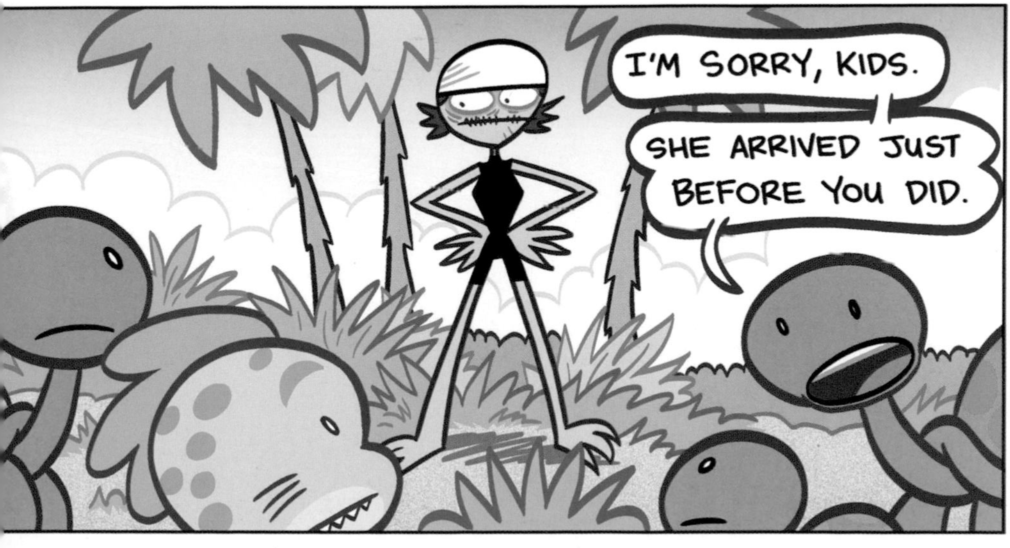
I'M SORRY, KIDS.
SHE ARRIVED JUST BEFORE YOU DID.

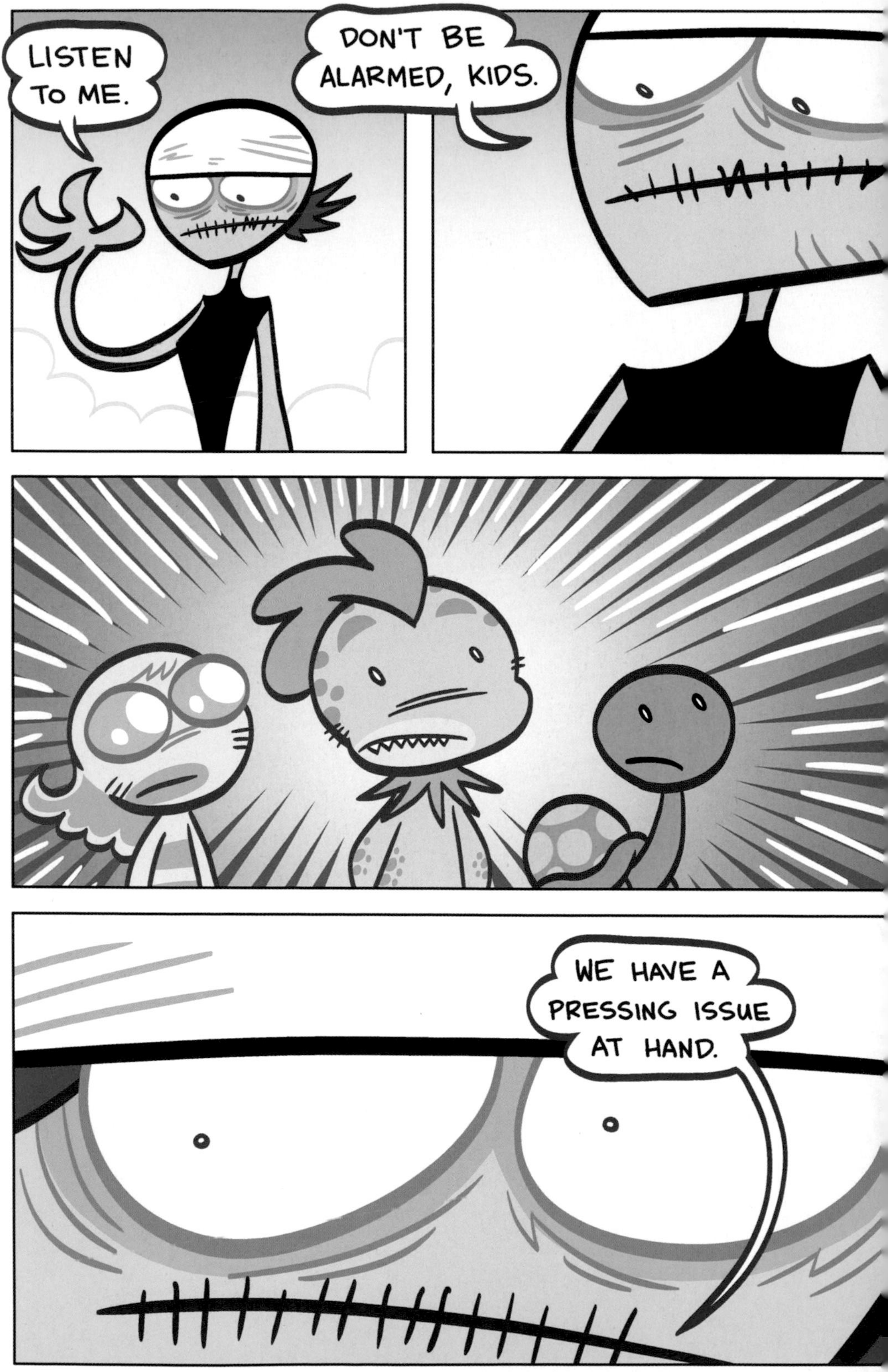
LISTEN TO ME.
DON'T BE ALARMED, KIDS.
WE HAVE A PRESSING ISSUE AT HAND.

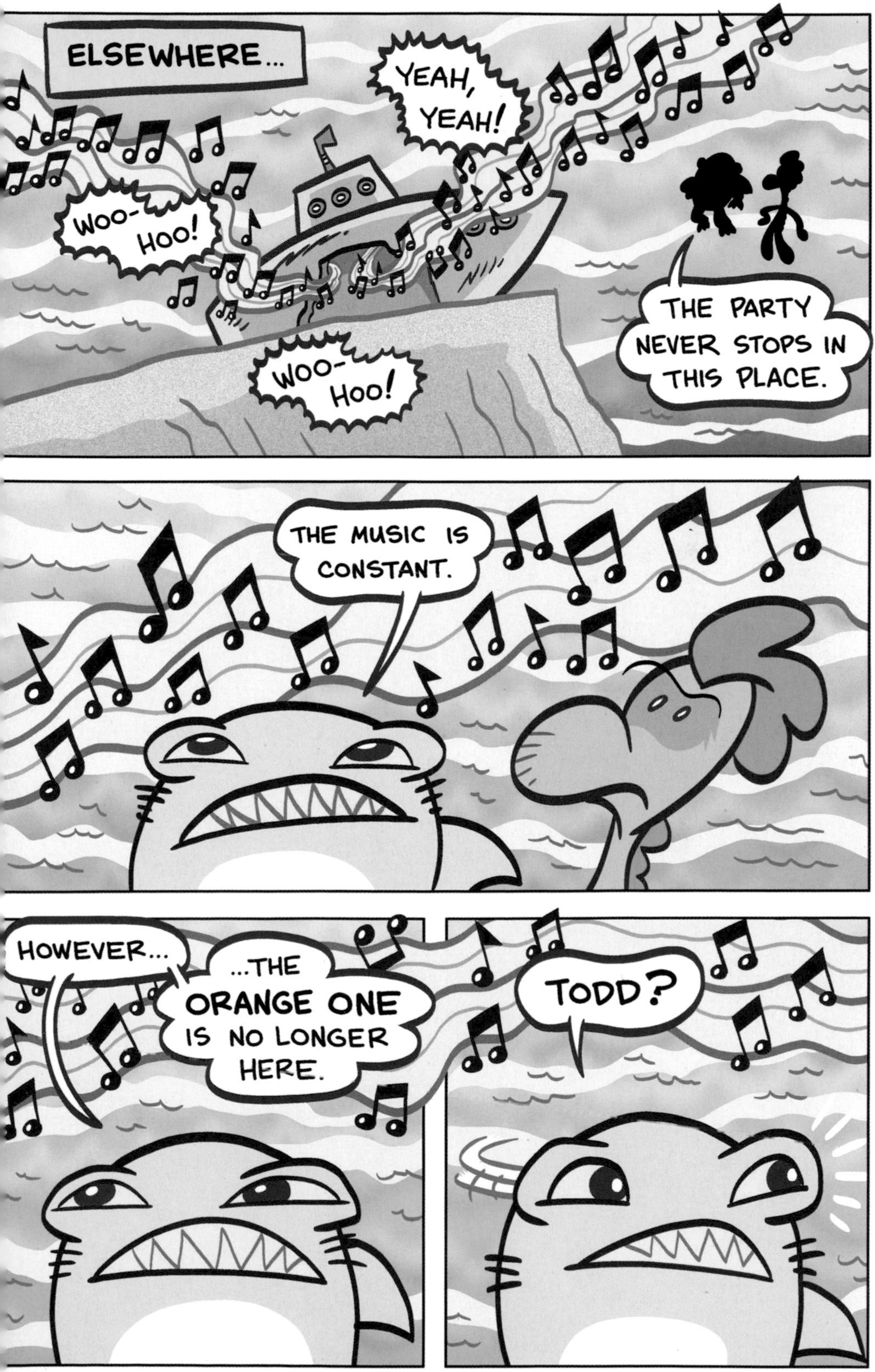
ELSEWHERE...
YEAH, YEAH!
WOO-HOO!
WOO-HOO!
THE PARTY NEVER STOPS IN THIS PLACE.
THE MUSIC IS CONSTANT.
HOWEVER...
...THE ORANGE ONE IS NO LONGER HERE.
TODD?

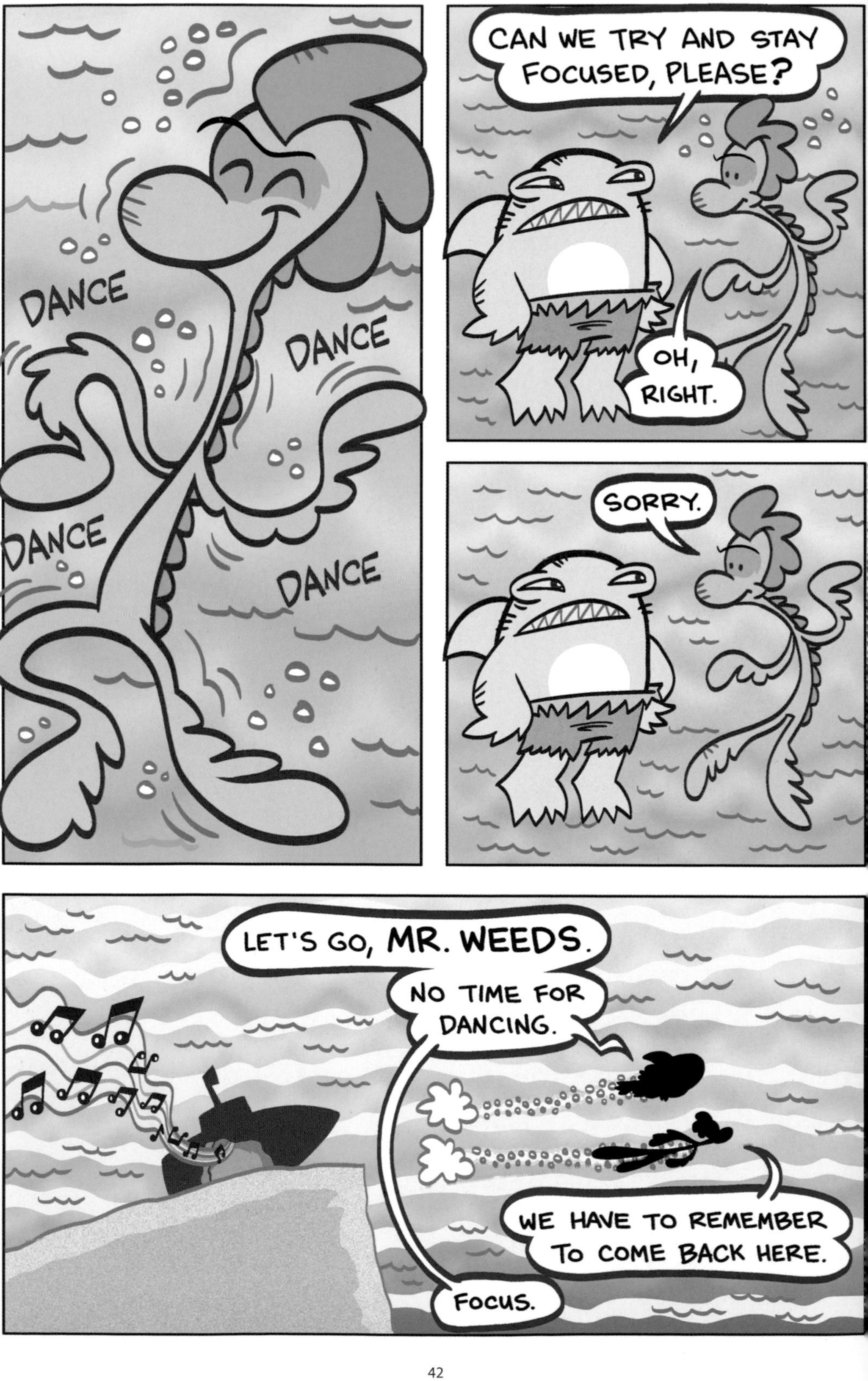

DANCE
DANCE
DANCE
DANCE
CAN WE TRY AND STAY FOCUSED, PLEASE?
OH, RIGHT.
SORRY.
LET'S GO, MR. WEEDS.
NO TIME FOR DANCING.
FOCUS.
WE HAVE TO REMEMBER TO COME BACK HERE.

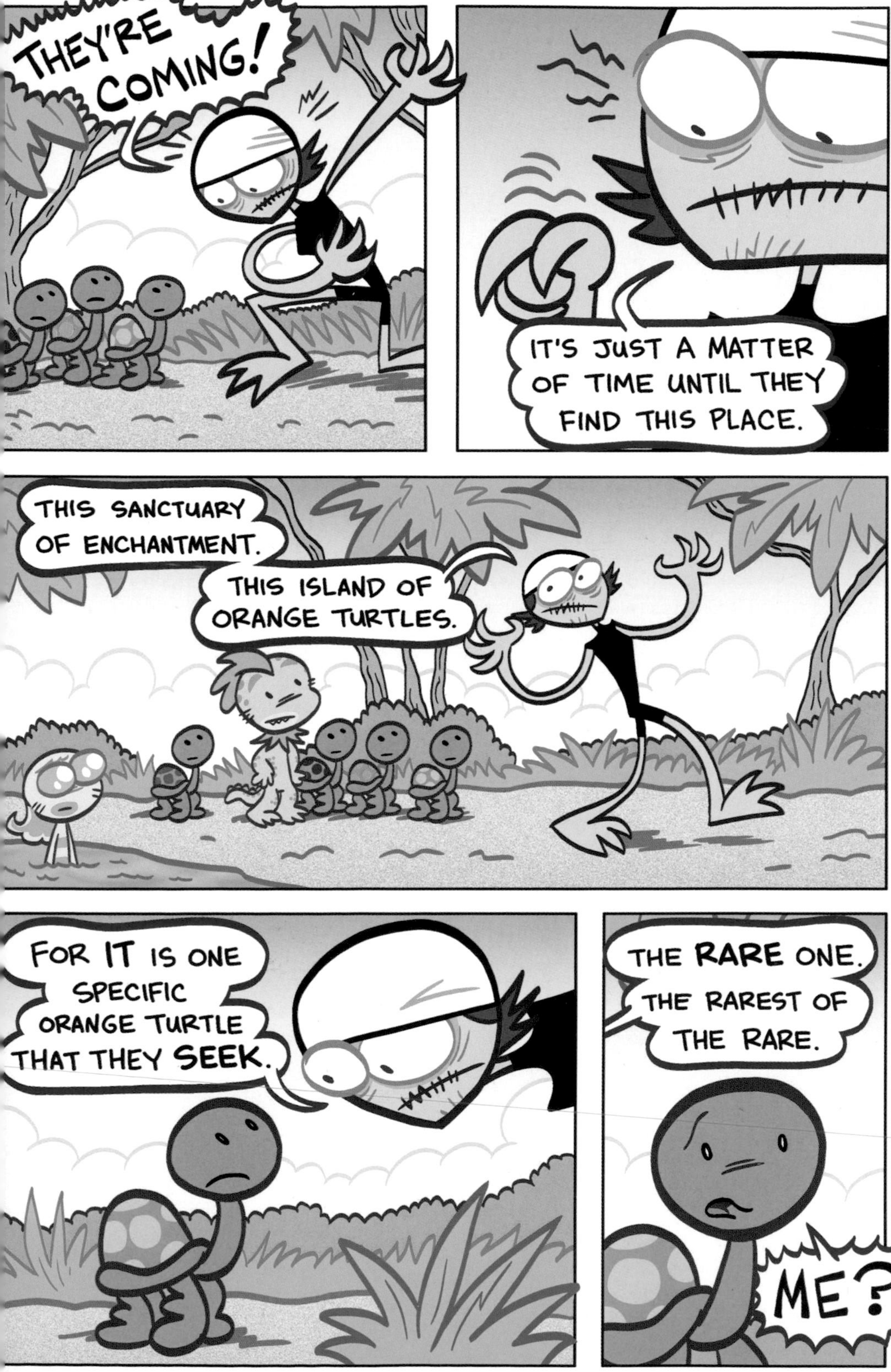
THEY'RE COMING!
IT'S JUST A MATTER OF TIME UNTIL THEY FIND THIS PLACE.
THIS SANCTUARY OF ENCHANTMENT.
THIS ISLAND OF ORANGE TURTLES.
FOR IT IS ONE SPECIFIC ORANGE TURTLE THAT THEY SEEK.
THE RARE ONE.
THE RAREST OF THE RARE.
ME?

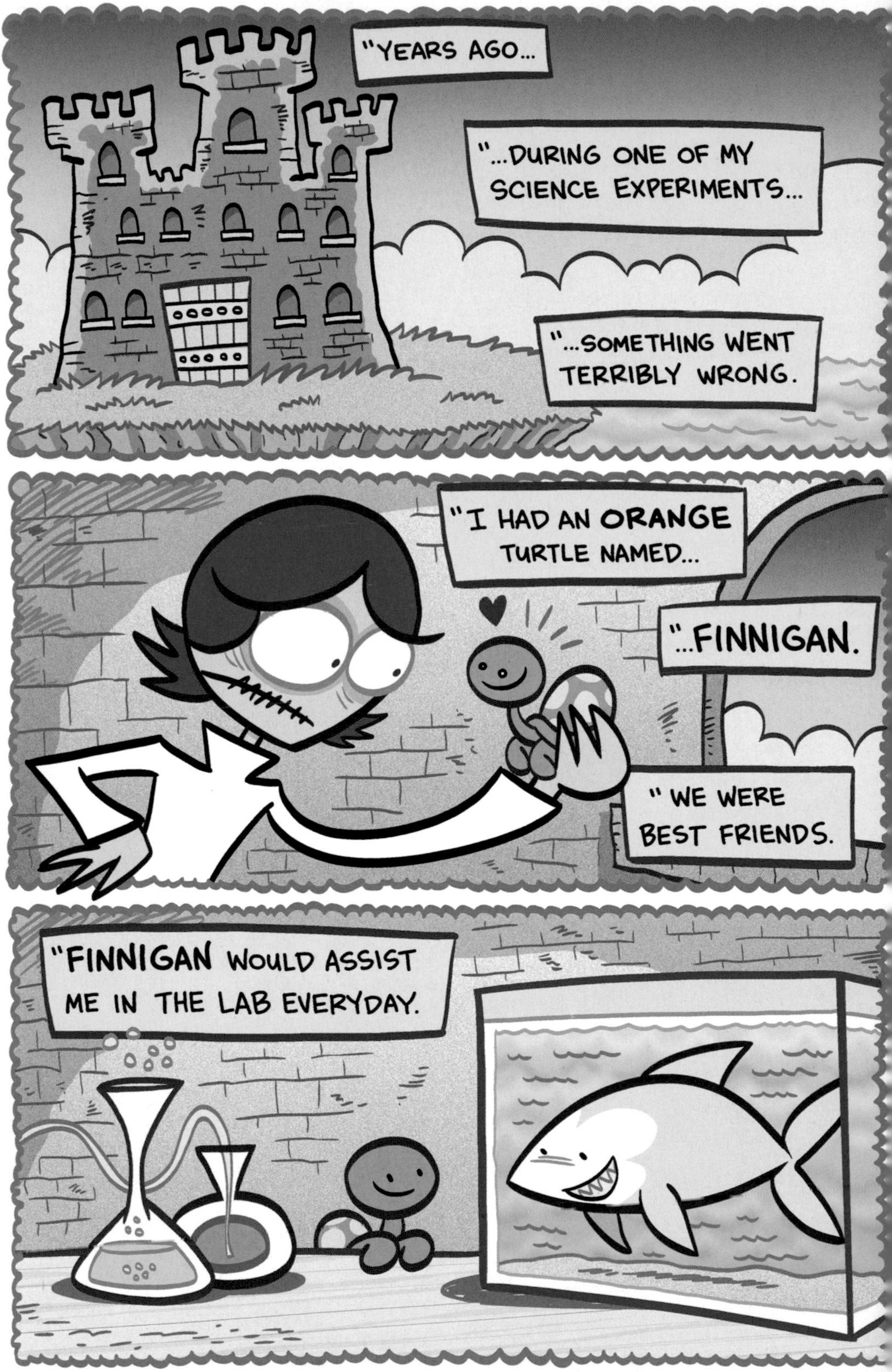
"YEARS AGO...
"...DURING ONE OF MY SCIENCE EXPERIMENTS...
"...SOMETHING WENT TERRIBLY WRONG.
"I HAD AN ORANGE TURTLE NAMED...
"...FINNIGAN.
"WE WERE BEST FRIENDS.
"FINNIGAN WOULD ASSIST ME IN THE LAB EVERYDAY.

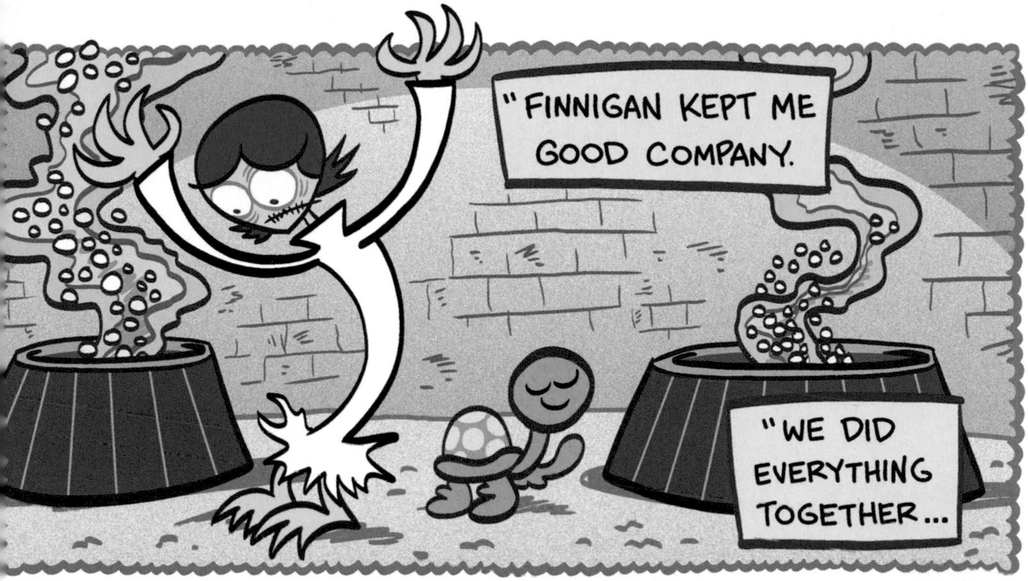
"FINNIGAN KEPT ME GOOD COMPANY.
"WE DID EVERYTHING TOGETHER...

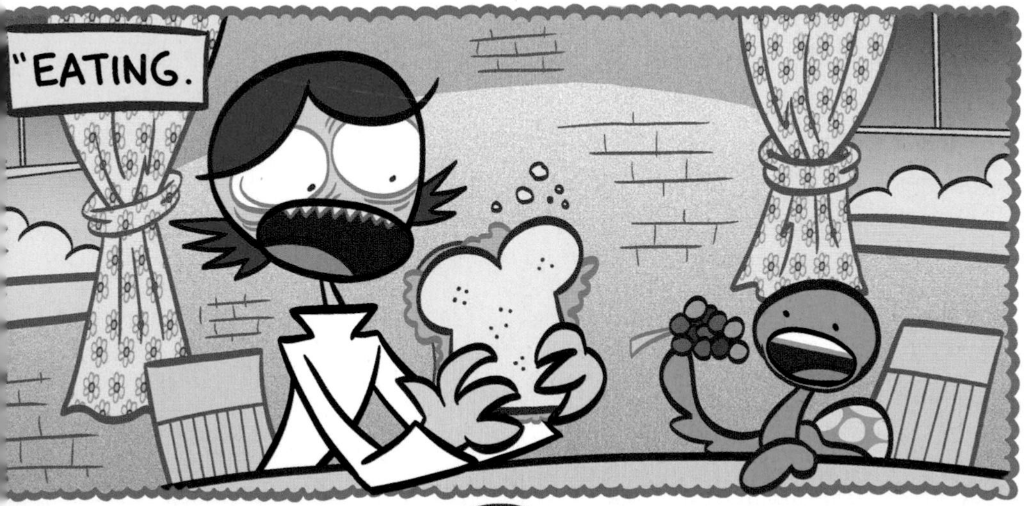
"EATING.

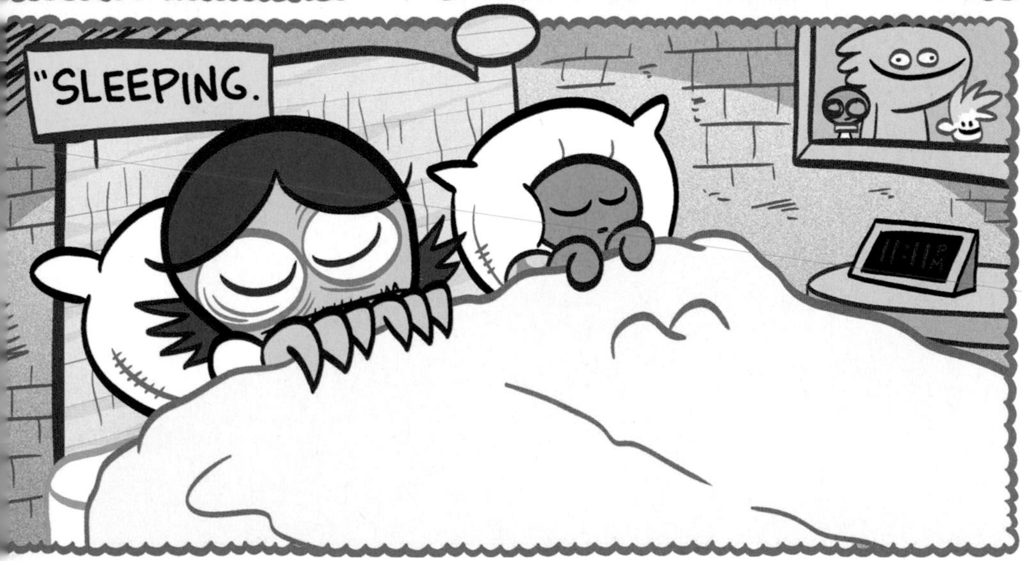
"SLEEPING.

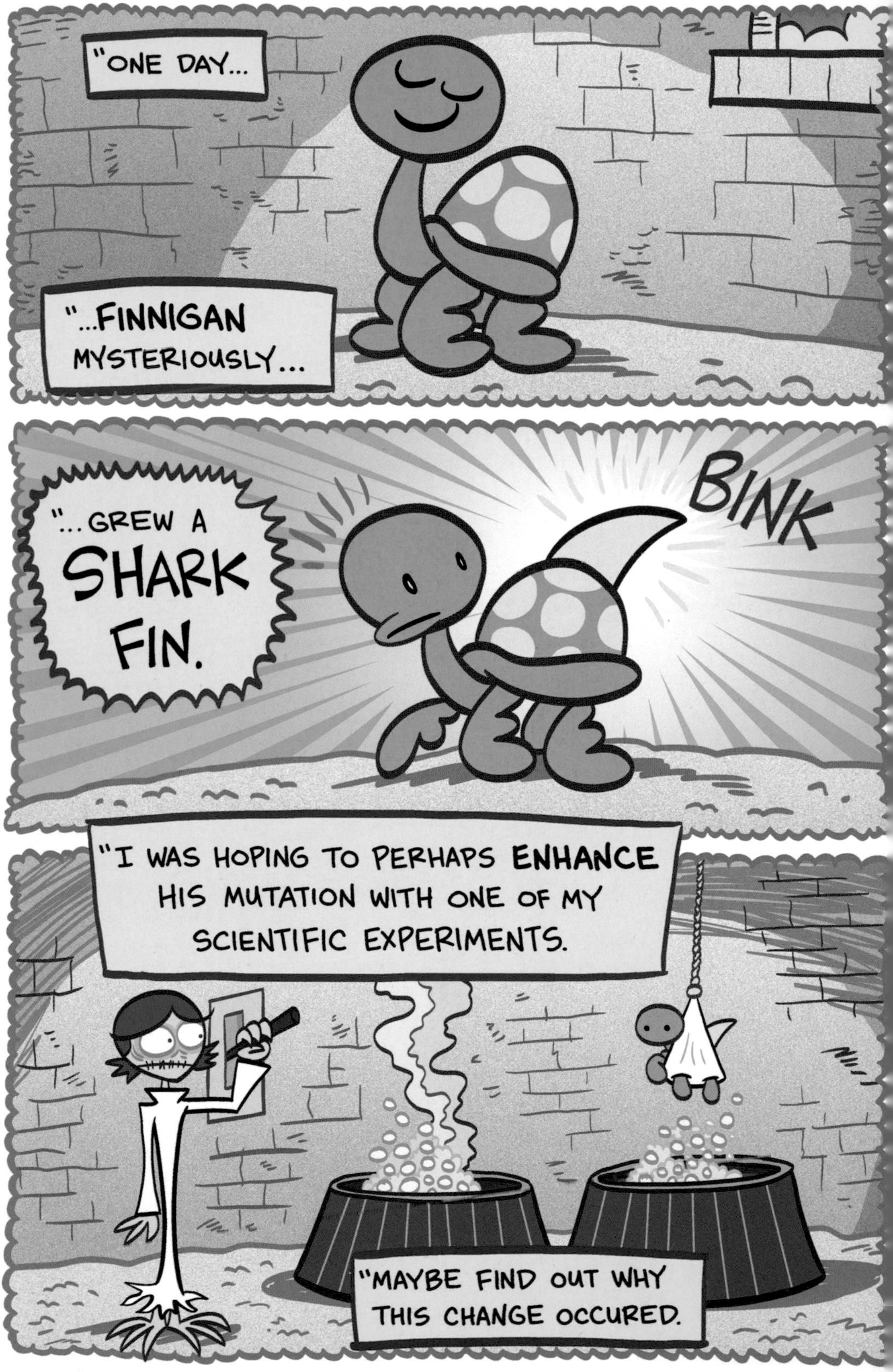
"ONE DAY...
"...FINNIGAN MYSTERIOUSLY...
"...GREW A SHARK FIN.
BINK
"I WAS HOPING TO PERHAPS ENHANCE HIS MUTATION WITH ONE OF MY SCIENTIFIC EXPERIMENTS.
"MAYBE FIND OUT WHY THIS CHANGE OCCURED.

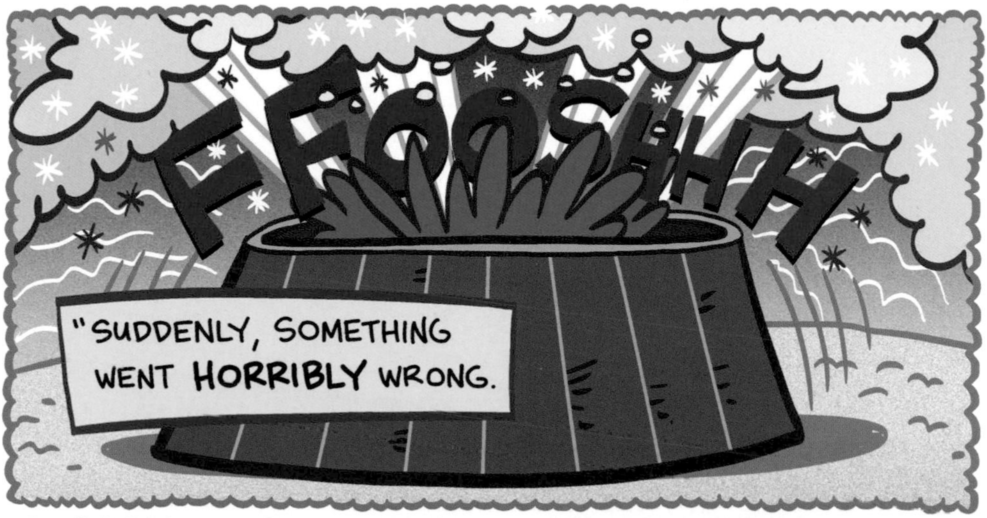
FFOOSHHH
"SUDDENLY, SOMETHING WENT HORRIBLY WRONG.

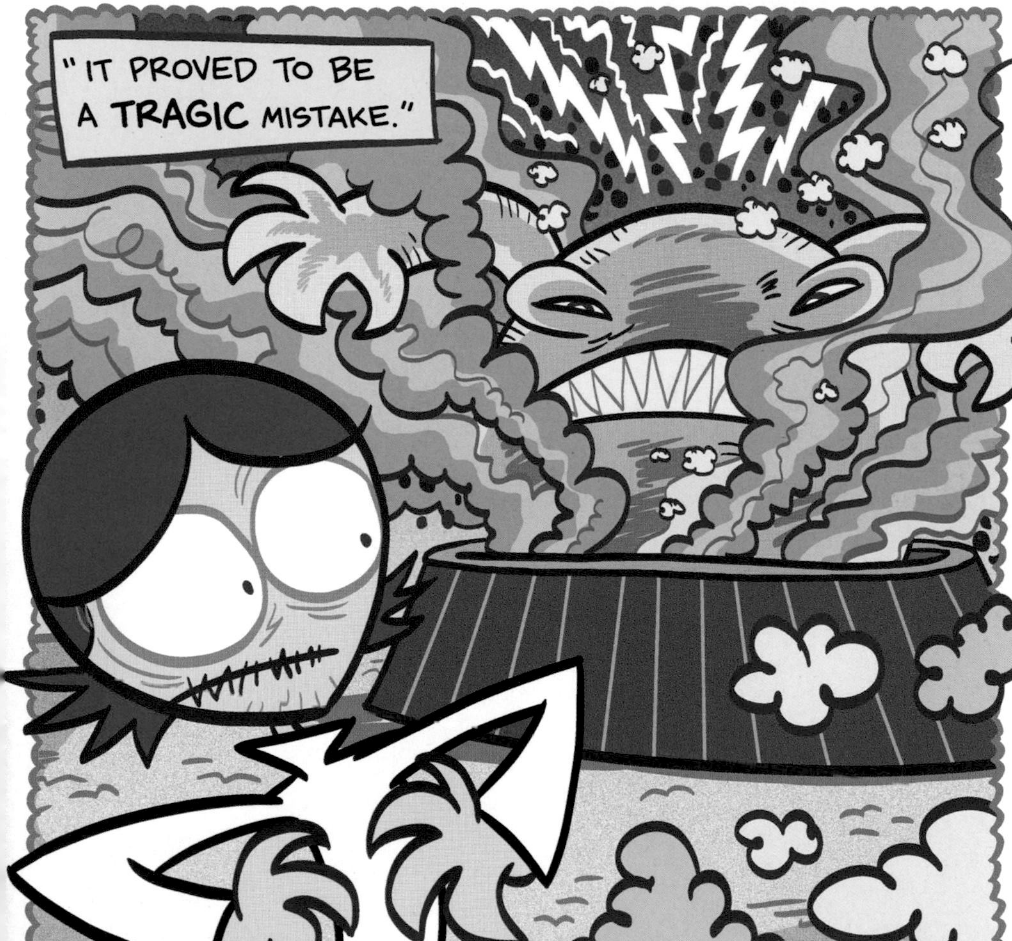
"IT PROVED TO BE A TRAGIC MISTAKE."

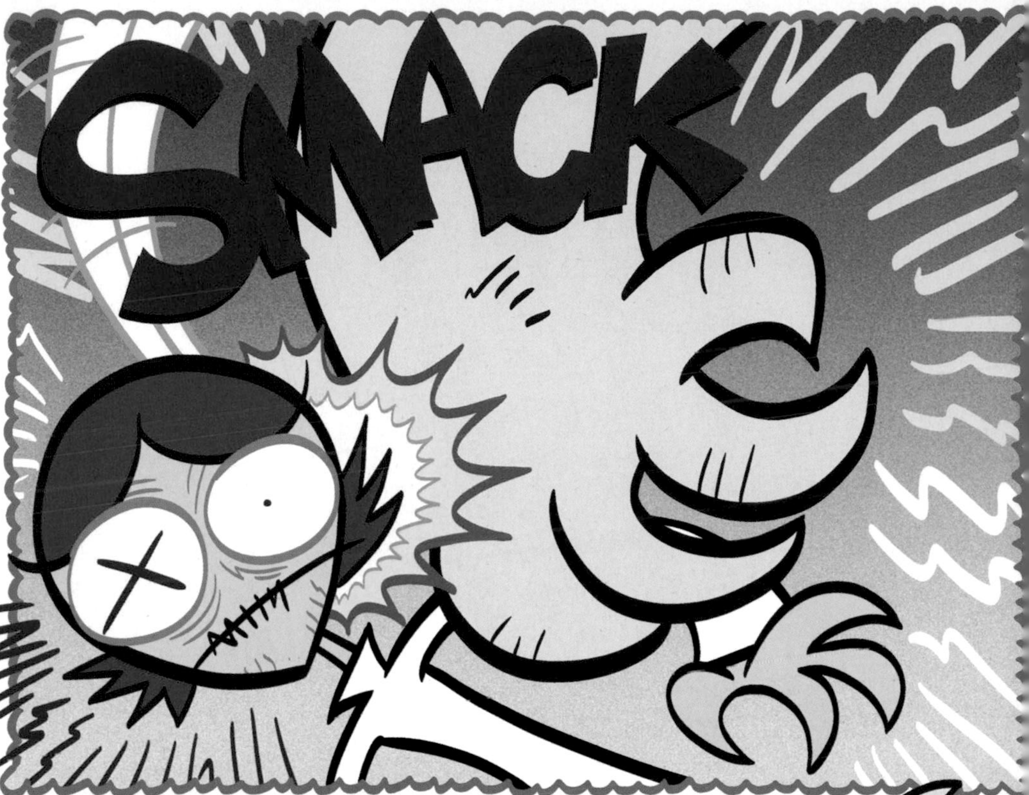
SMACK

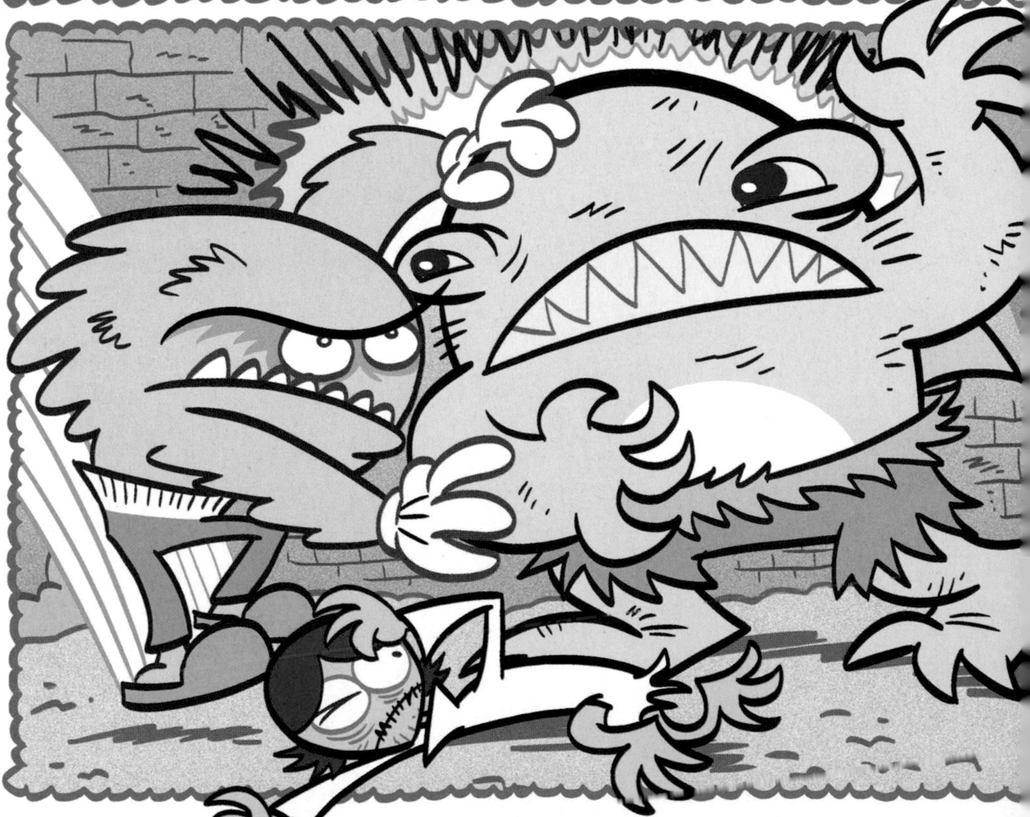

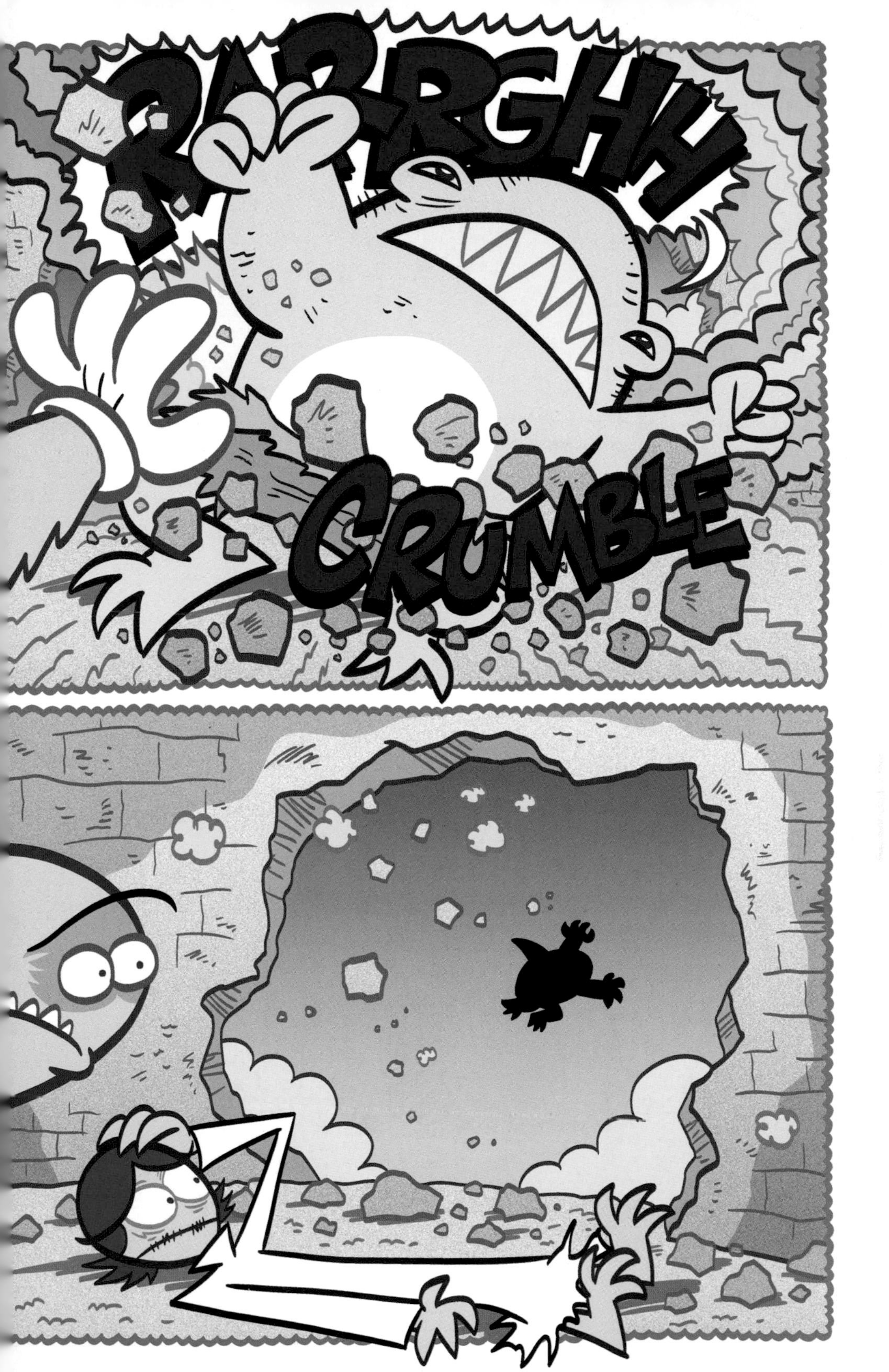
RAARGHH
CRUMBLE

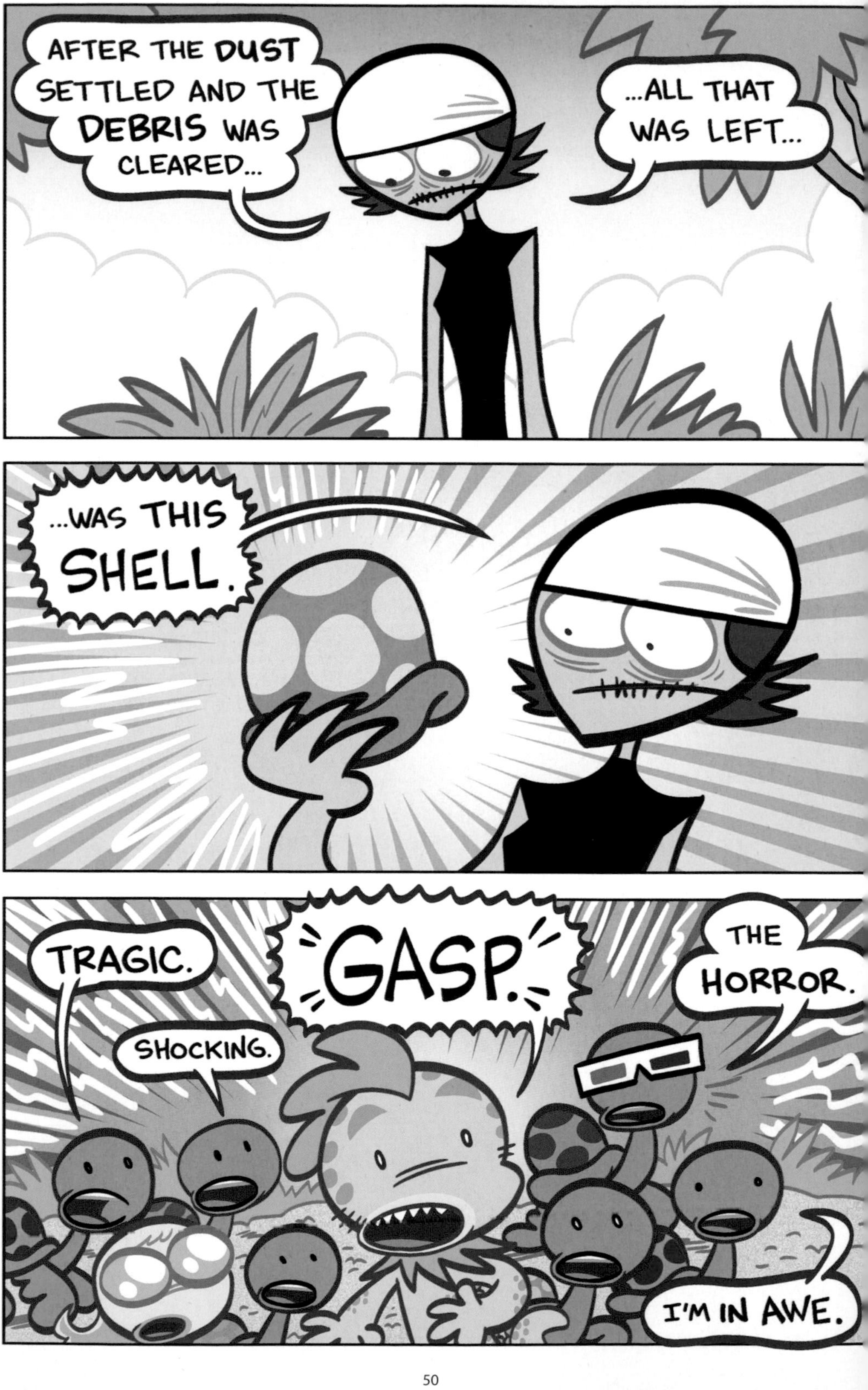
AFTER THE DUST SETTLED AND THE DEBRIS WAS CLEARED...
...ALL THAT WAS LEFT...
...WAS THIS SHELL.
TRAGIC.
SHOCKING.
GASP.
THE HORROR.
I'M IN AWE.

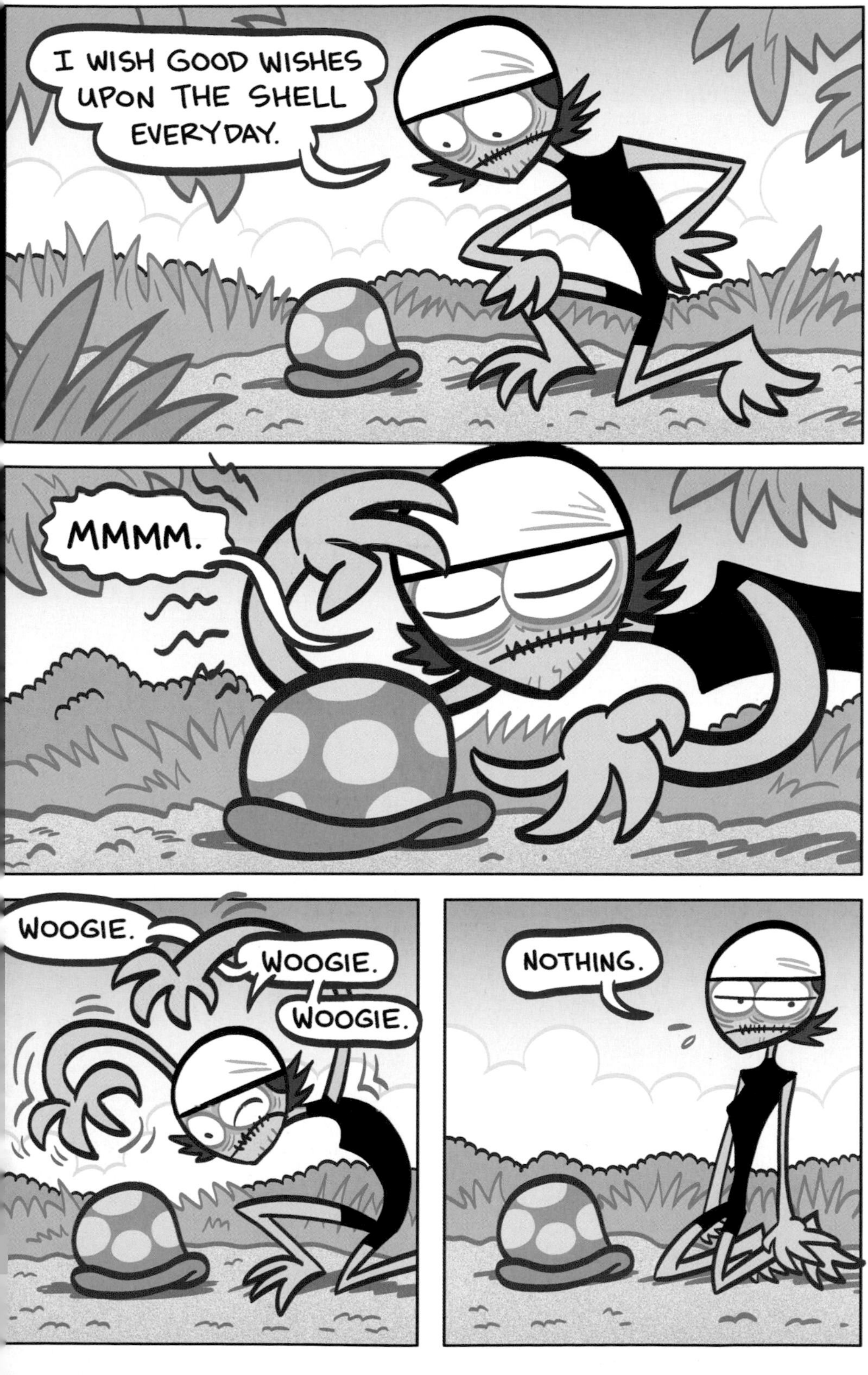
I WISH GOOD WISHES UPON THE SHELL EVERYDAY.
MMMM.
WOOGIE.
WOOGIE.
WOOGIE.
NOTHING.

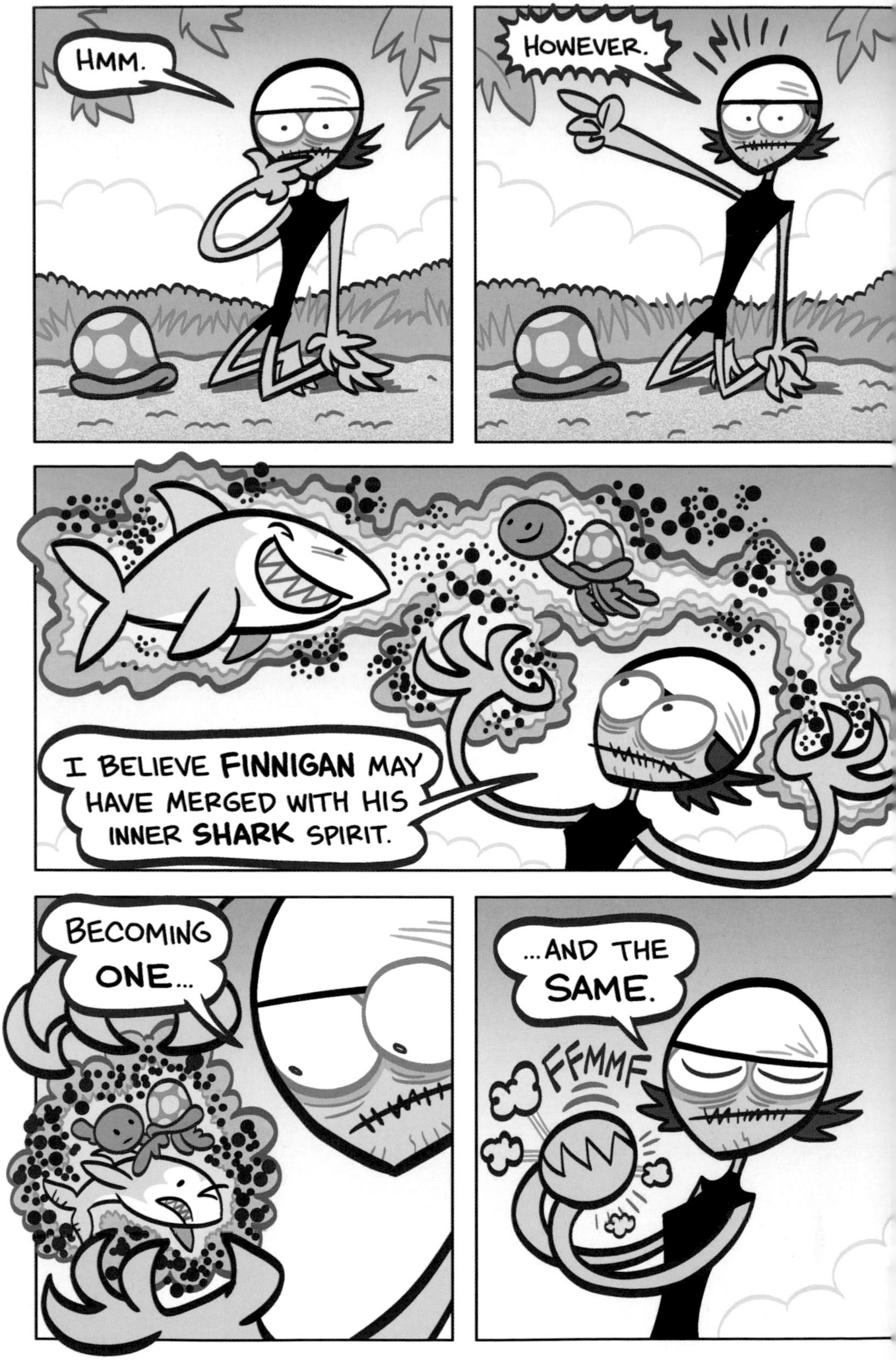
HMM.
HOWEVER.
I BELIEVE FINNIGAN MAY HAVE MERGED WITH HIS INNER SHARK SPIRIT.
BECOMING ONE...
...AND THE SAME.
FFMMF

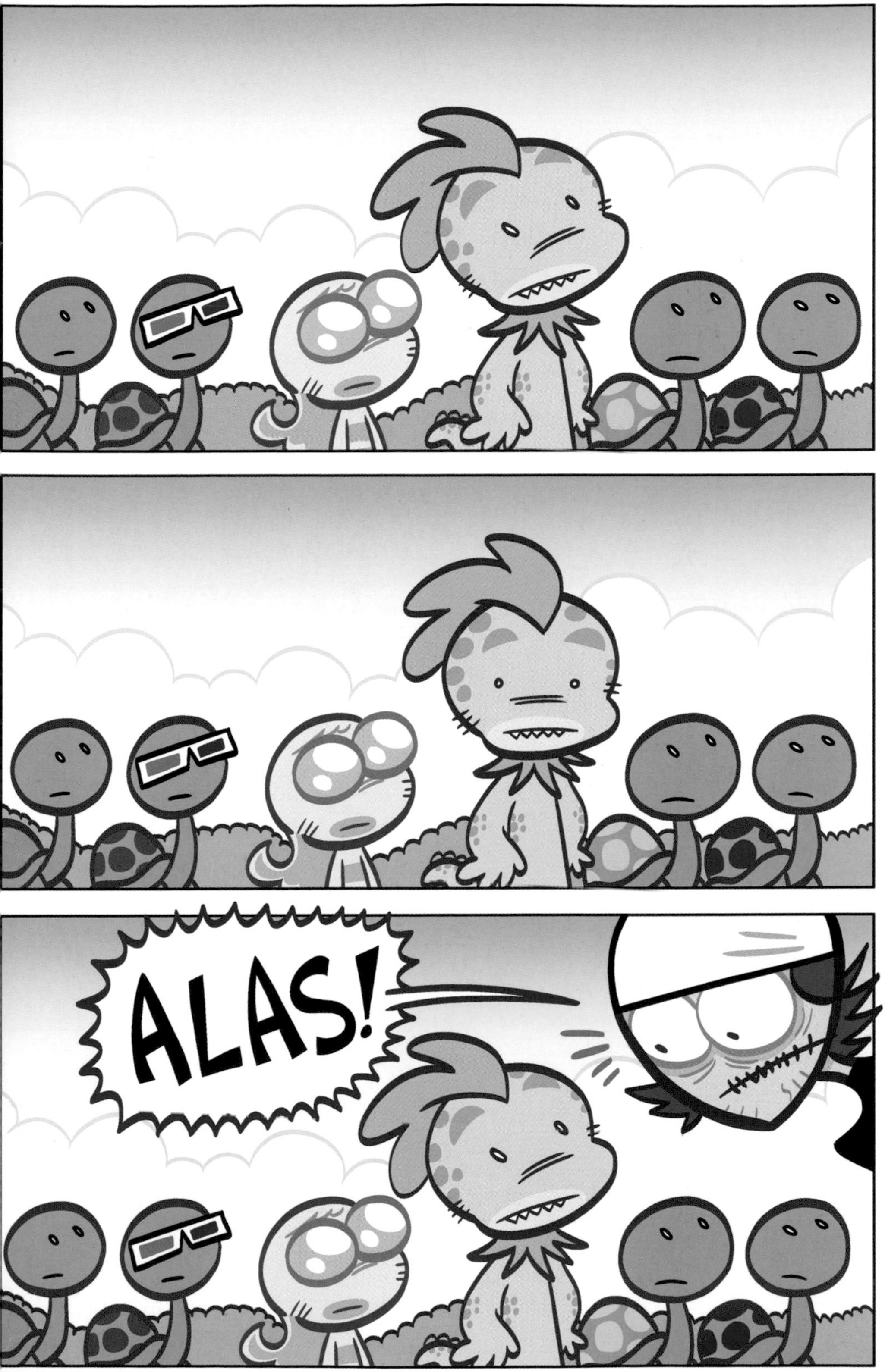
ALAS!

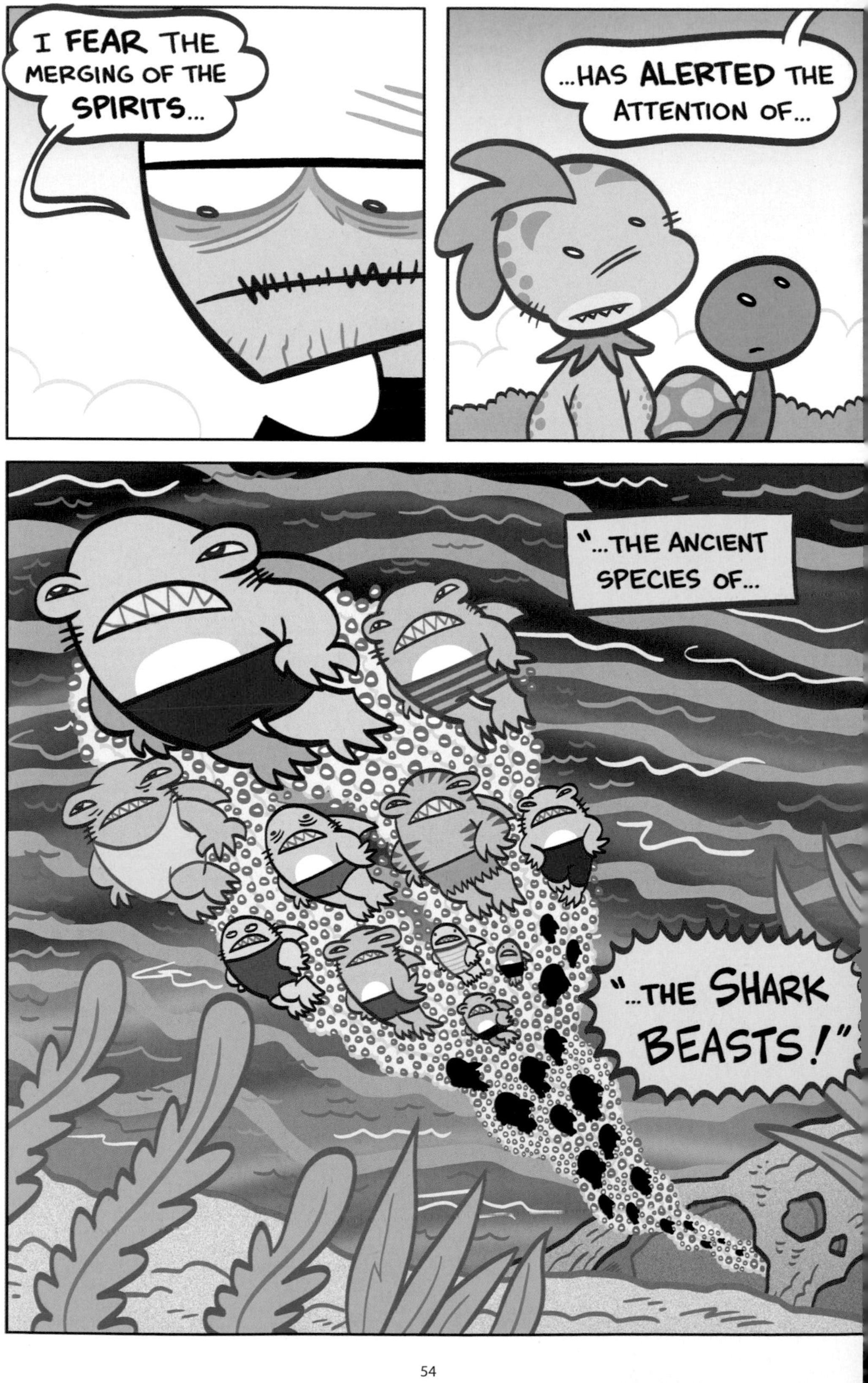
I FEAR THE MERGING OF THE SPIRITS...
...HAS ALERTED THE ATTENTION OF...
"...THE ANCIENT SPECIES OF...
"...THE SHARK BEASTS!"

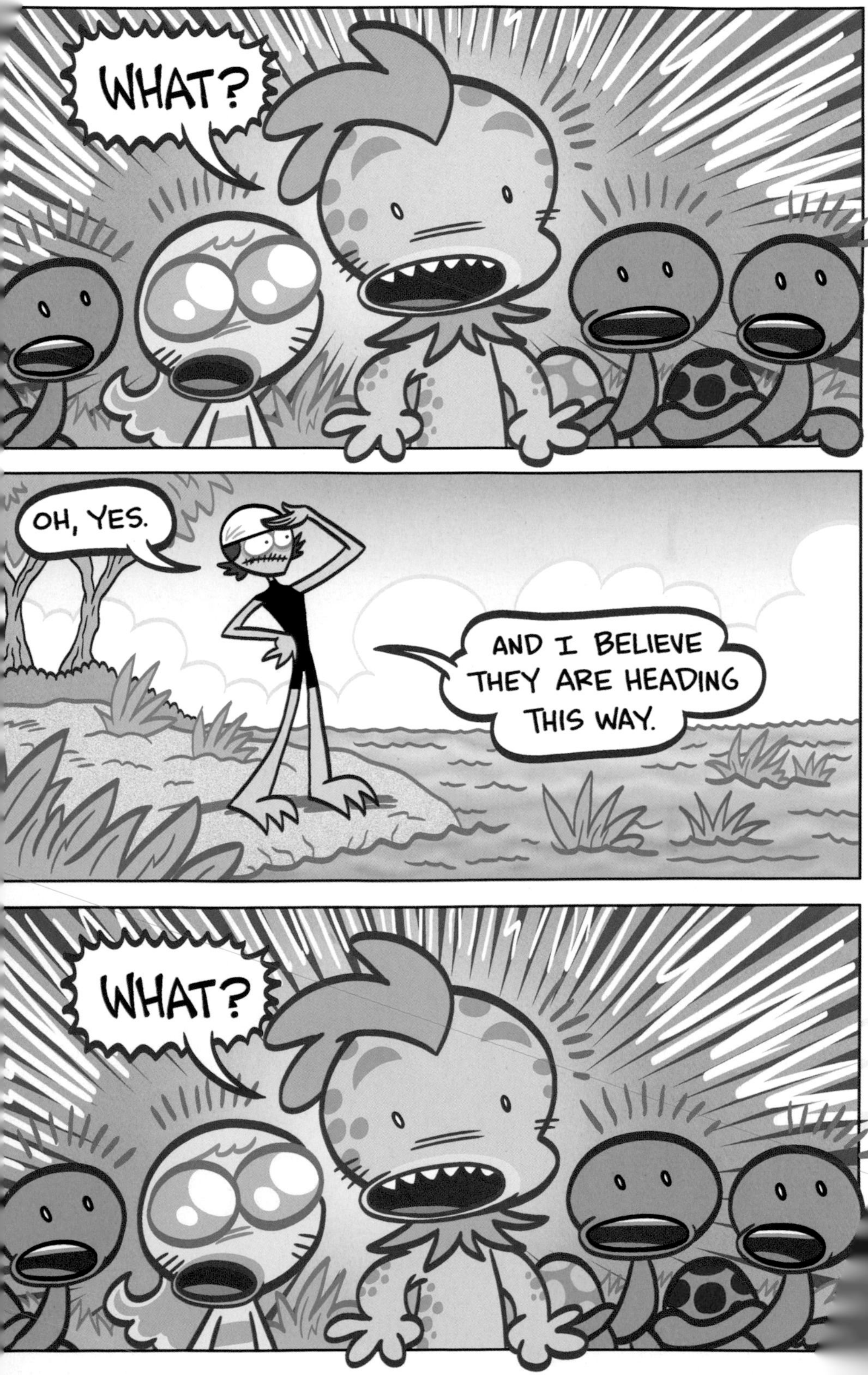
WHAT?
OH, YES.
AND I BELIEVE THEY ARE HEADING THIS WAY.
WHAT?

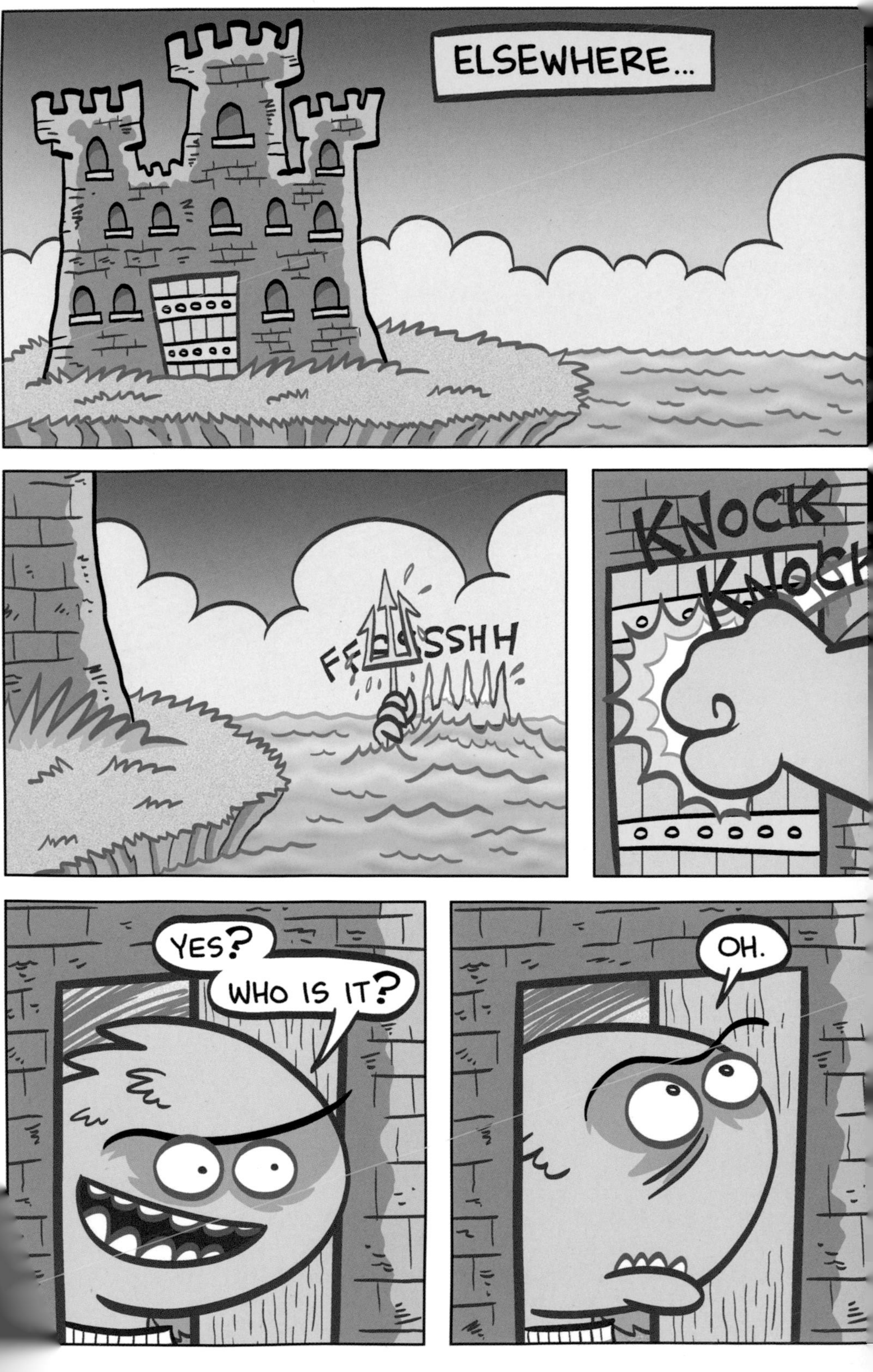
ELSEWHERE...
FFSSHH
KNOCK
KNOCK
YES?
WHO IS IT?
OH.

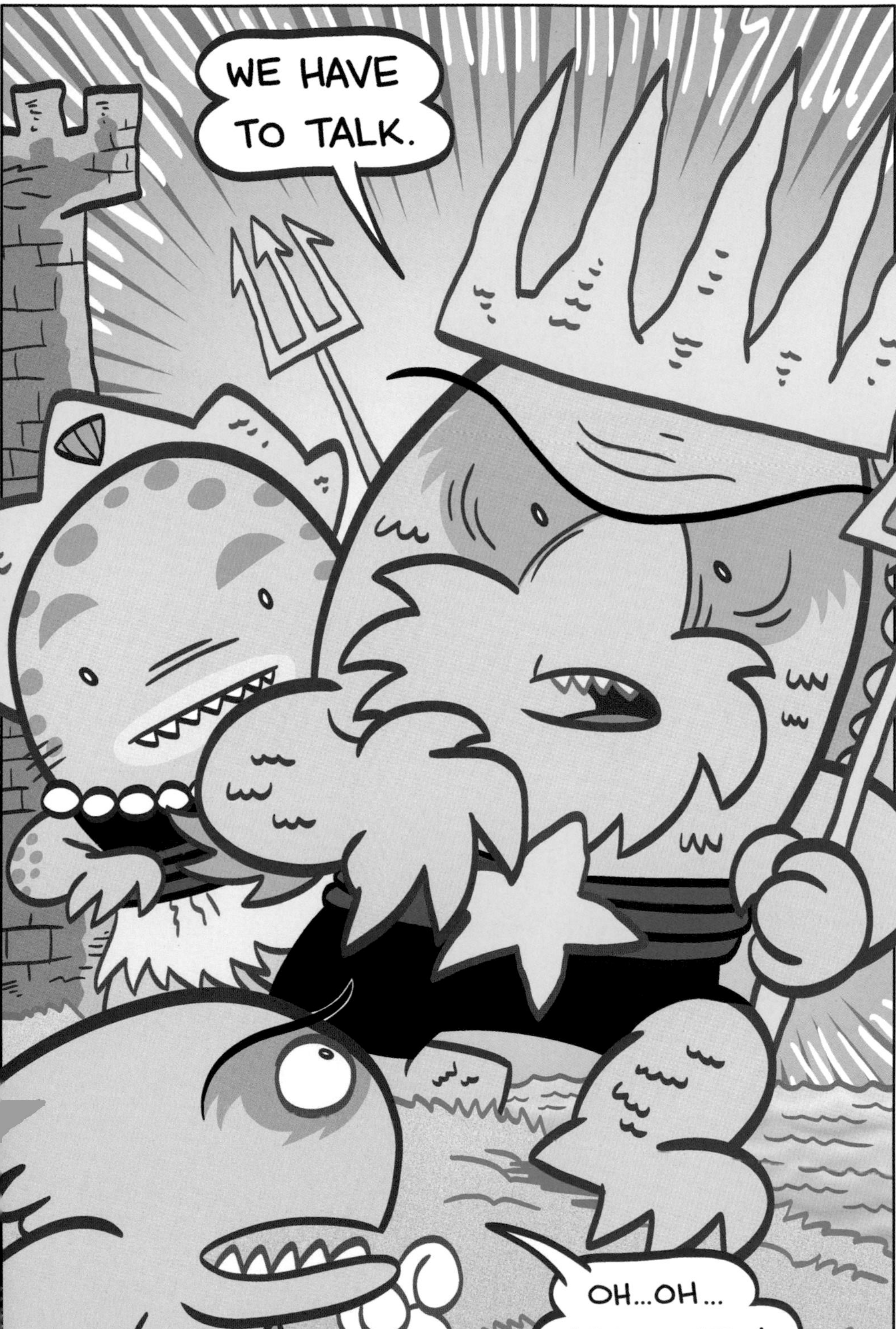
WE HAVE TO TALK.
OH...OH... ABSOLUTELY.

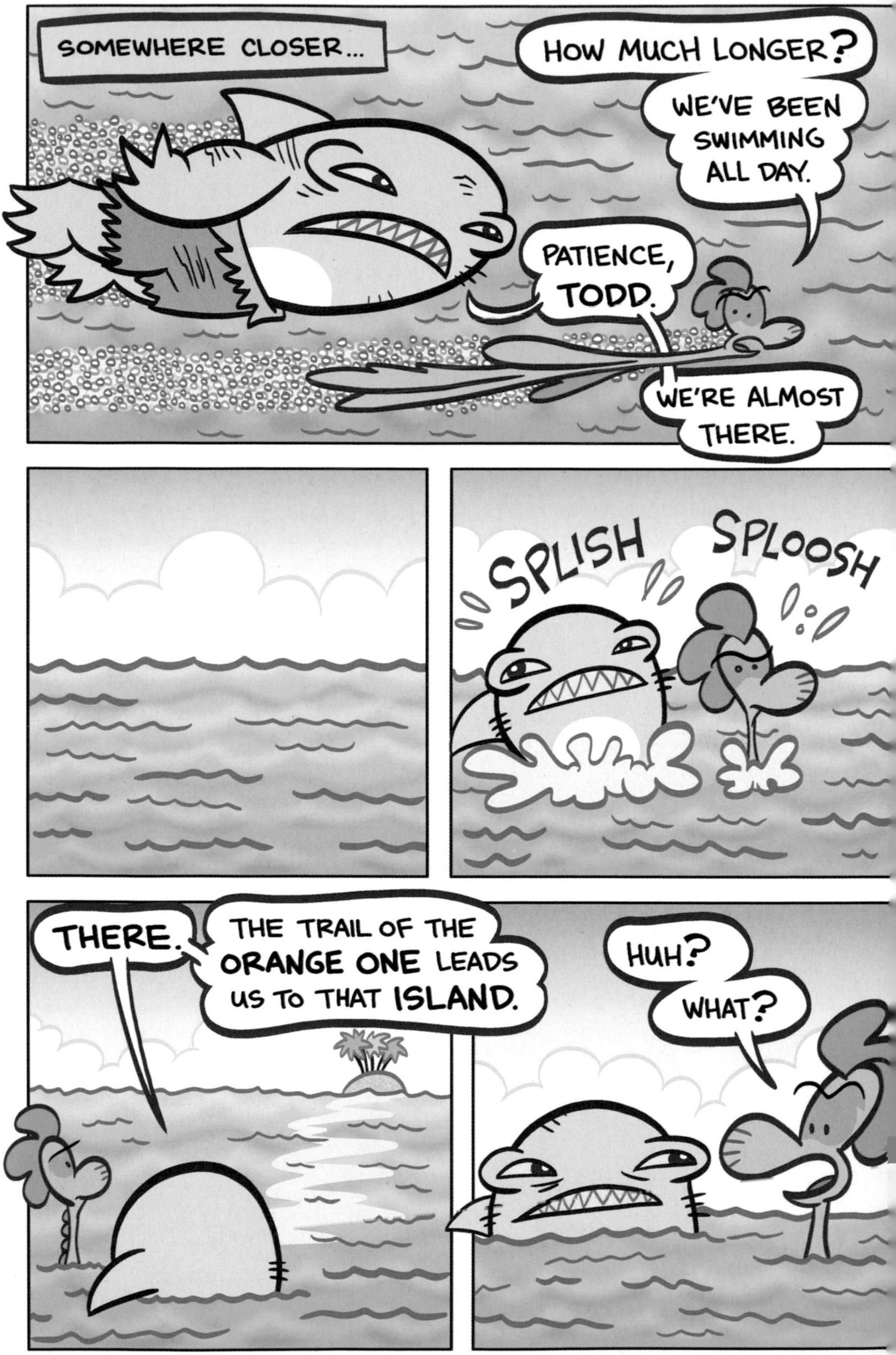
SOMEWHERE CLOSER...
HOW MUCH LONGER?
WE'VE BEEN SWIMMING ALL DAY.
PATIENCE, TODD.
WE'RE ALMOST THERE.
SPLISH
SPLOOSH
THERE.
THE TRAIL OF THE ORANGE ONE LEADS US TO THAT ISLAND.
HUH?
WHAT?

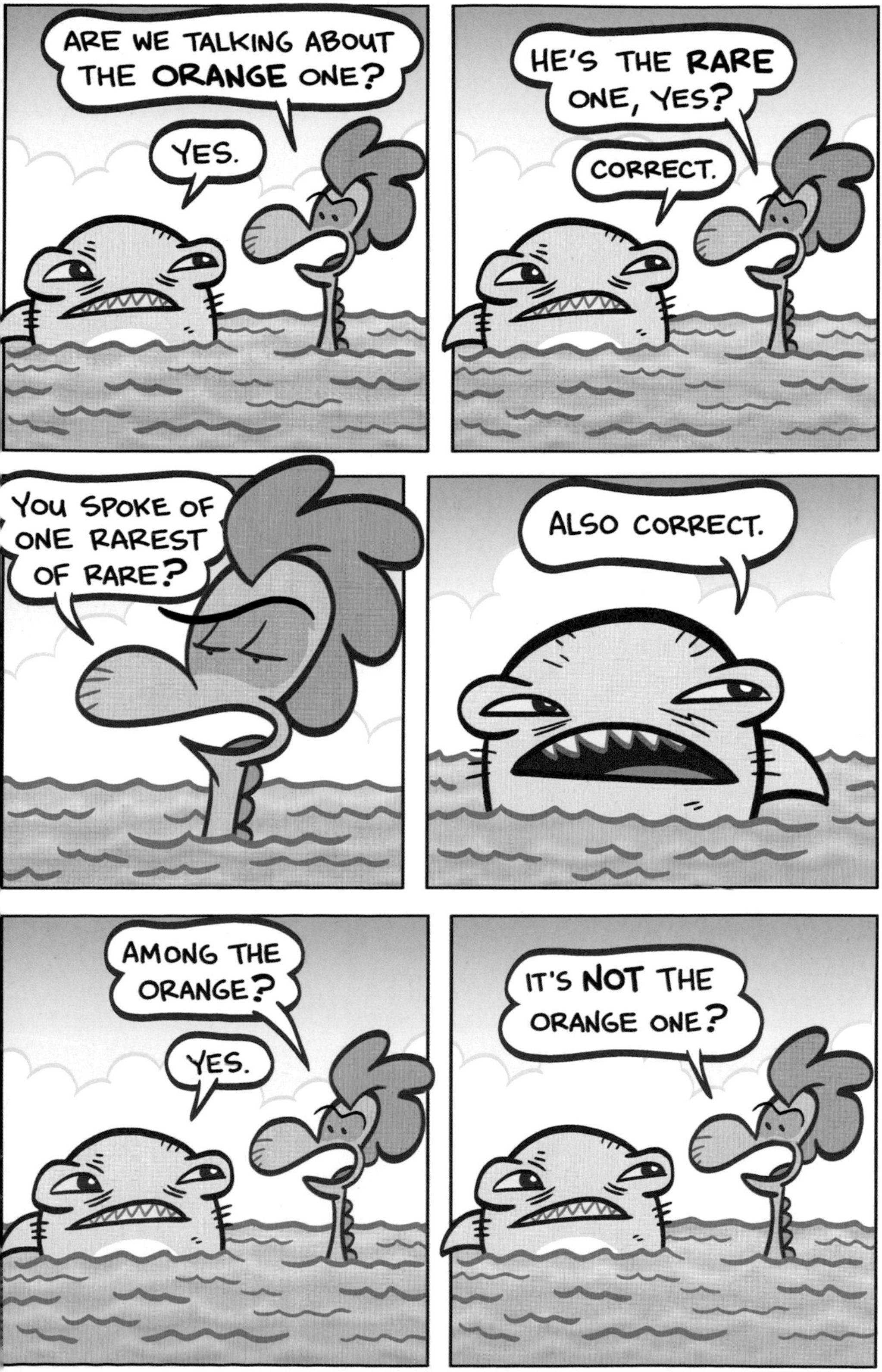
ARE WE TALKING ABOUT THE ORANGE ONE?
YES.
HE'S THE RARE ONE, YES?
CORRECT.
YOU SPOKE OF ONE RAREST OF RARE?
ALSO CORRECT.
AMONG THE ORANGE?
YES.
IT'S NOT THE ORANGE ONE?

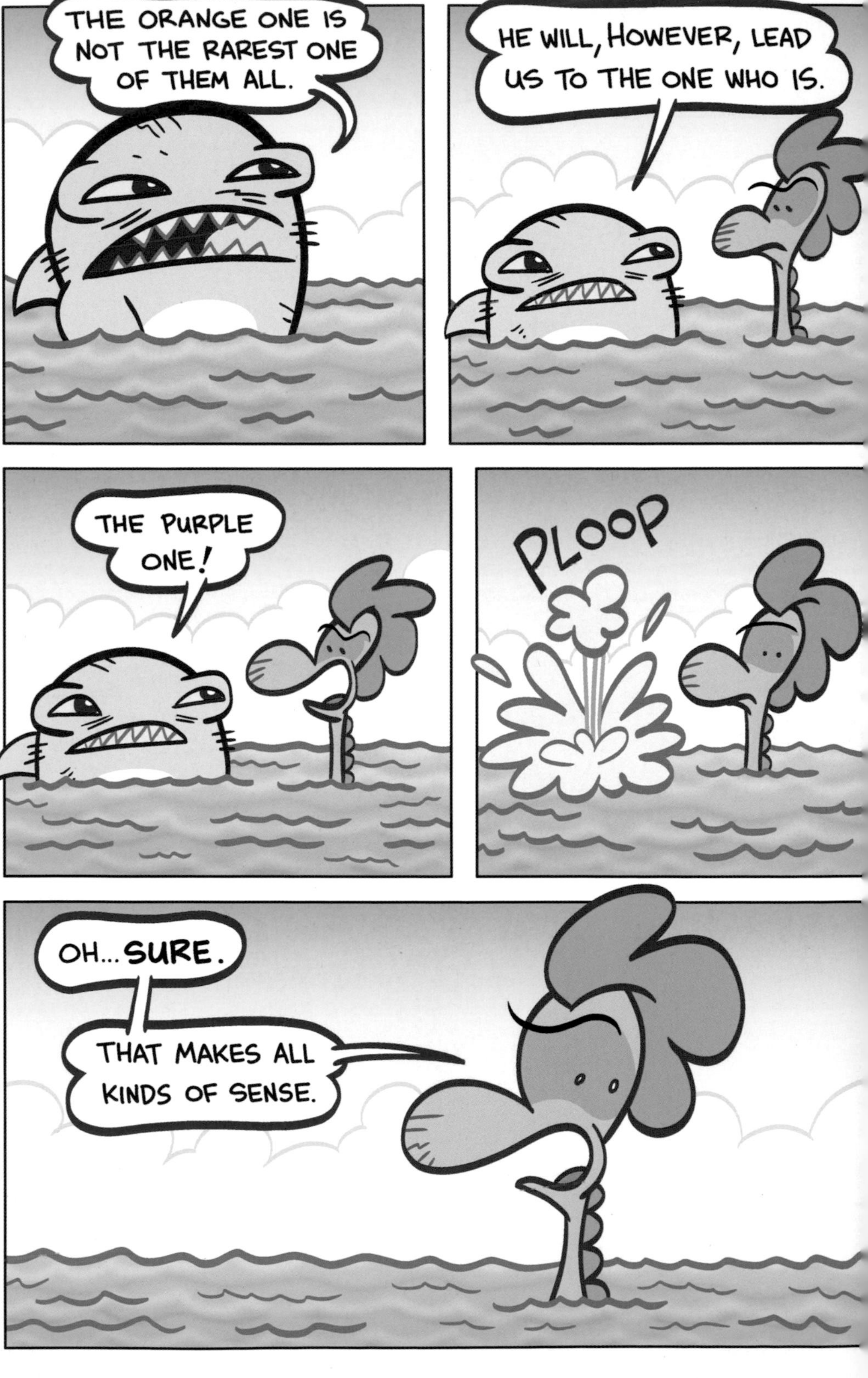
THE ORANGE ONE IS NOT THE RAREST ONE OF THEM ALL.
HE WILL, HOWEVER, LEAD US TO THE ONE WHO IS.
THE PURPLE ONE!
PLOOP
OH... SURE.
THAT MAKES ALL KINDS OF SENSE.

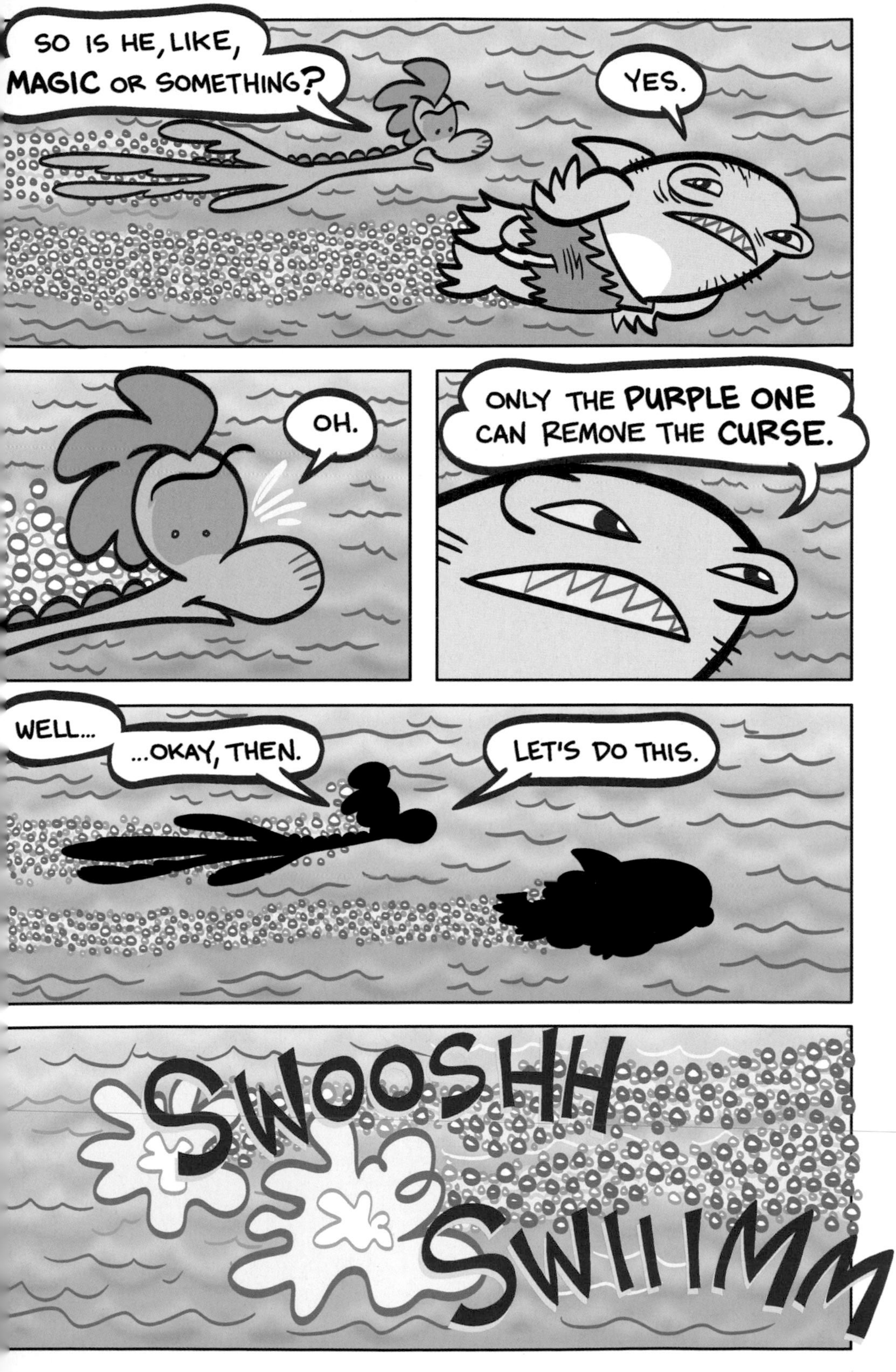
SO IS HE, LIKE, MAGIC OR SOMETHING?
YES.
OH.
ONLY THE PURPLE ONE CAN REMOVE THE CURSE.
WELL...
...OKAY, THEN.
LET'S DO THIS.
SWOOSHH
SWIIIMM

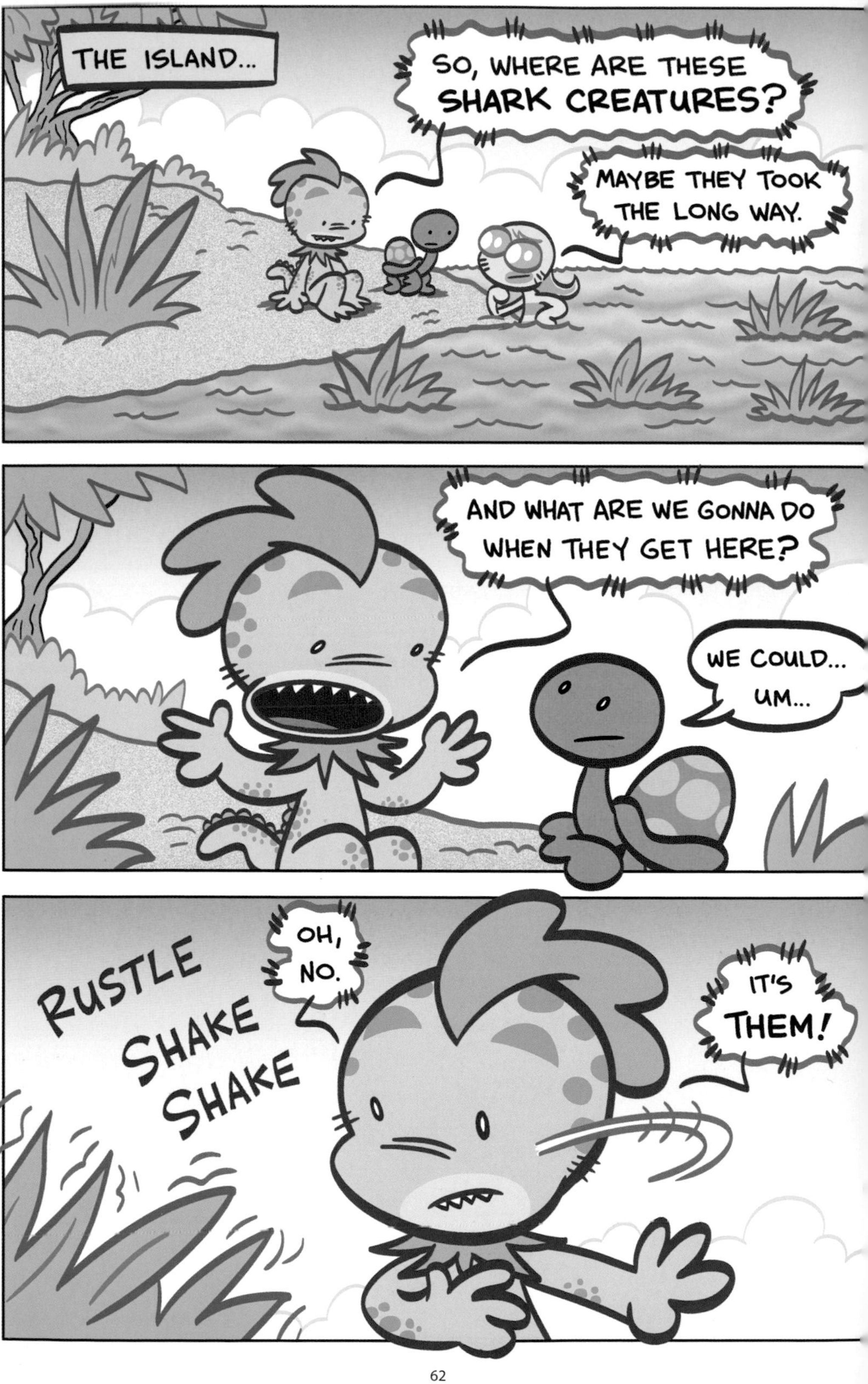
THE ISLAND...
SO, WHERE ARE THESE SHARK CREATURES?
MAYBE THEY TOOK THE LONG WAY.
AND WHAT ARE WE GONNA DO WHEN THEY GET HERE?
WE COULD... UM...
RUSTLE
SHAKE
SHAKE
OH, NO.
IT'S THEM!

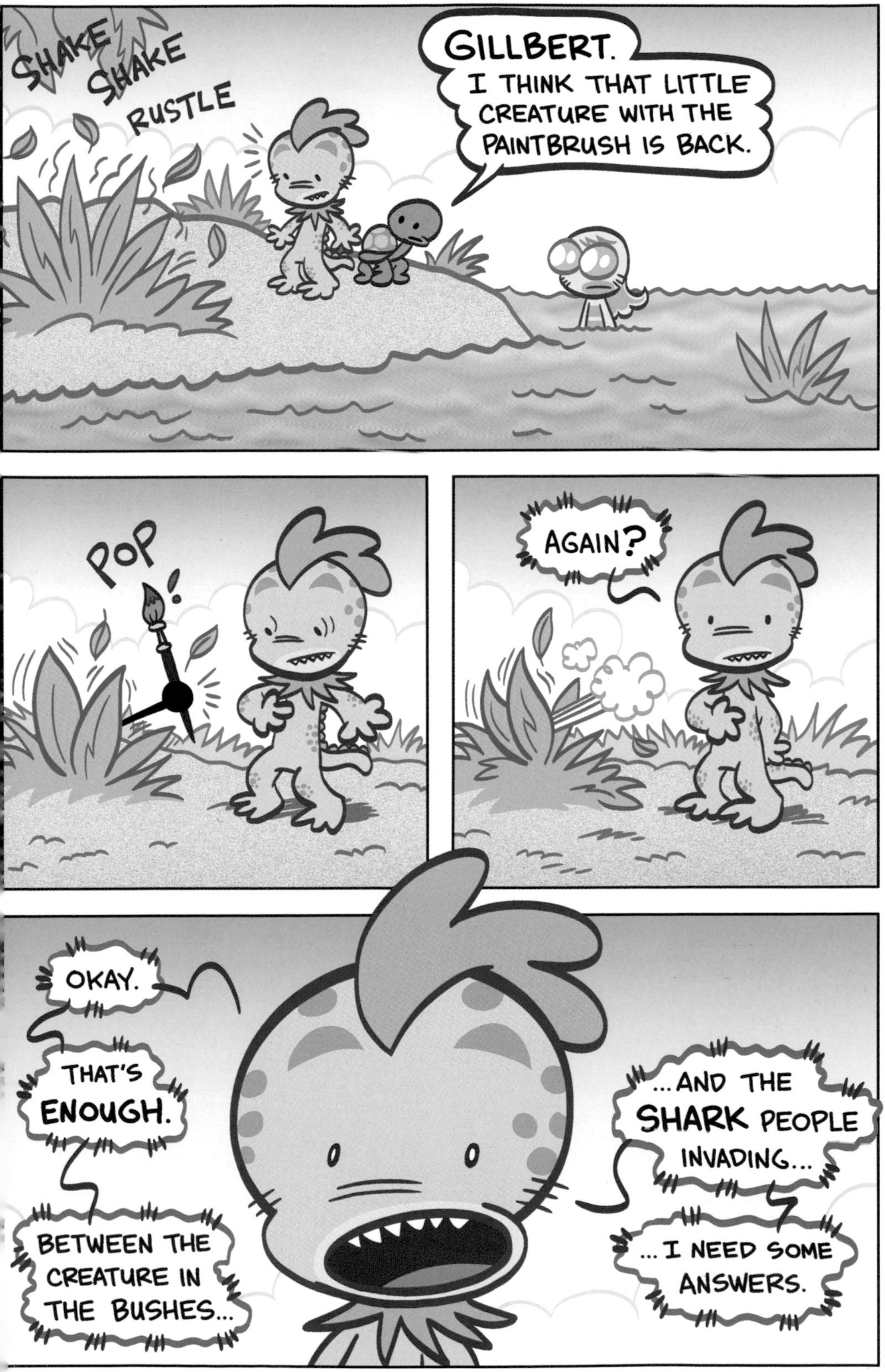
SHAKE
SHAKE
RUSTLE
GILLBERT.
I THINK THAT LITTLE CREATURE WITH THE PAINTBRUSH IS BACK.
POP
AGAIN?
OKAY.
THAT'S ENOUGH.
BETWEEN THE CREATURE IN THE BUSHES...
...AND THE SHARK PEOPLE INVADING...
...I NEED SOME ANSWERS.

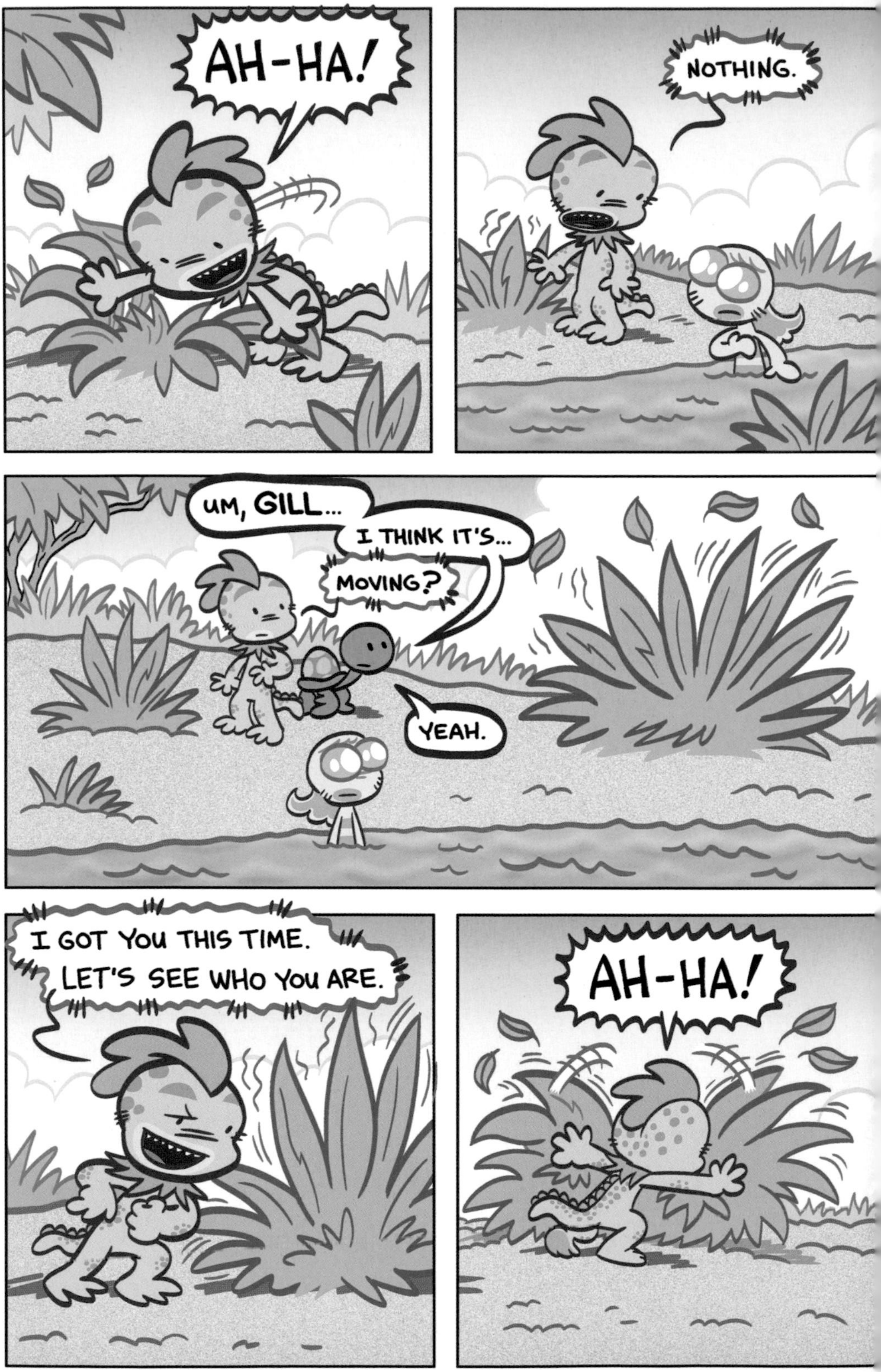
AH-HA!
NOTHING.
UM, GILL...
I THINK IT'S...
MOVING?
YEAH.
I GOT YOU THIS TIME.
LET'S SEE WHO YOU ARE.
AH-HA!

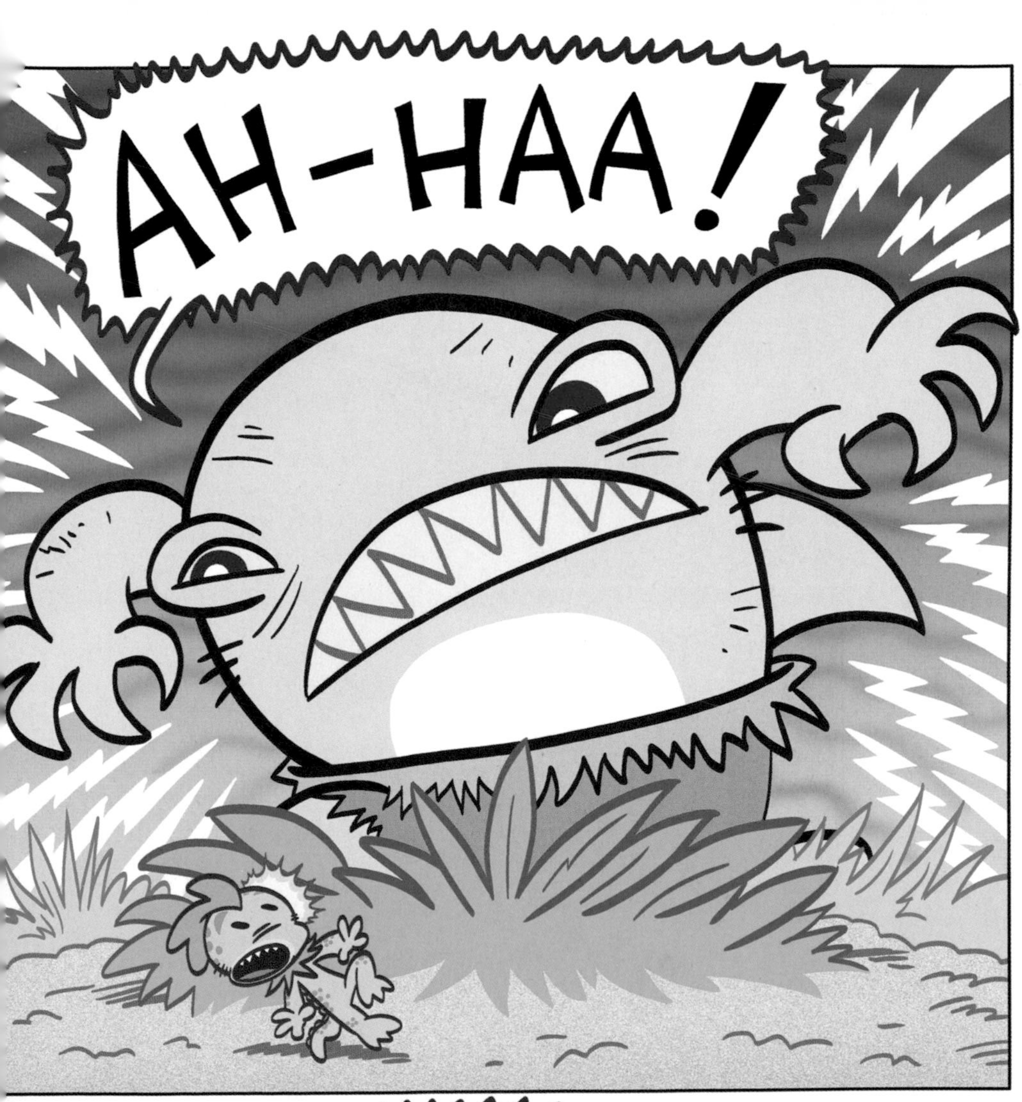
AH-HAA!

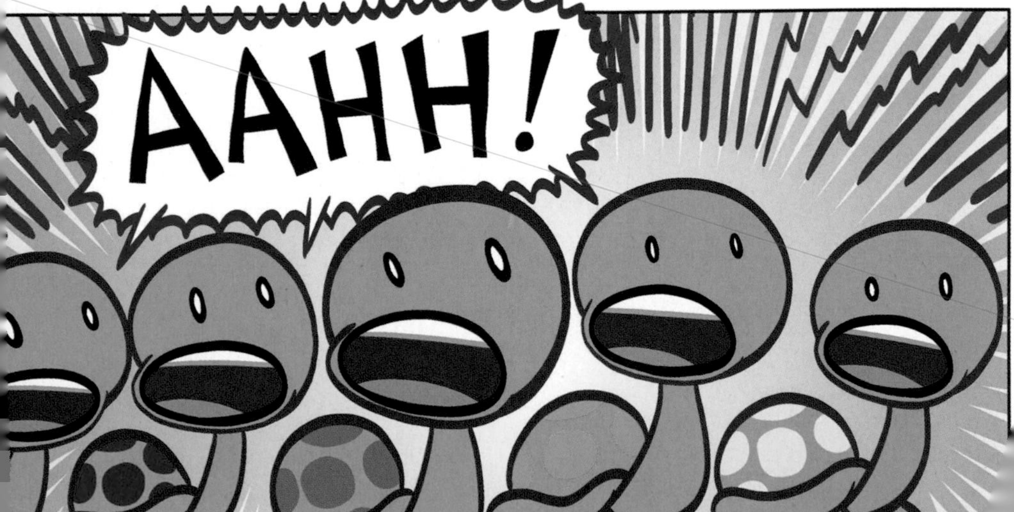
AAHH!

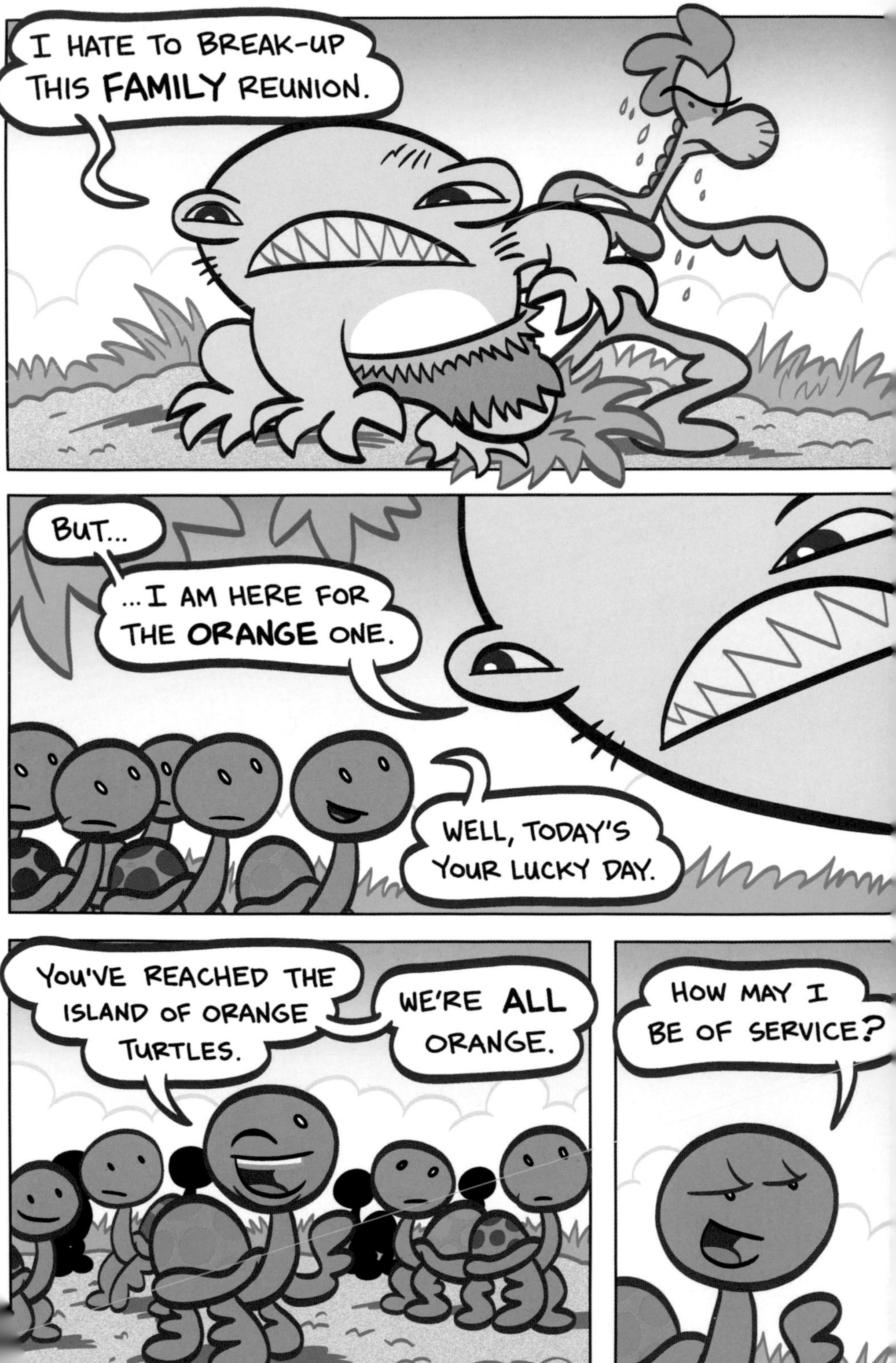
I HATE TO BREAK-UP THIS FAMILY REUNION.
BUT...
...I AM HERE FOR THE ORANGE ONE.
WELL, TODAY'S YOUR LUCKY DAY.
YOU'VE REACHED THE ISLAND OF ORANGE TURTLES.
WE'RE ALL ORANGE.
HOW MAY I BE OF SERVICE?

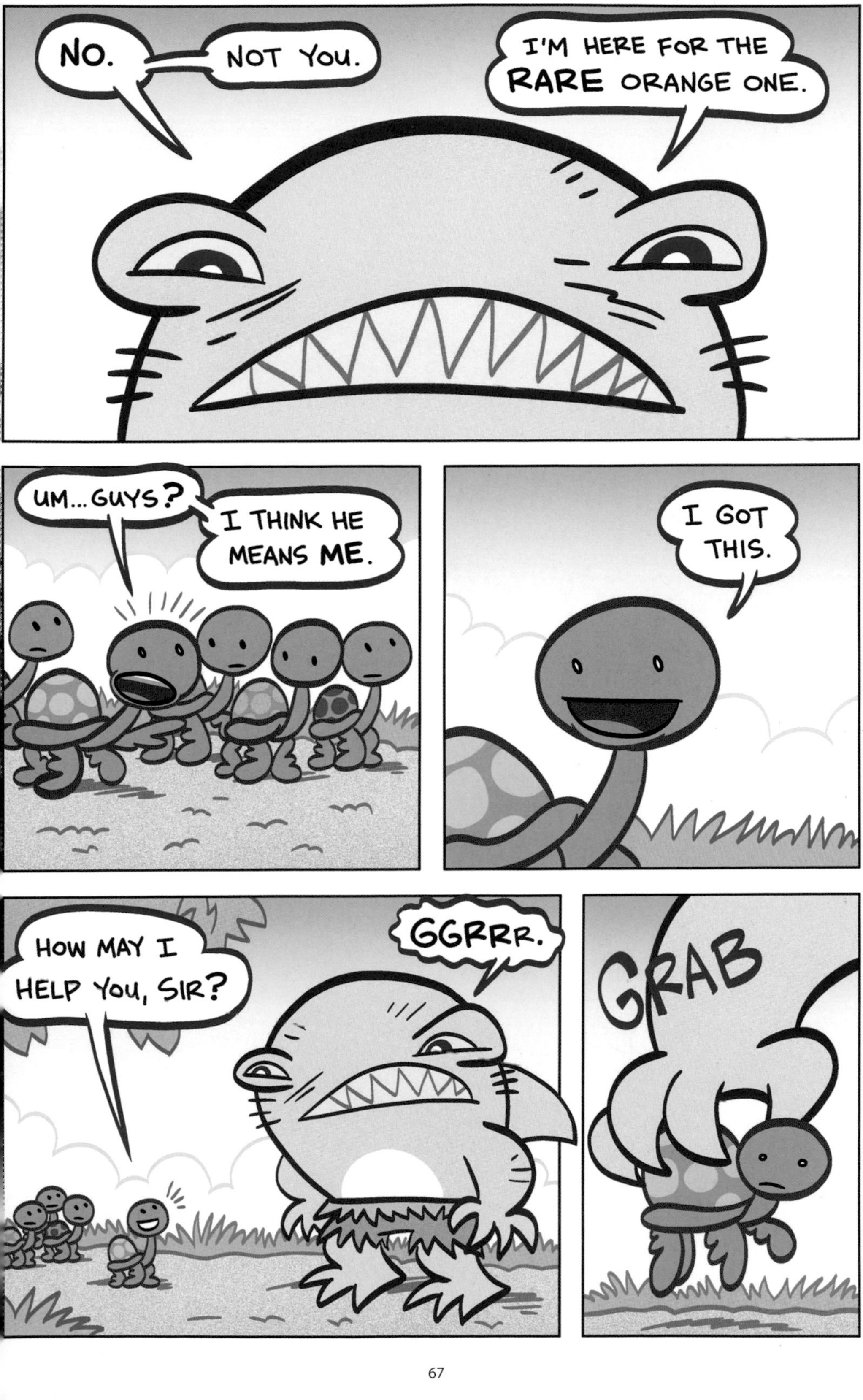
NO.
NOT YOU.
I'M HERE FOR THE RARE ORANGE ONE.
UM... GUYS?
I THINK HE MEANS ME.
I GOT THIS.
HOW MAY I HELP YOU, SIR?
GGRRR.
GRAB

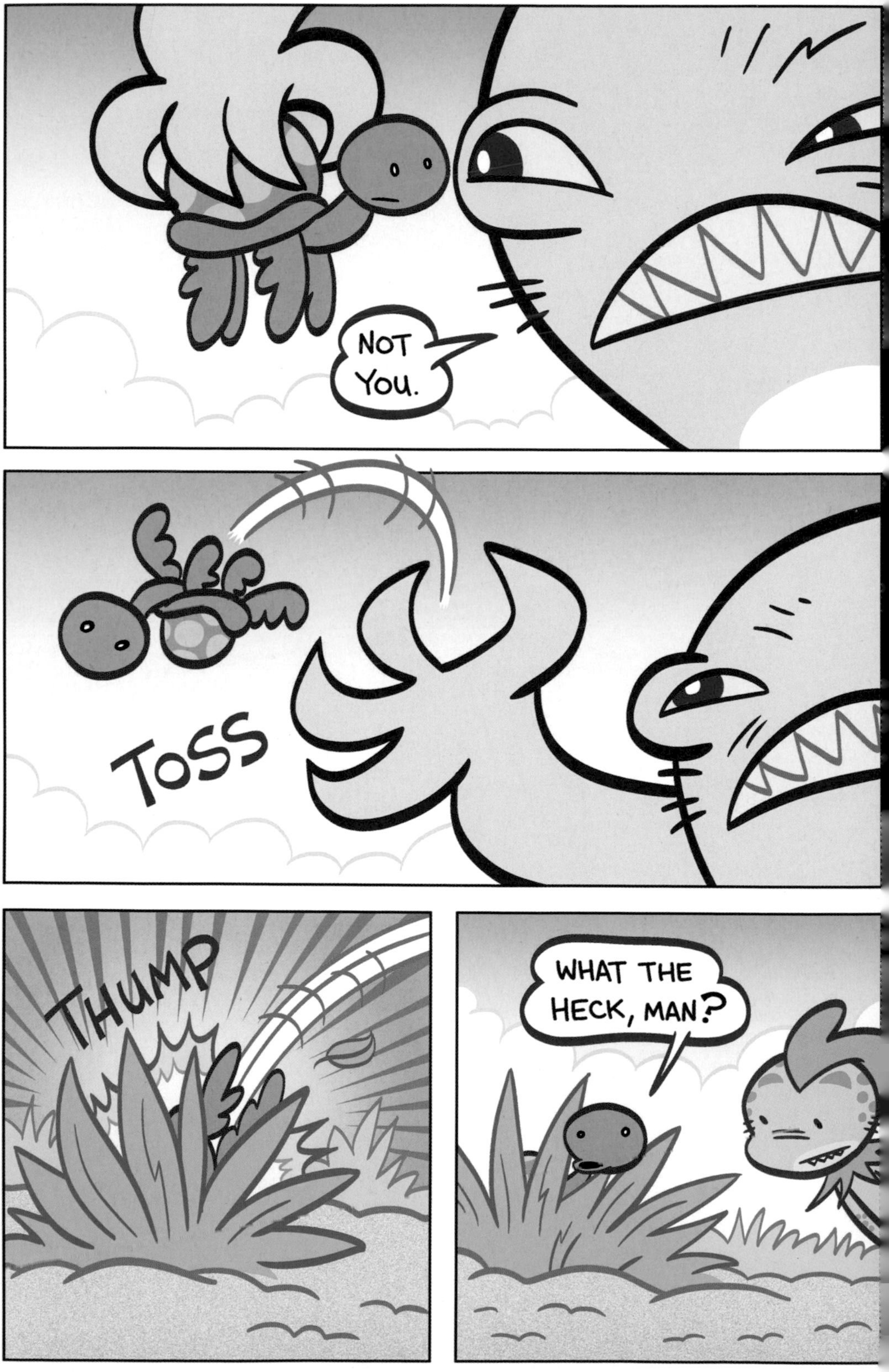
NOT YOU.
TOSS
THUMP
WHAT THE HECK, MAN?

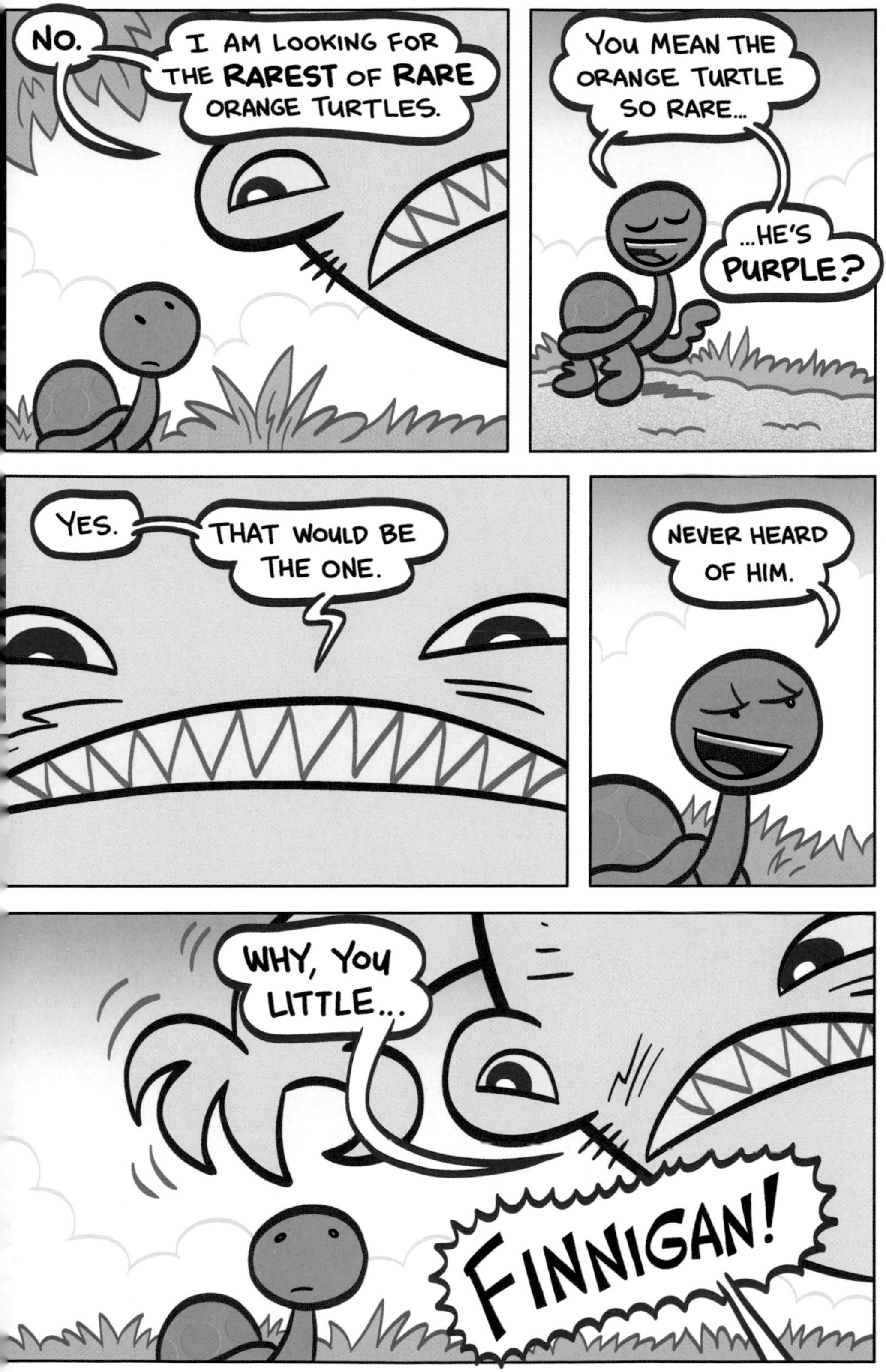
NO.
I AM LOOKING FOR THE RAREST OF RARE ORANGE TURTLES.
YOU MEAN THE ORANGE TURTLE SO RARE...
...HE'S PURPLE?
YES.
THAT WOULD BE THE ONE.
NEVER HEARD OF HIM.
WHY, YOU LITTLE...
FINNIGAN!

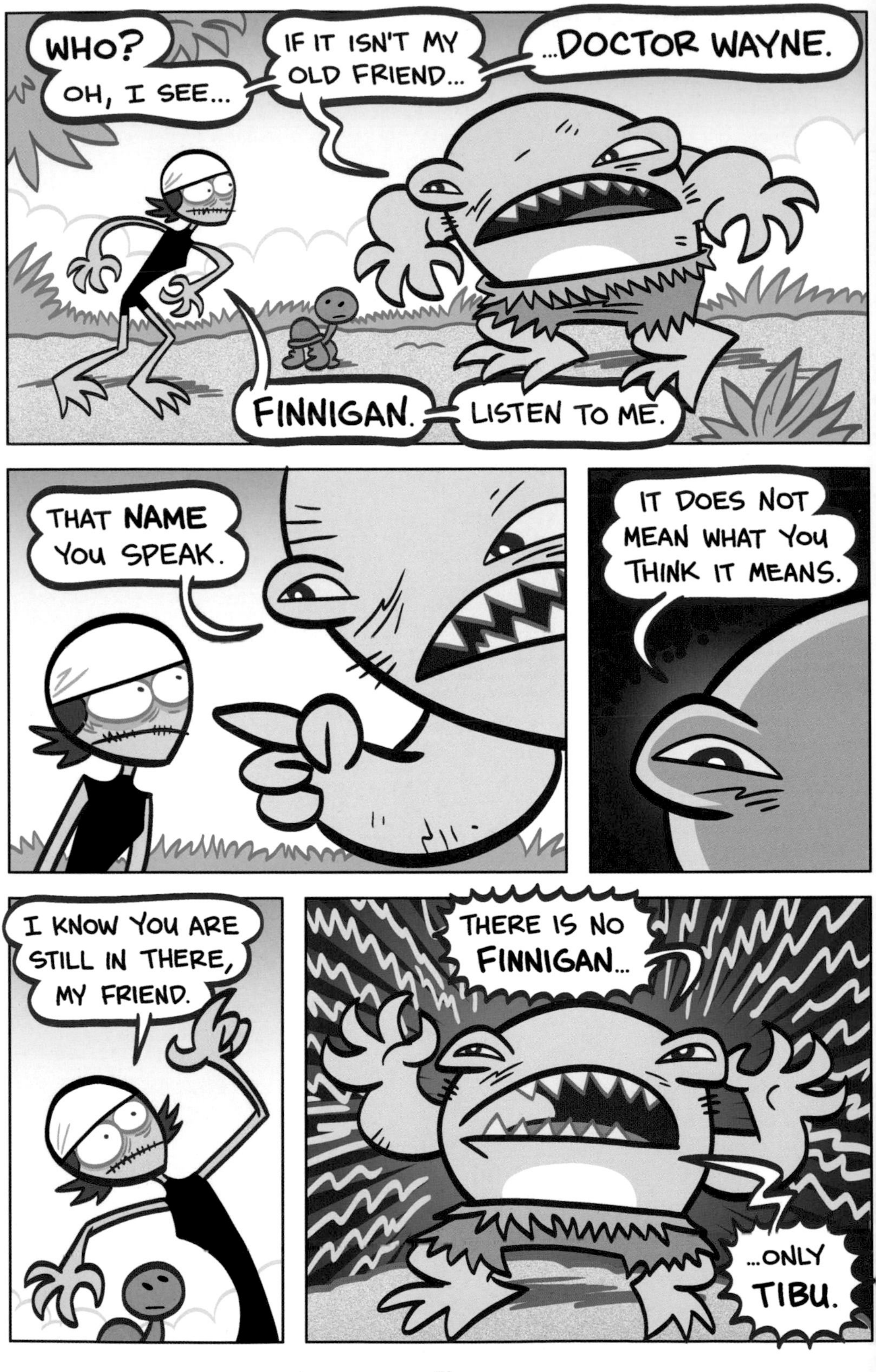
WHO?
OH, I SEE...
IF IT ISN'T MY OLD FRIEND...
...DOCTOR WAYNE.
FINNIGAN.
LISTEN TO ME.
THAT NAME YOU SPEAK.
IT DOES NOT MEAN WHAT YOU THINK IT MEANS.
I KNOW YOU ARE STILL IN THERE, MY FRIEND.
THERE IS NO FINNIGAN...
...ONLY TIBU.

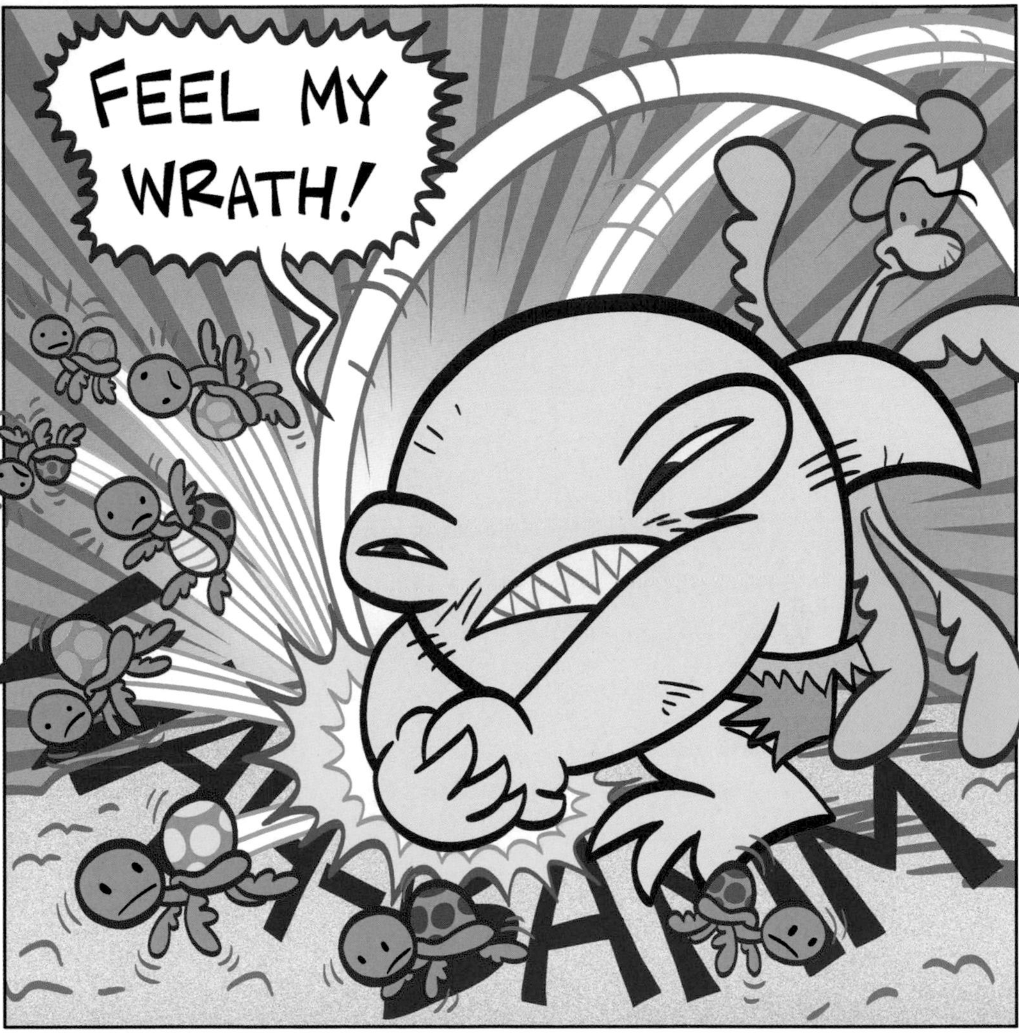
FEEL MY WRATH!

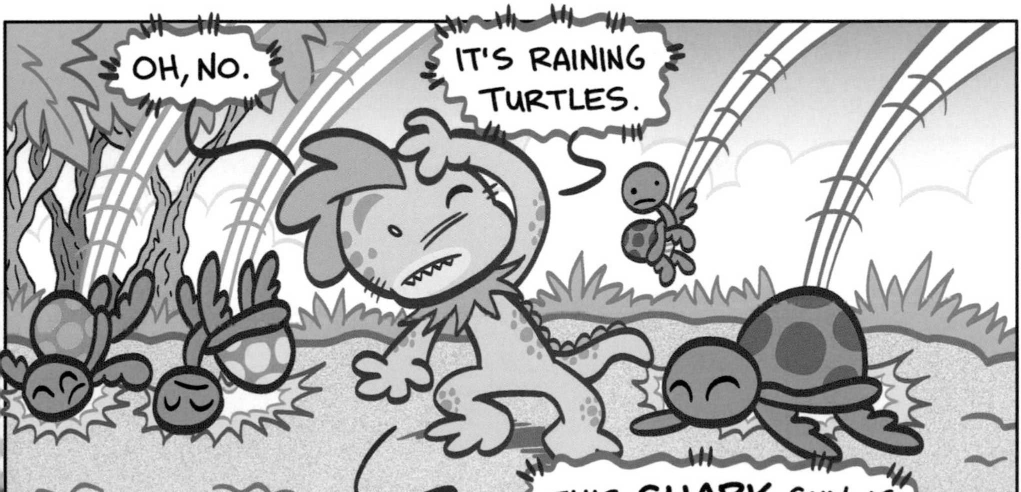
OH, NO.
IT'S RAINING TURTLES.
THIS **SHARK** GUY IS **WAY** OUT OF CONTROL.

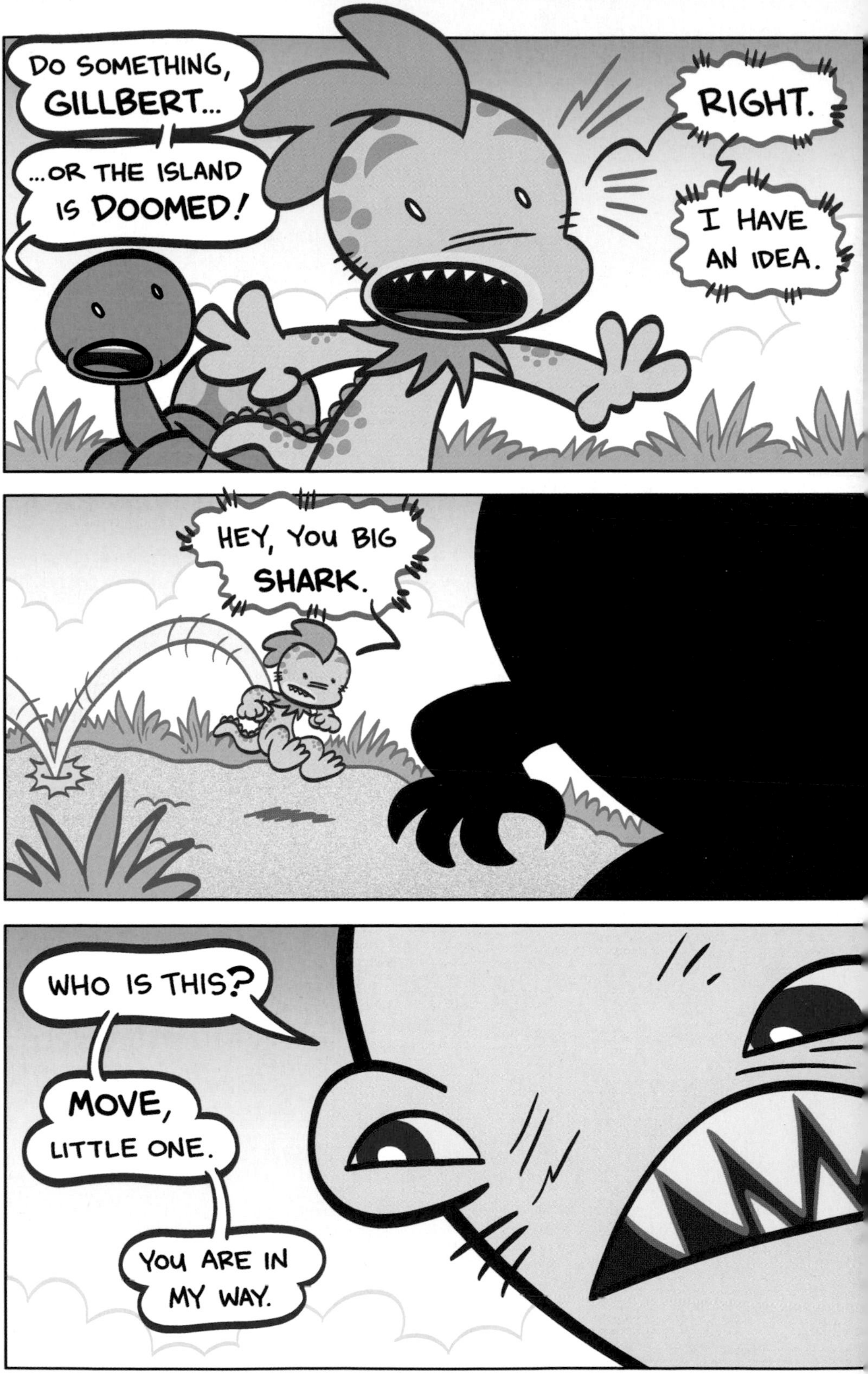
DO SOMETHING, GILLBERT...
...OR THE ISLAND IS DOOMED!
RIGHT.
I HAVE AN IDEA.
HEY, YOU BIG SHARK.
WHO IS THIS?
MOVE, LITTLE ONE.
YOU ARE IN MY WAY.

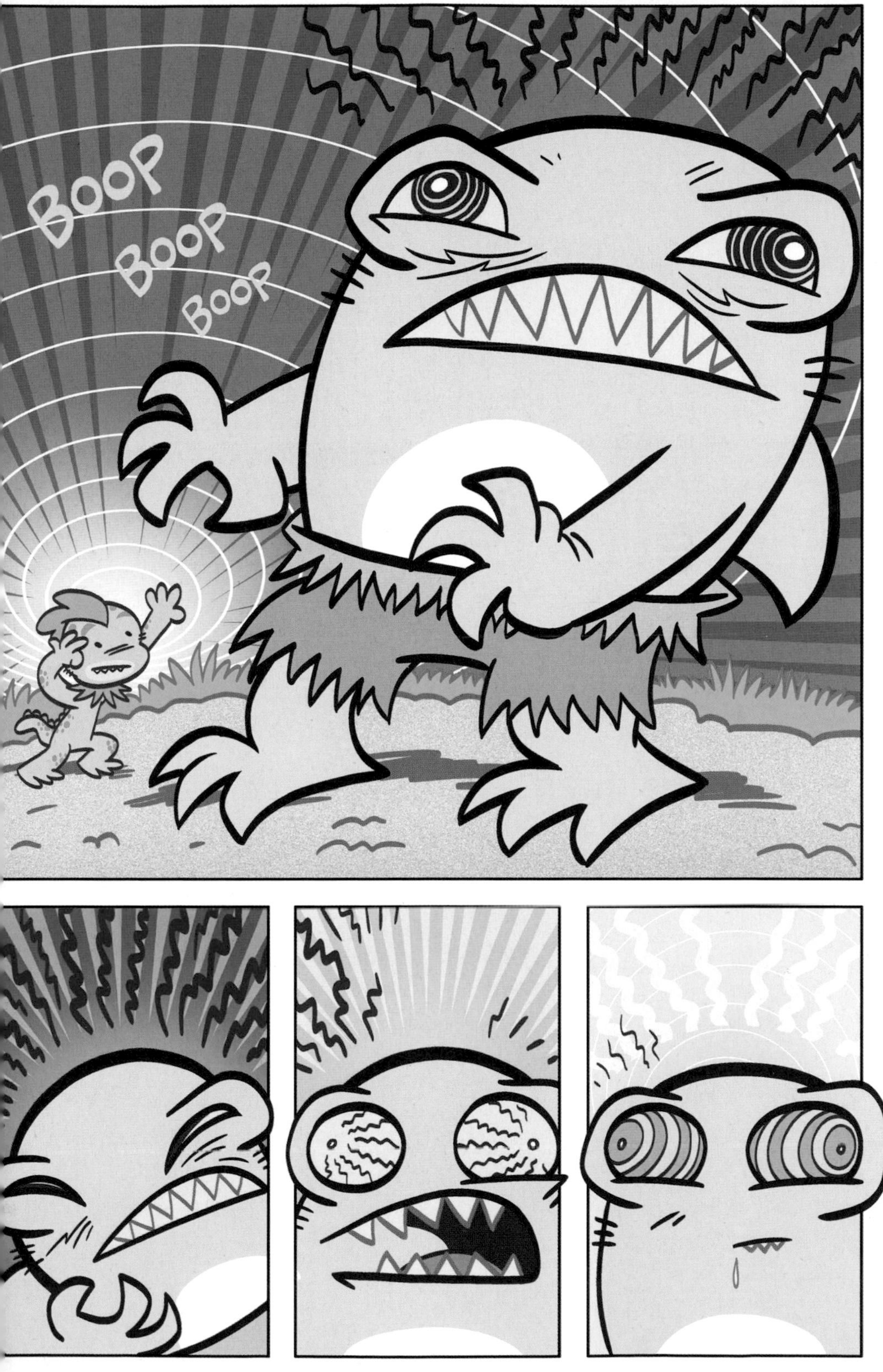
BOOP
BOOP
BOOP

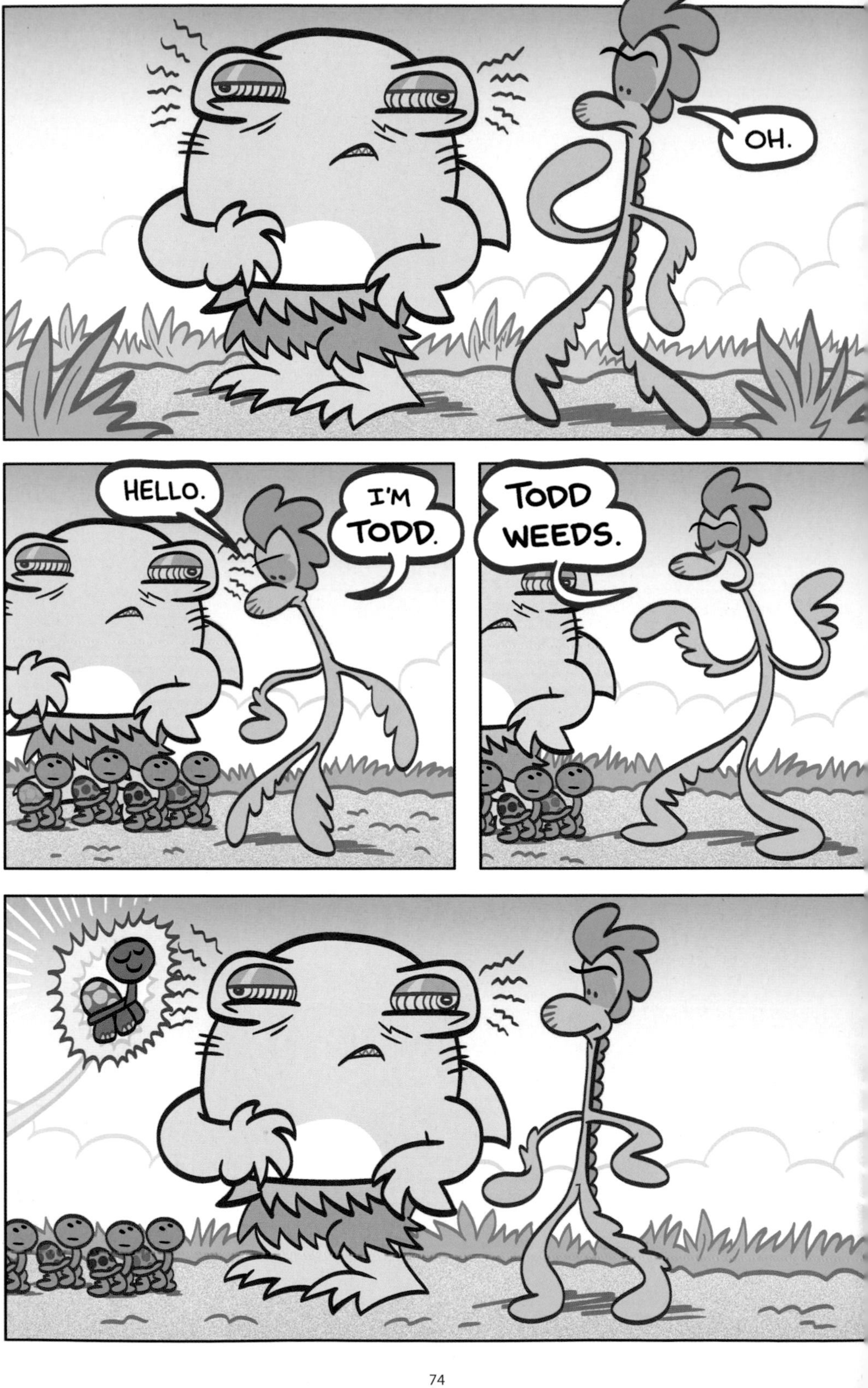
OH.
HELLO.
I'M TODD.
TODD WEEDS.

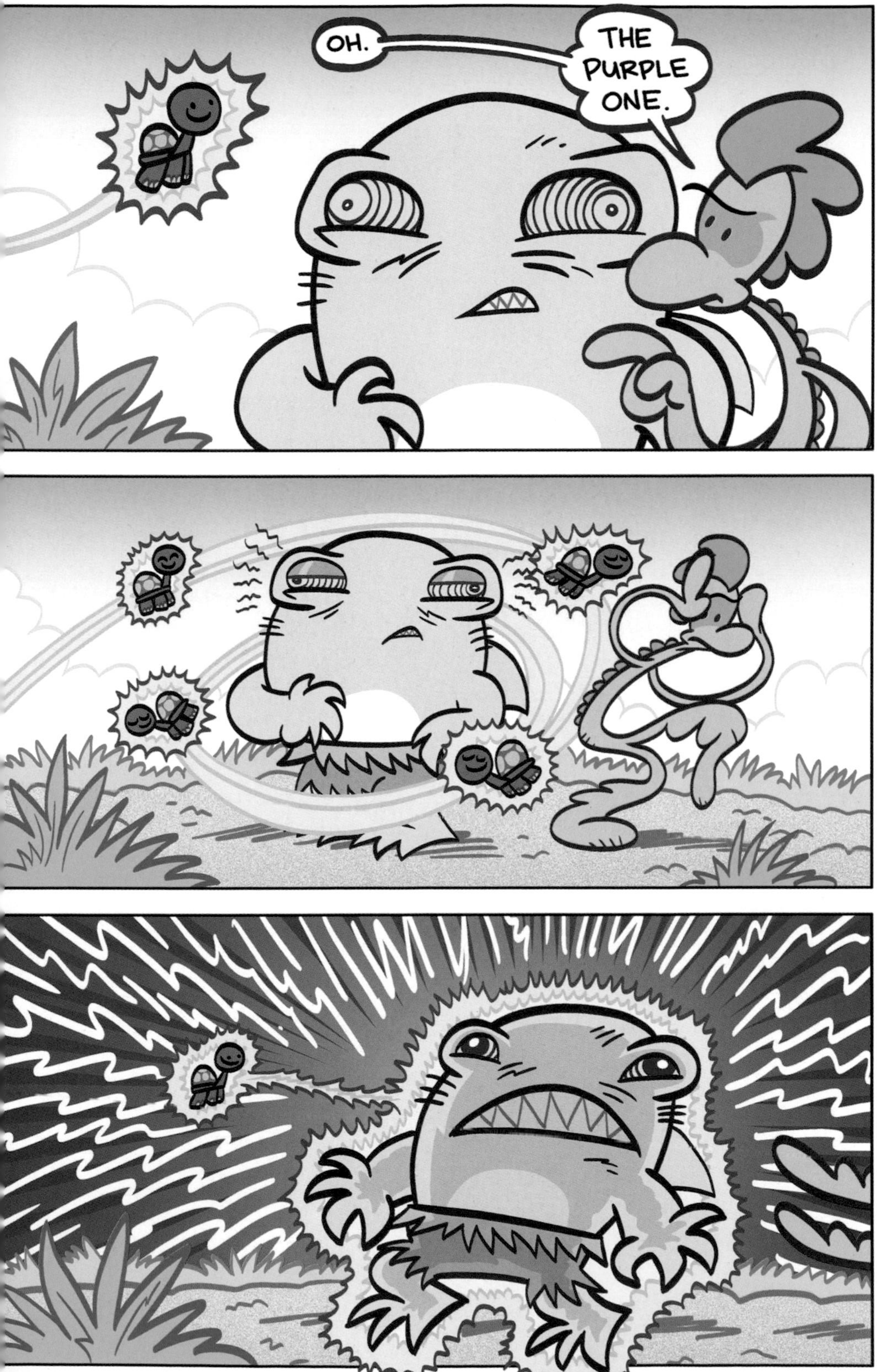
OH.
THE PURPLE ONE.

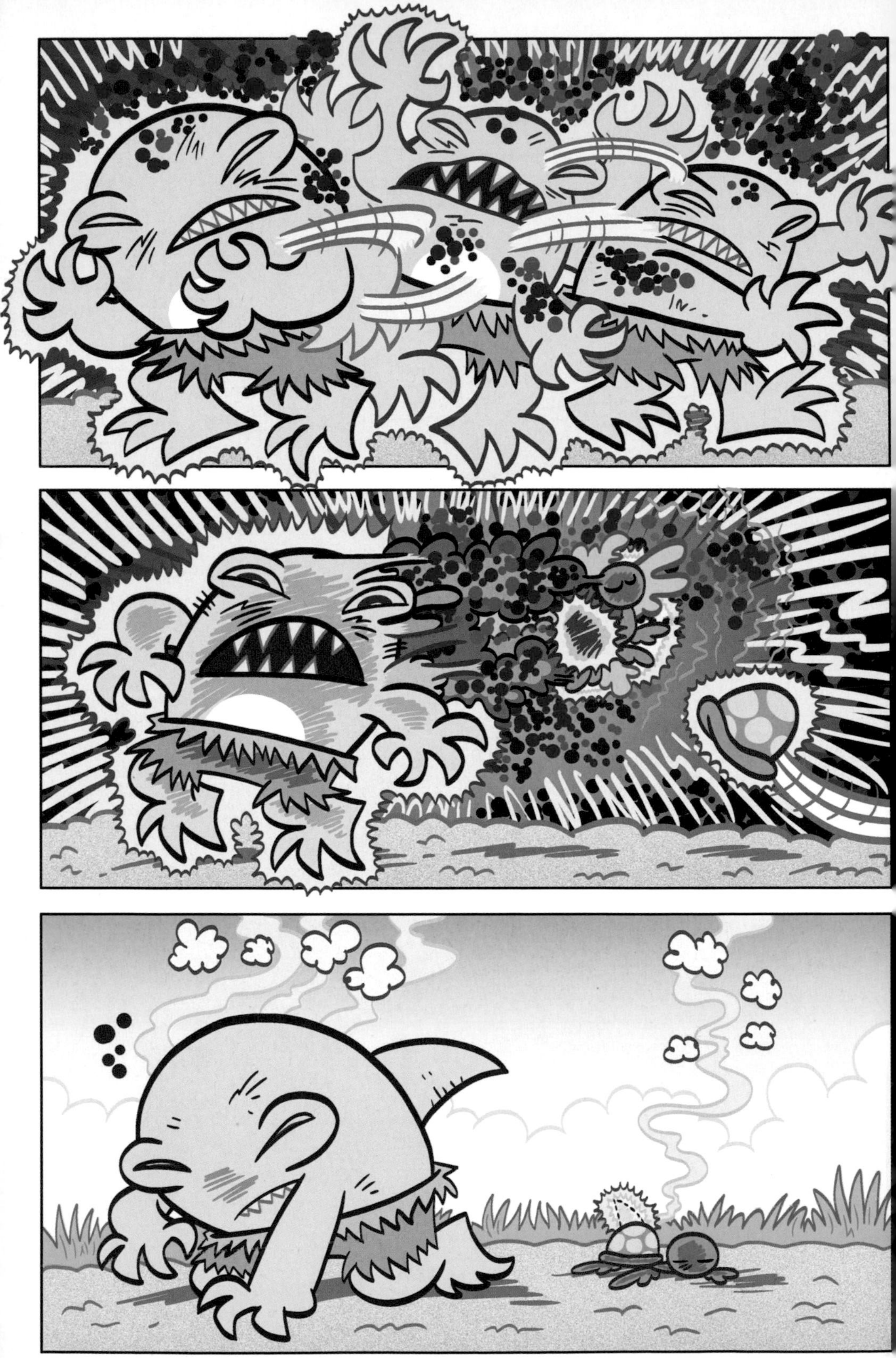

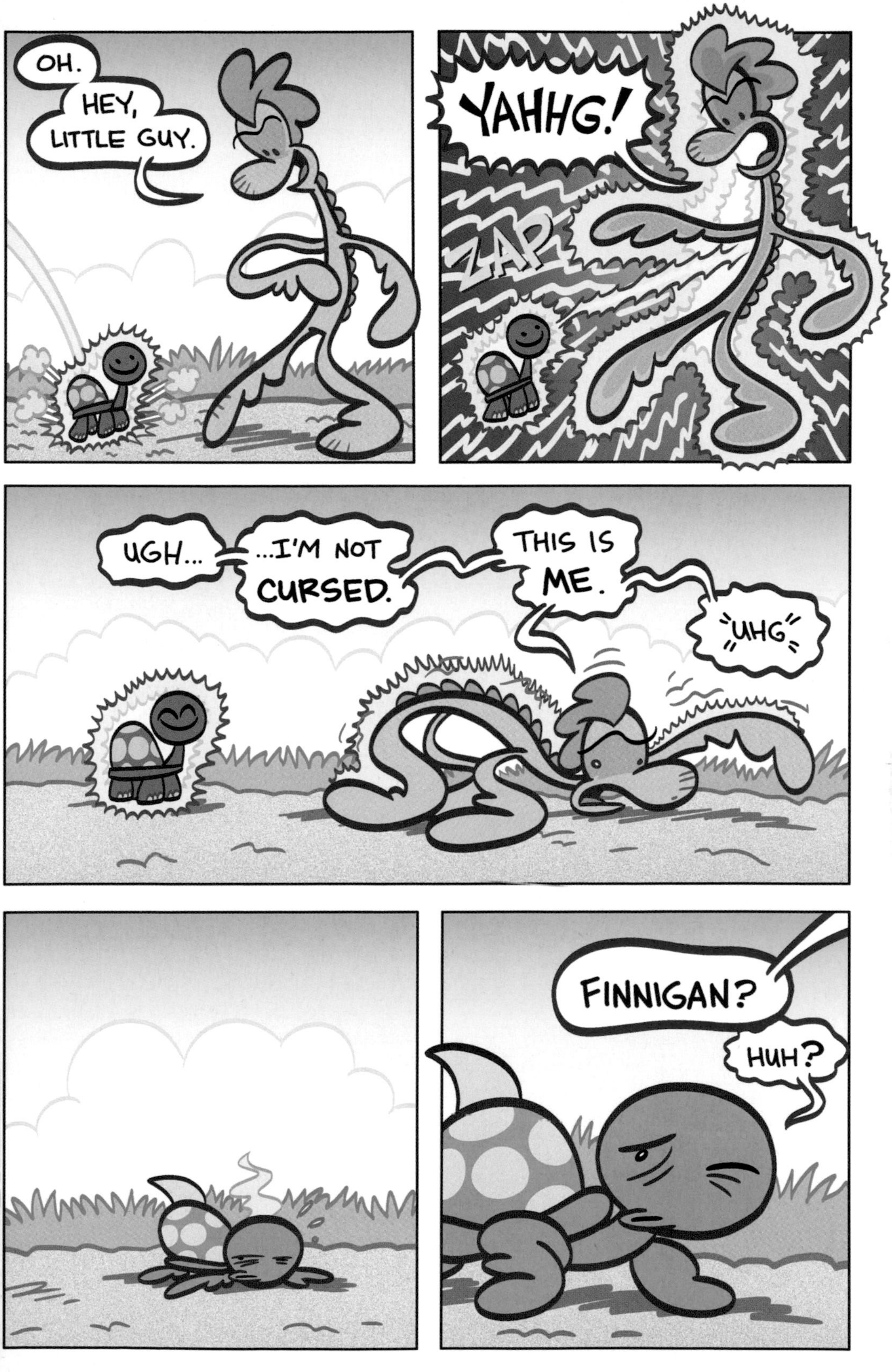
OH.
HEY, LITTLE GUY.
YAHHG!
ZAP
UGH...
...I'M NOT CURSED.
THIS IS ME.
UHG
FINNIGAN?
HUH?

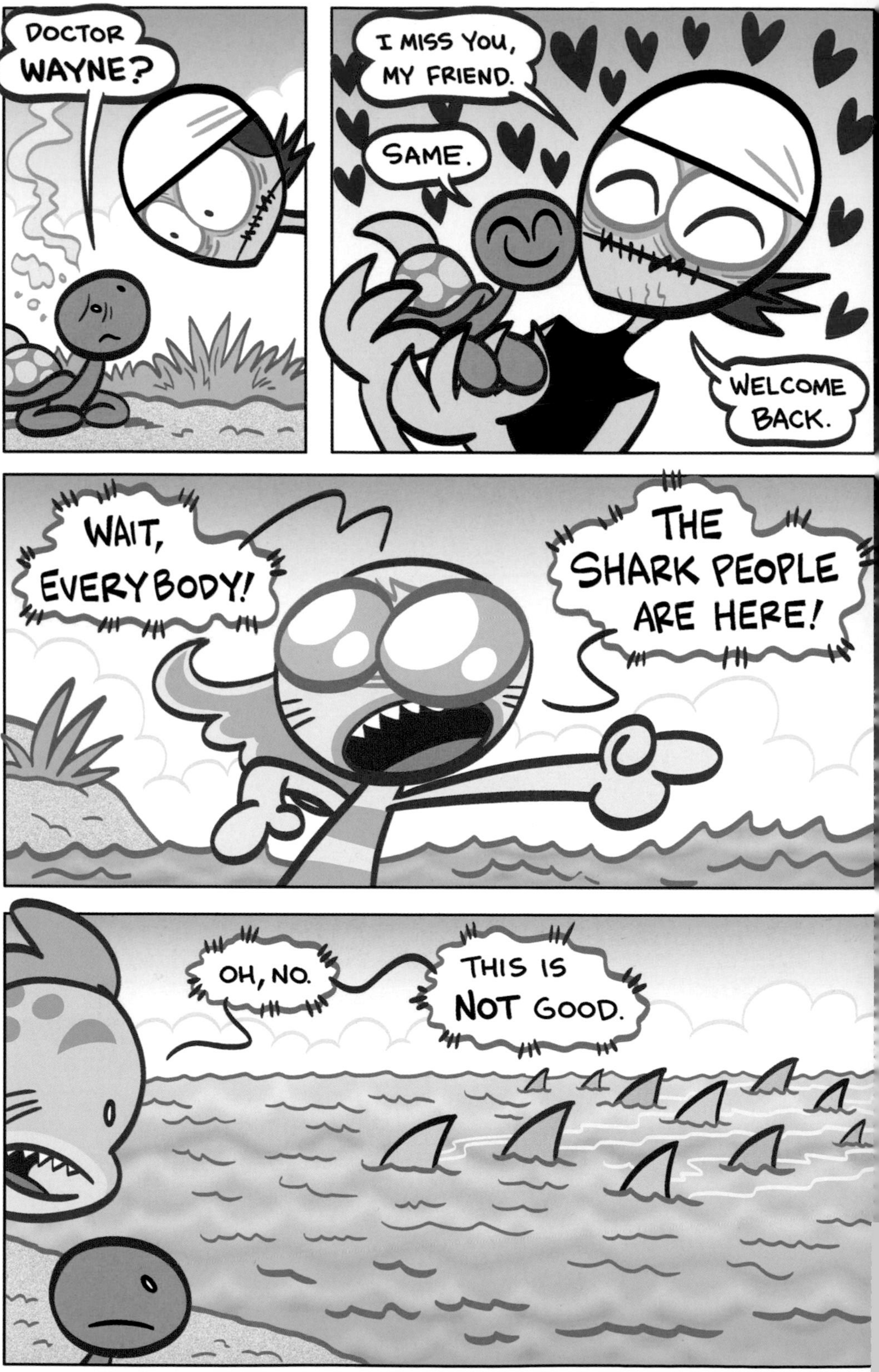
DOCTOR WAYNE?
I MISS YOU, MY FRIEND.
SAME.
WELCOME BACK.
WAIT, EVERYBODY!
THE SHARK PEOPLE ARE HERE!
OH, NO.
THIS IS NOT GOOD.

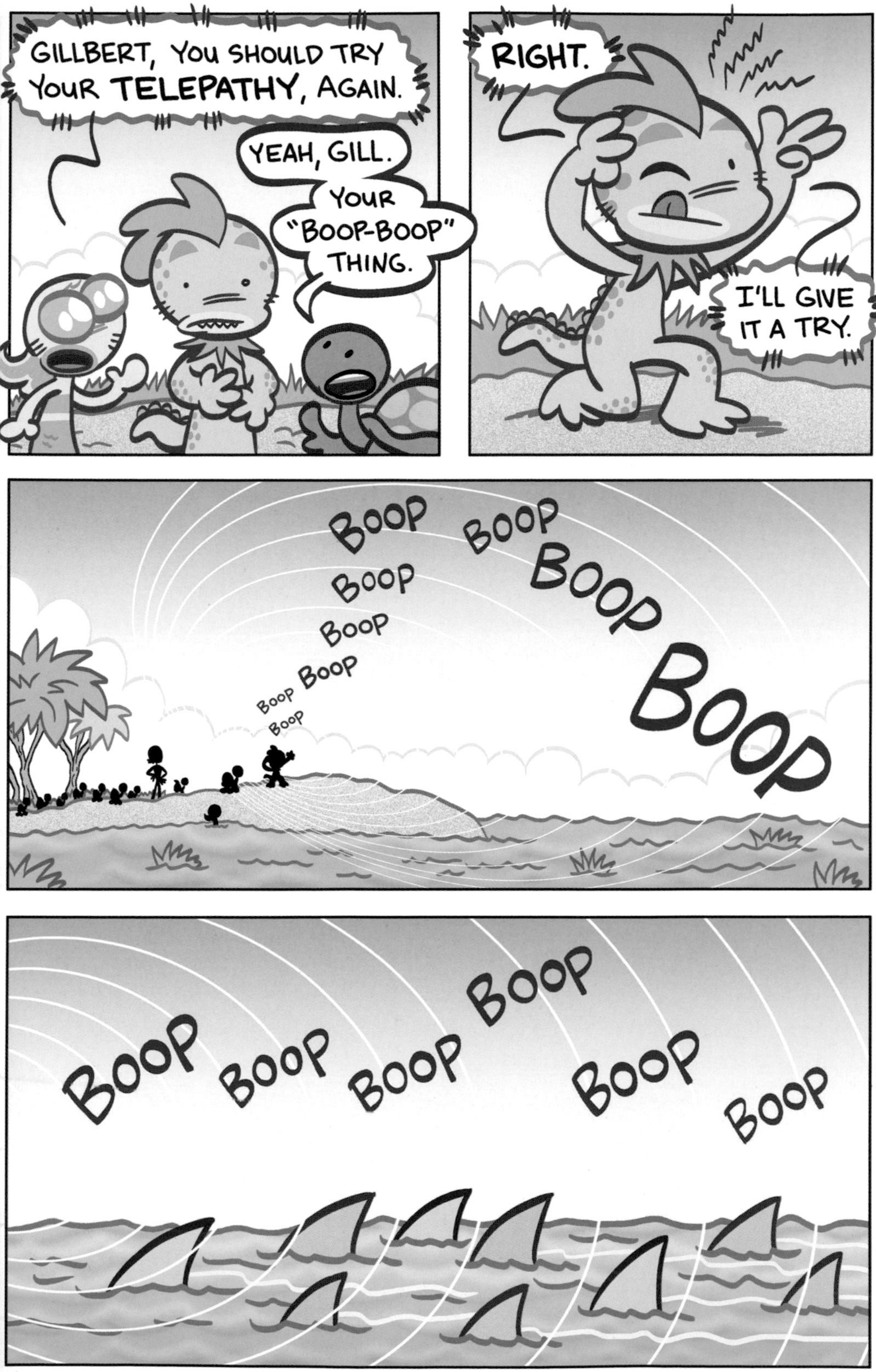
GILLBERT, YOU SHOULD TRY YOUR TELEPATHY, AGAIN.
YEAH, GILL.
YOUR "BOOP-BOOP" THING.
RIGHT.
I'LL GIVE IT A TRY.
BOOP BOOP BOOP BOOP BOOP BOOP BOOP BOOP BOOP
BOOP BOOP BOOP BOOP BOOP BOOP

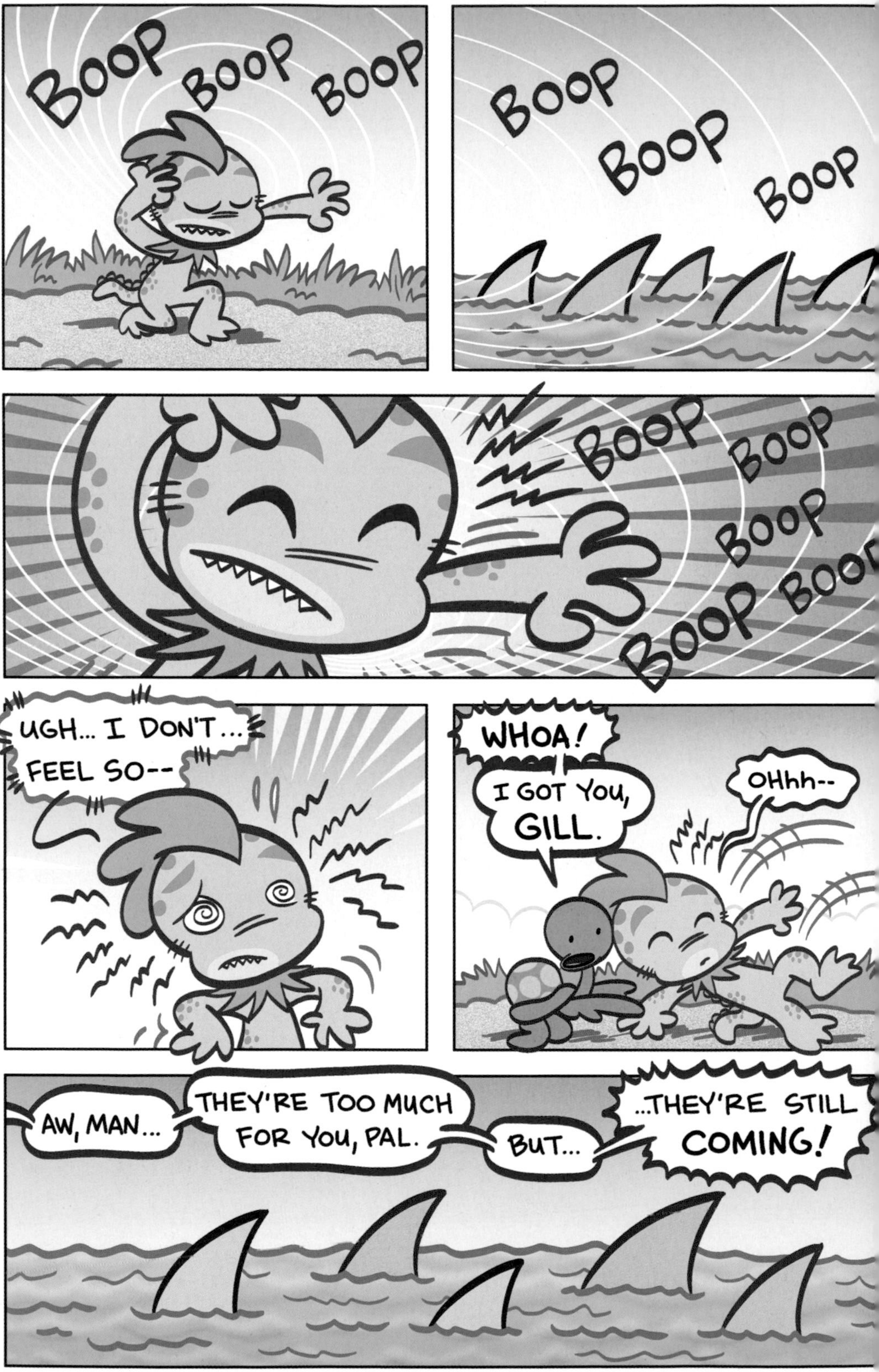
BOOP BOOP BOOP
BOOP BOOP BOOP
BOOP BOOP BOOP BOOP BOOP
UGH... I DON'T... FEEL SO--
WHOA!
I GOT YOU, GILL.
OHhh--
AW, MAN...
THEY'RE TOO MUCH FOR YOU, PAL.
BUT...
...THEY'RE STILL COMING!

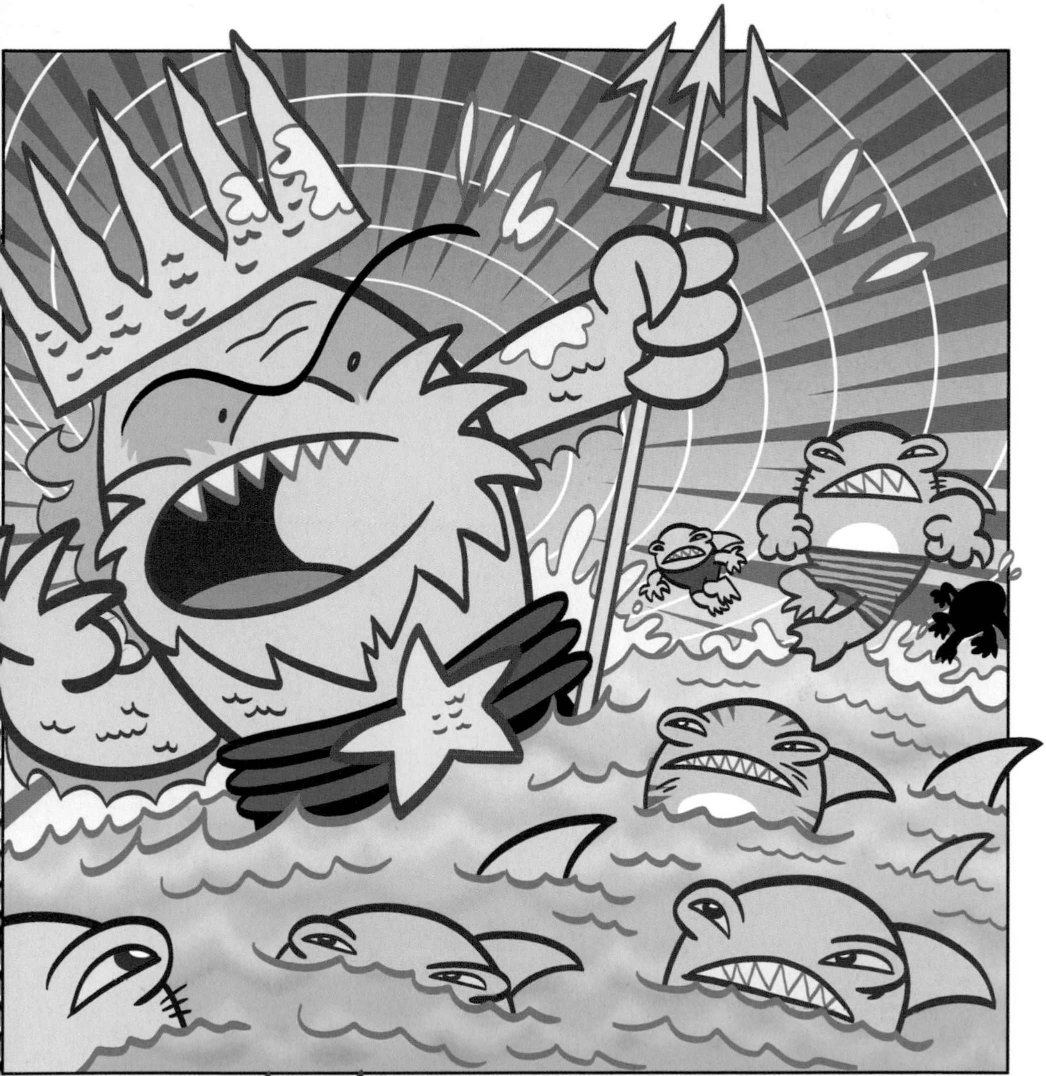

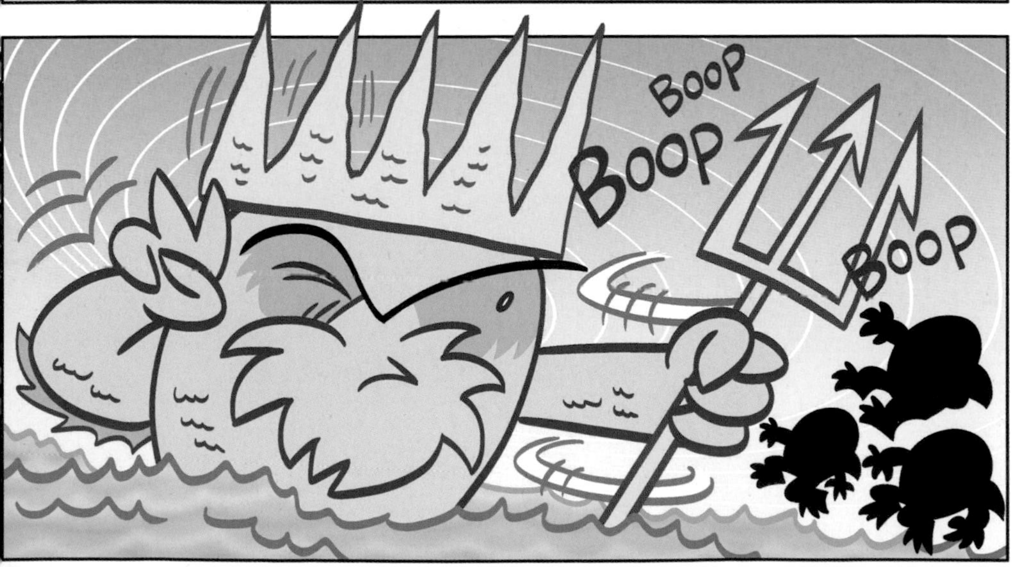
BOOP
BOOP
BOOP

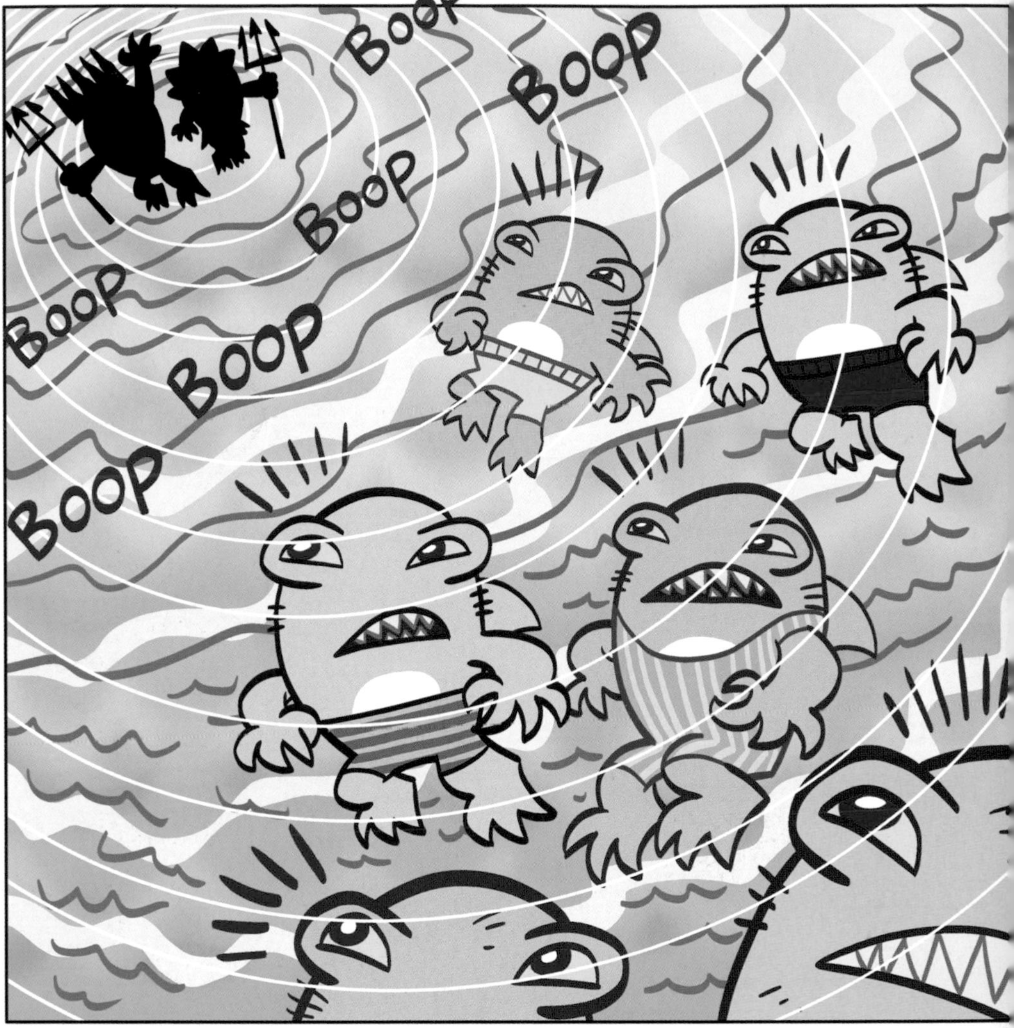
Boop
Boop
Boop
Boop
Boop
Boop

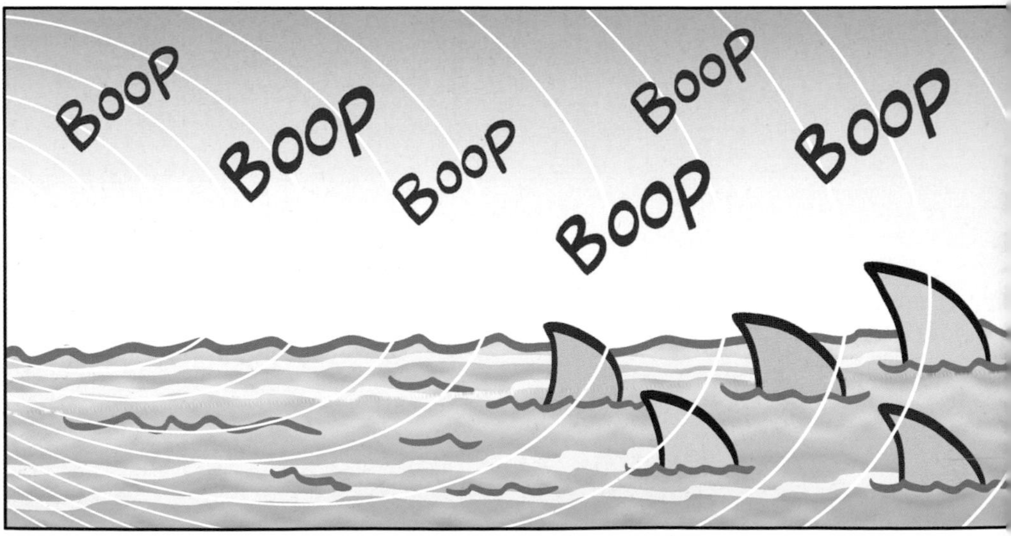
Boop
Boop
Boop
Boop
Boop
Boop

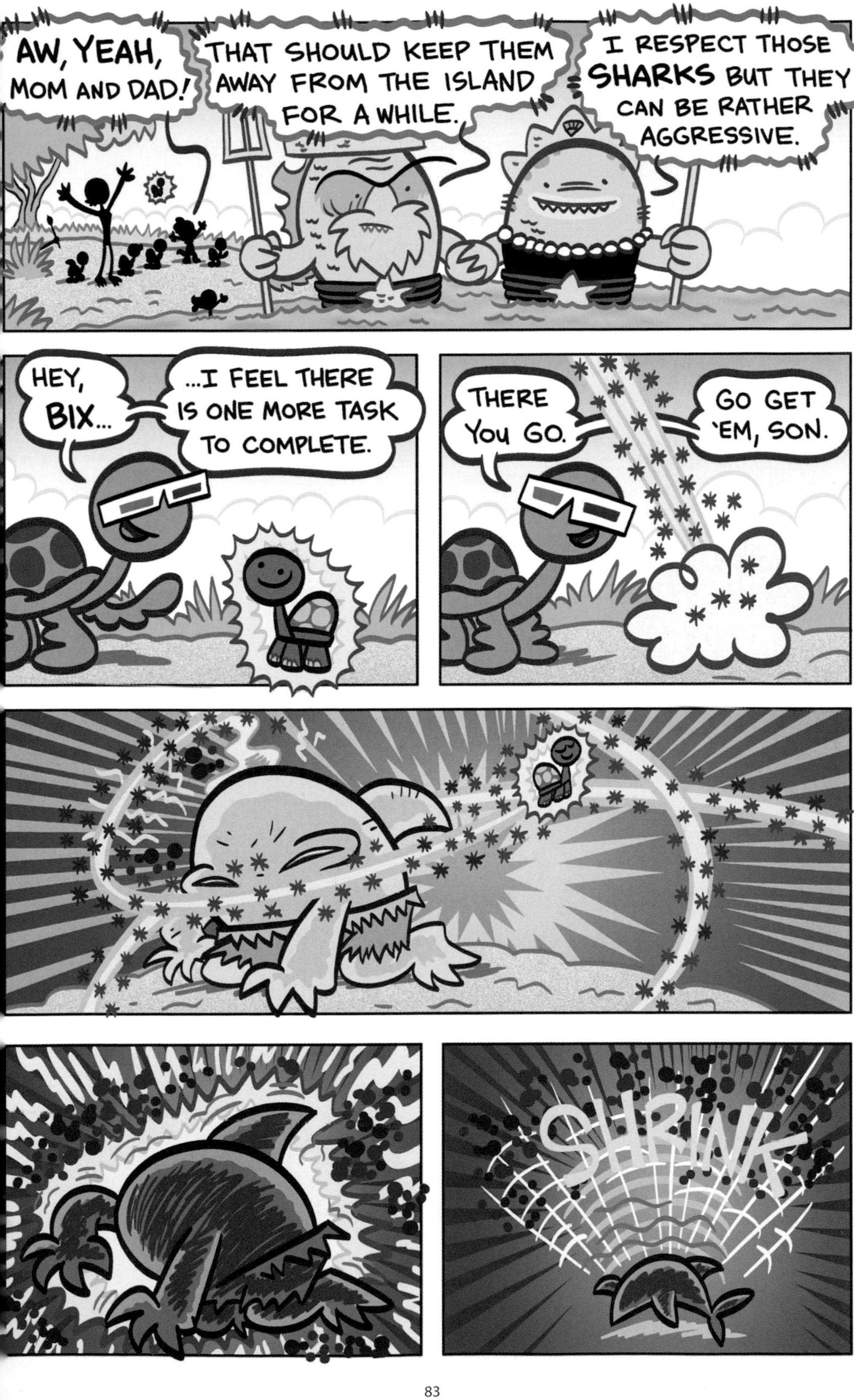
AW, YEAH, MOM AND DAD!
THAT SHOULD KEEP THEM AWAY FROM THE ISLAND FOR A WHILE.
I RESPECT THOSE SHARKS BUT THEY CAN BE RATHER AGGRESSIVE.
HEY, BIX...
...I FEEL THERE IS ONE MORE TASK TO COMPLETE.
THERE YOU GO.
GO GET 'EM, SON.
SHRINK

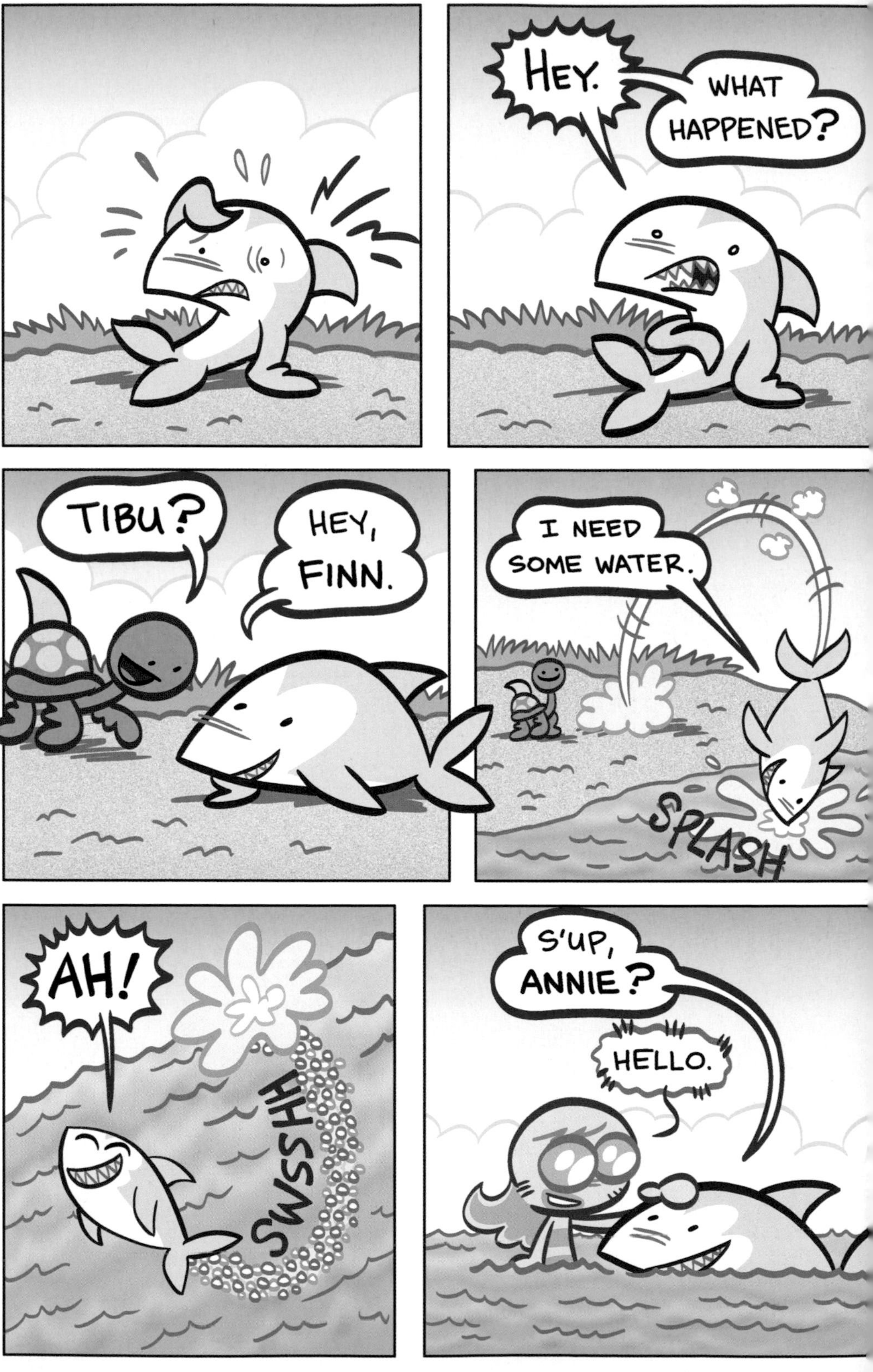
HEY.
WHAT HAPPENED?
TIBU?
HEY, FINN.
I NEED SOME WATER.
SPLASH
AH!
SWSSHHH
S'UP, ANNIE?
HELLO.

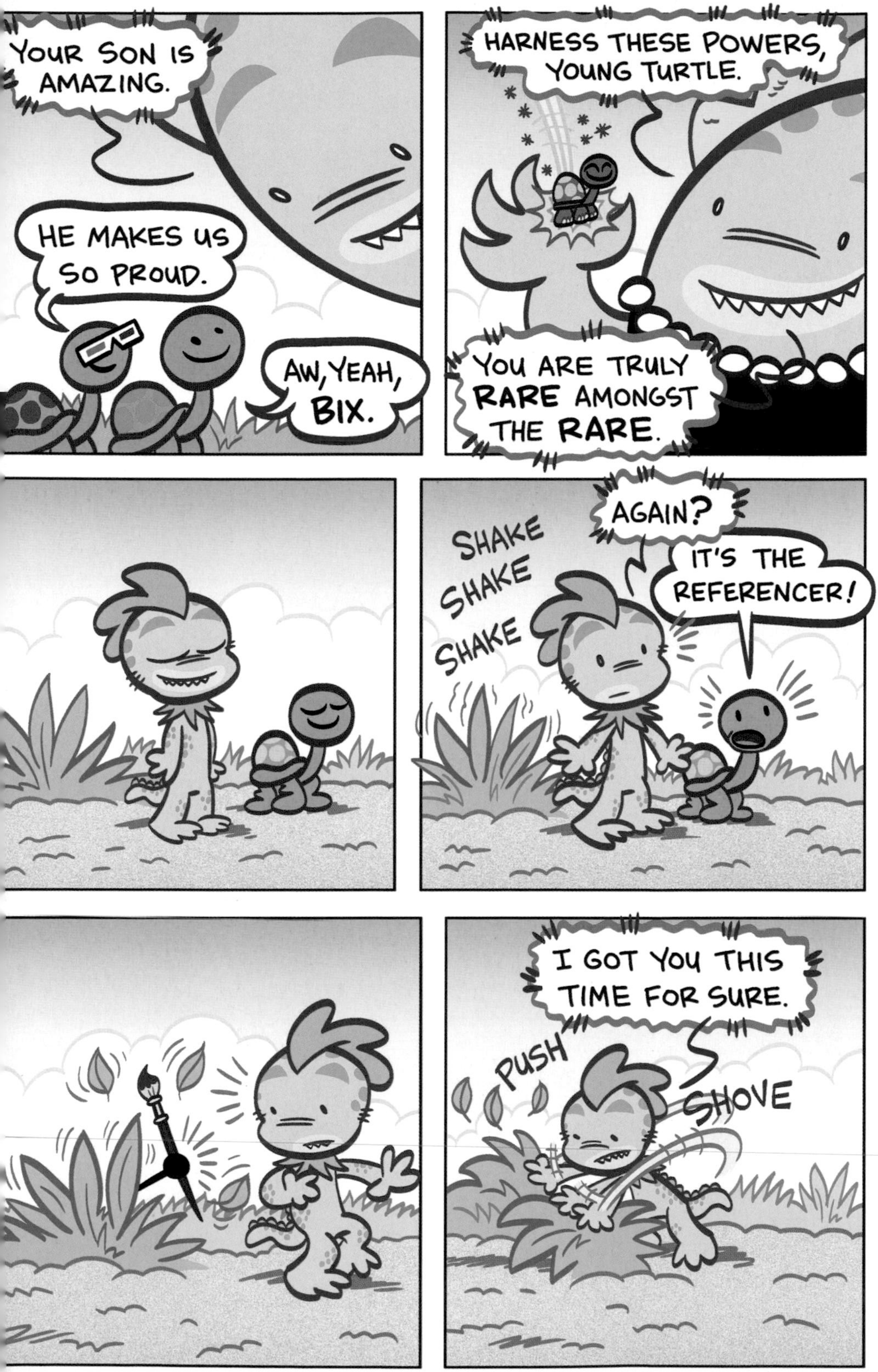
YOUR SON IS AMAZING.
HE MAKES US SO PROUD.
AW, YEAH, BIX.
HARNESS THESE POWERS, YOUNG TURTLE.
YOU ARE TRULY RARE AMONGST THE RARE.
SHAKE SHAKE SHAKE
AGAIN?
IT'S THE REFERENCER!
I GOT YOU THIS TIME FOR SURE.
PUSH
SHOVE

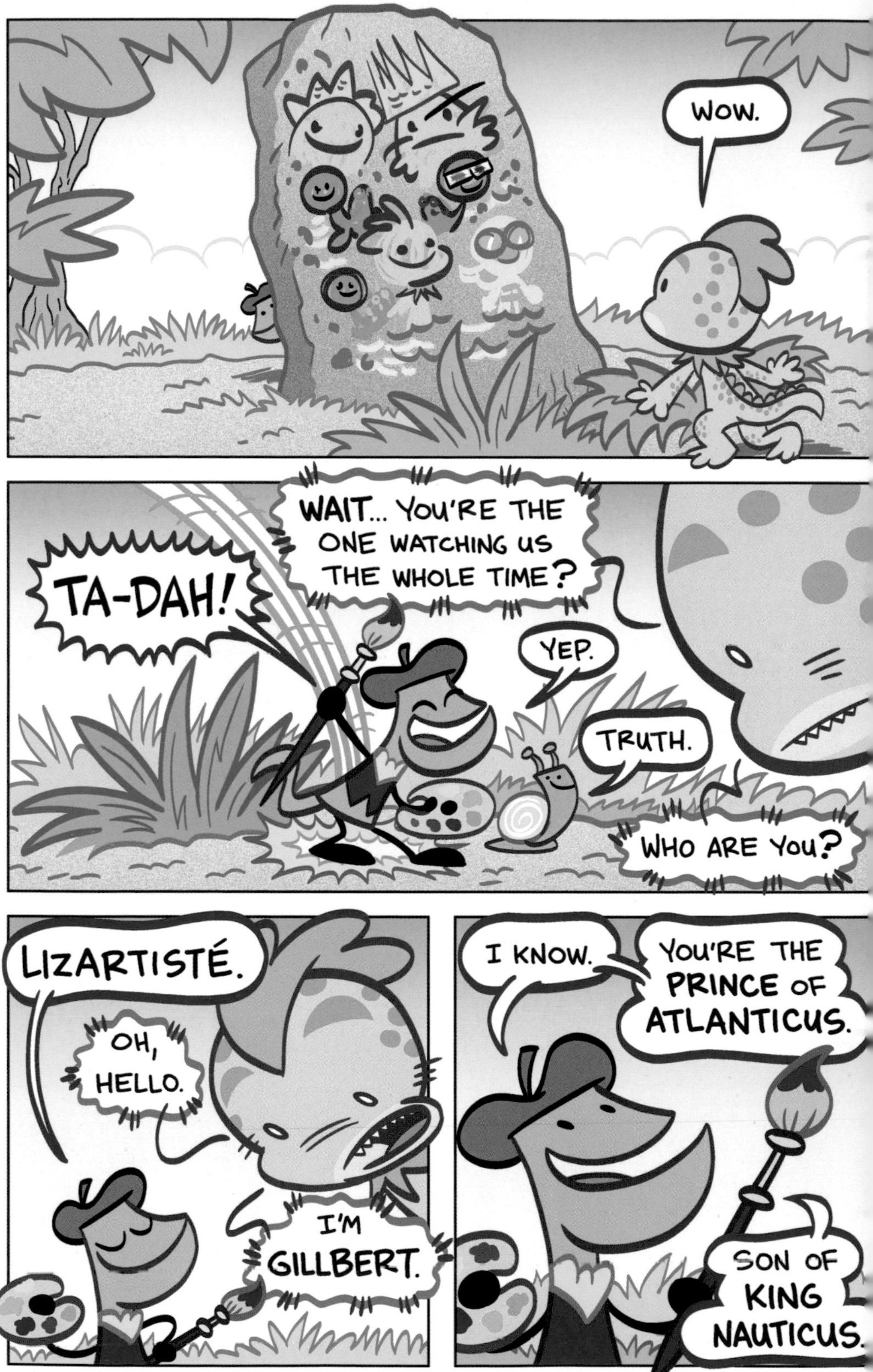
WOW.
TA-DAH!
WAIT... YOU'RE THE ONE WATCHING US THE WHOLE TIME?
YEP.
TRUTH.
WHO ARE YOU?
LIZARTISTÉ.
OH, HELLO.
I'M GILLBERT.
I KNOW.
YOU'RE THE PRINCE OF ATLANTICUS.
SON OF KING NAUTICUS.

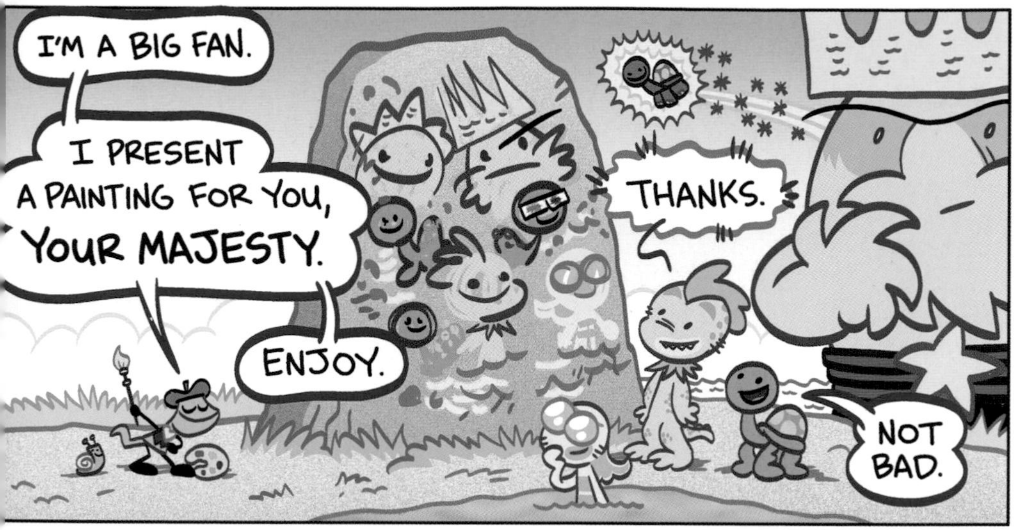
I'M A BIG FAN.
I PRESENT A PAINTING FOR YOU, YOUR MAJESTY.
ENJOY.
THANKS.
NOT BAD.

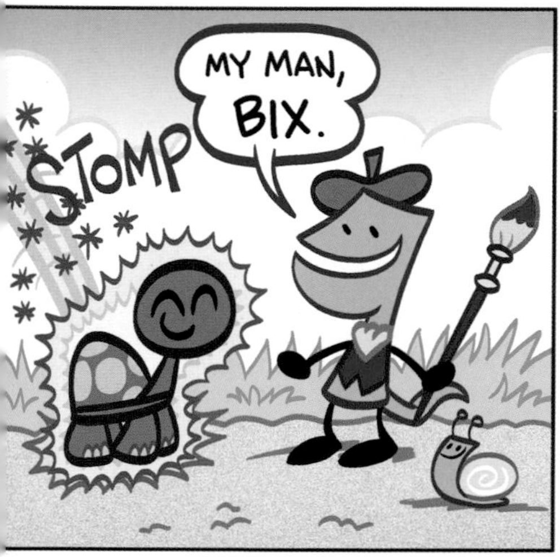
STOMP
MY MAN, BIX.

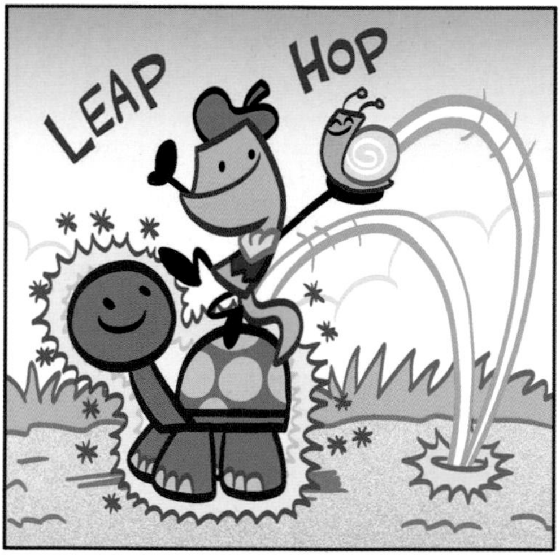
LEAP
HOP

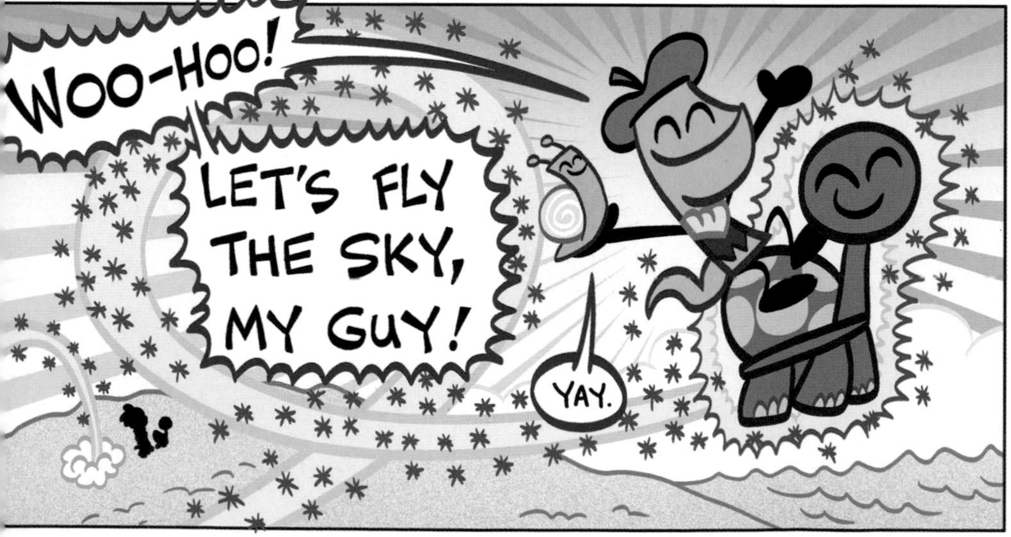
WOO-HOO!
LET'S FLY THE SKY, MY GUY!
YAY.

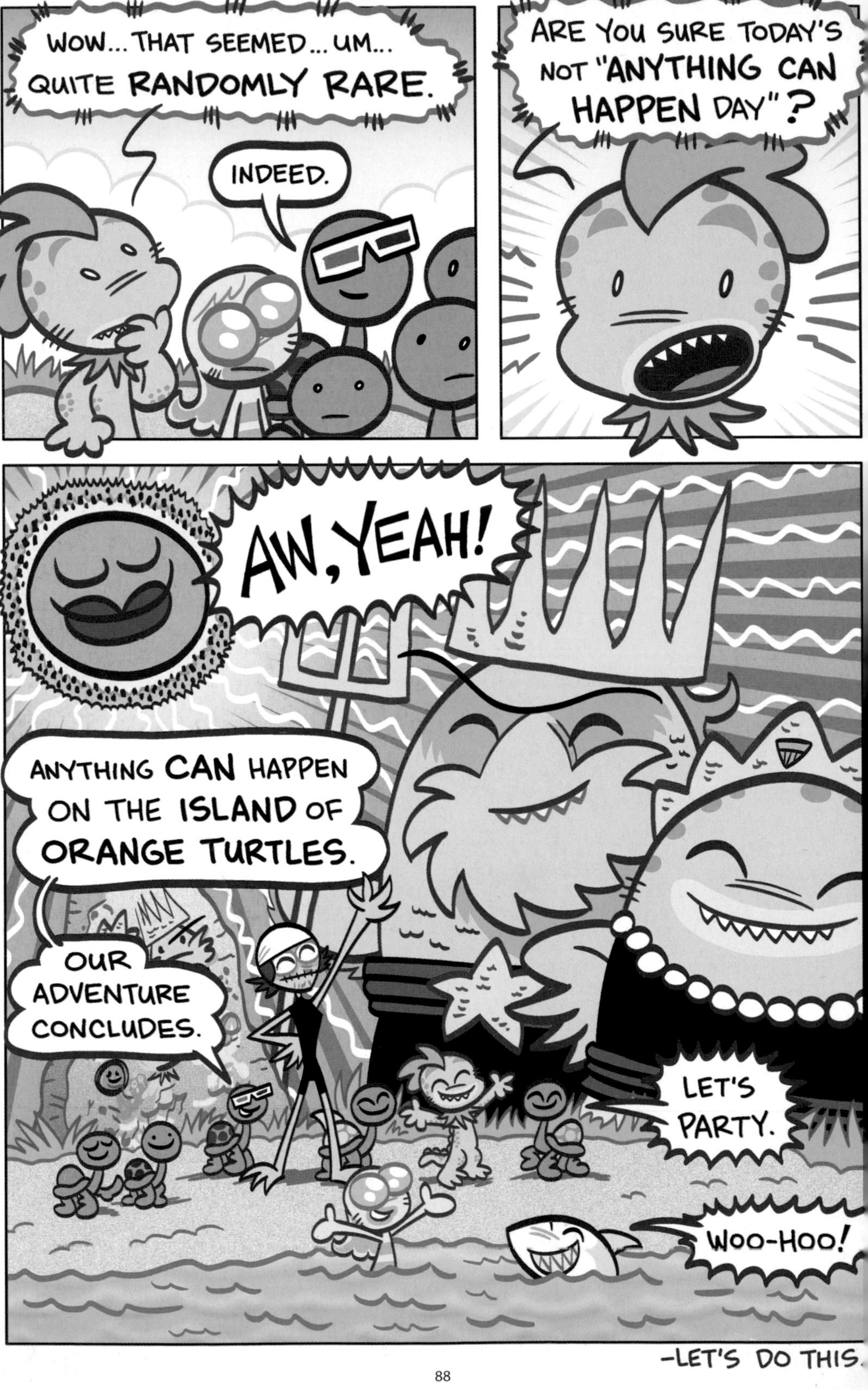
WOW... THAT SEEMED... UM... QUITE RANDOMLY RARE.
INDEED.
ARE YOU SURE TODAY'S NOT "ANYTHING CAN HAPPEN DAY"?
AW, YEAH!
ANYTHING CAN HAPPEN ON THE ISLAND OF ORANGE TURTLES.
OUR ADVENTURE CONCLUDES.
LET'S PARTY.
WOO-HOO!

-LET'S DO THIS.